Penguin Science Fiction
The Night of Kadar

Evacuated from London during the bombing, Garry Kilworth's mother produced him in York in 1941. His parents were travellers, and his teenage years were spent in Southern Arabia.

After two years at an Air Force technical college, he was sent to the Far East to immerse himself in the heady orientalism of Malaya and Singapore. He also spent a year drifting on a tiny coral island in the Maldives of the Indian Ocean.

Later years saw Garry Kilworth enjoying prolonged periods in Germany, Africa, Bahrain, Aden, Malta and Cyprus. It was during those years that he began to write fiction and poetry, and in 1974 he won the Gollancz/*Sunday Times* Science Fiction competition.

He is now a Senior Telecommunications Executive with a communications firm that operates on a world-wide basis. Apart from delving into new communications developments and writing, he enjoys the family activities of canoeing, camping in the wilds, ornithology and collecting anything useless to nature or Man. He is married to a social worker and they have two teenage children.

Garry Kilworth's first novel, *In Solitary*, is also published in Penguins.

Garry Kilworth

The Night of Kadar

Penguin Books

Penguin Books Ltd, Harmondsworth,
Middlesex, England
Penguin Books, 625 Madison Avenue,
New York, New York 10022, U.S.A.
Penguin Books Australia Ltd, Ringwood,
Victoria, Australia
Penguin Books Canada Ltd, 2801 John Street,
Markham, Ontario, Canada L3R 1B4
Penguin Books (N.Z.) Ltd, 182–190 Wairau Road,
Auckland 10, New Zealand

First published by Faber & Faber Ltd 1978
Published in Penguin Books 1979

Copyright © Garry Kilworth, 1978
All rights reserved

Made and printed in Great Britain by
Richard Clay (The Chaucer Press) Ltd
Bungay, Suffolk
Set in Linotype Plantin

Except in the United States of America, this book is
sold subject to the condition that it shall not, by
way of trade or otherwise, be lent, re-sold, hired out,
or otherwise circulated without the publisher's prior
consent in any form of binding or cover other than
that in which it is published and without a similar
condition including this condition being imposed on
the subsequent purchaser

Nothing but respect is intended in this novel towards the religion of Islam

Better is the Night of Kadar (Glory) than a thousand months . . .

THE KORAN

To my mother and father
(and to Rosemary Burns and Graham Maxwell)

Part One

*They cannot scare me with their empty spaces
Between the stars – on stars where no human race is.
I have it in me so much nearer home
To scare myself with my own desert places.*

Robert Frost, 'Desert Places'

One

There is a click. A thousand years have passed since such a sound echoed through the starship. It is a lonely sound, limited by the volume of air which surrounds it and, it could be argued, no sound at all since it falls on no ears. *If there is no one to hear the tree toppling in the forest, then the fall is silent.* Suns are the mute lions of the universe, their roaring contained by the vacuum that envelops them. Like the roaring of the suns, the starship's click is contained within its producer and goes unheard by any form of organic life.

But the ship itself hears the click, or rather feels it which is the same thing, and it knows that its ancillary homers have found and locked-on to the solar system which is likely to contain the Earthworld. The ship begins its analysis of the available data: number of planets, size of sun, destiny of individual worlds, planes of ellipses. Eventually for the first time since launching, and through several of those sudden clicks, a world has appeared on the tapes which is suitable for habitation. If it had been capable of such an act the ship would have heaved a long sigh of relief. The timeless journey seemed near its end. The final duty could begin.

Only the low electrical hum of the wide-awake equipment plays around the empty cabins and gangways. In the lightless storage quarters, food containers are stacked squarely and held fast to walls by strong clips; unused styli fill the drawers, and strapped reference tapes line the walls. Everything is clean and neat and was last touched by the hand of a Final Checker not long before the ship had broken clear of Earth's atmosphere – thousands of years in the past. Throughout the ship cocooned equipment, from the largest crane engine to the smallest needle, awaits the manipulations of non-existent human fingers. The first steps have already been taken towards forming those fingers and the ship begins the continuance of that process.

Deep in their artificial uteri embryos rapidly begin to warm to life from their previously frozen state. The process of birth to the yet unborn two thousand residents of the starship's mother units is accelerated and each embryo in turn becomes a foetus. Eyes, noses and mouths begin to form. Fluids begin flowing, pulses press against elastic arteries, lungs begin to draw breath from the rich air.

The click is no longer alone. It is joined by the noise that issues from hundreds of small throats. A banshee screaming that would send any aware person on board the ship stark raving mad. But there is no awareness – only unconscious children who race towards adolescence and puberty in their plastic cells. Growth rate is accelerated to forty times its normal speed.

Education is in progress. The adults who finally emerge from the cells must be aware of the planet that spawned them. They require a general knowledge of its history. They need their own specialized information which will make them skilled professionals. Above all, they need the knowledge of their purpose for being alive at all.

It is well. Everything moves smoothly towards the finalization of the overall plan. All is in order. The incubator cossets its young; the intelligence units feed their captive pupils with knowledge; the teacher presents them with stimulating material and searches for the expected behavioural changes in their simulated childhoods; voices cry out from dreams with all the babbling of Nimrod's tower; ears hear; fingers grasp; the integument encircles the whole, and carries it towards a promised world. Good. Harmony prevails ... Harmony?

Question? No. No. Then, yes. A vague disturbance. Unease? Search and, nothing. Where? Uncertainty. Inspection and correction – the proper procedure. But what? And where? Alert the defences. Tell them ... tell them ...

The incubator continues its work of weaning and rearing its new batch of charges, the teacher still teaches. What, then, is wrong?

The ship automatically checks its shell for a breach, beginning at one end and working along to the other. The process takes several minutes to complete and when it is over the result is negative. There has been no breach.

Yet there is a positive alien identification somewhere on board.

The registration in the defence system is definite and unmistakable. Not an accident; not an explosion, fissure, escape of gas. There is no drive malfunction to correct, no corrosion in the power storage units, no fires, no floods. The problem is not from any inherent source. It is from the outside, and it has entered. A small, indefinable trace of alien presence.

The defence mechanism comes into action. Torpedo motors spring to life, missile launchers swivel their snouts searching for their target, armaments bristle over the whole shell. The ship is a porcupine of destructive tubes.

What? Where? Who?

Nothing. They can find nothing. The ship is as puzzled as a piece of semi-intelligent machinery can be. It continues to search for the foe, testing the space for several thousand kiloms around the area of the ship for anything positive.

Suddenly the sniffing weapons find a target, two thousand kiloms away, and almost joyfully blast it out of existence. The dust cloud spreads out into space. It was a large innocent passing meteor and now it is many minute meteors, but it is not the intruder. The intruder is still on board the ship. No hairline crack is too narrow for the alien presence, no wire too thin. It slides between closed hatchways, it travels like a current through the wires and along the metal walls. The ship cannot stop it for there is nothing tangible to grapple with. It is as insubstantial as a ray of light, yet with microsecond speed it changes its direction, retreats, dissipates and reforms.

The current travels throughout the ship cataloguing all that it discovers and transmitting it back to its remote users. Finally the knowledge is acquired and the decision taken. The ray re-enters the intelligence units and fuses the internal circuitry into one coagulate mass of plastic and metal. The teachers cease to function halfway through delivering a crucial piece of information – they are irreparable.

Two

Othman was born in the middle of the day's third quarter at the age of thirty Earthyears. He was aware of the sun's rays, warm upon his olive skin, and he opened his eyes slowly to look down the large beak-like nose, past the bearded chin, at his feet some two metres away.

The feet were also large and Othman regarded them thoughtfully before deciding he knew what they were and for what purpose they were designed. He swung himself into a sitting position and full-face into the direct glare of the sunlight making his head spin. After a while he was able to disconnect the various tubes and electrodes from his body leaving small, temporary white scars in their places.

Others were also coming to life on the great wheel of the open-lidded uteri which the ship had gently detached from itself and laid in the long grasses. Some were attempting to find their feet – others were merely lying inside the transparent cocoons staring at the yellow sky, adjusting themselves to their new state of awareness.

Yellow? It should be blue – or – no, that was some other

sky. A sky Othman had been shown in his dreams, but one he would never see in reality. His head began to clear and he climbed unsteadily to his feet to observe his surroundings.

The starship was busy dismembering itself on a grassy clearing not far from the shores of a vast sea. Behind the starship stretched a forest, mountainous and thick with green and other, brighter colours.

Large waxy leaves of some of the plants denoted the infrequency of rain during part of the planet's year and rich blooms, unless they were self-pollinating, suggested the presence of at least insect life. Othman studied the blooms intently – some of them were over eighty centimetres in diameter. He hoped the local insects did not follow the same size pattern. But if that boded ill, the fruit harvest would compensate for the danger. He nodded with satisfaction. Someone spoke to him in his native Arabic tongue. It was a woman.

'This is a beautiful place, but so cold!'

She turned her dark eyes upon Othman and his response was almost immediate. He said quickly, 'How do you know what *cold* is? Beauty yes, you have seen beauty in your mind – but coldness? Perhaps that is a normal temperature for our bodies to cope with but they have not yet adjusted to being outside the uterus?'

When she saw his hostility she was puzzled but reacted similarly.

'I can tell it's cool because I feel uncomfortable. You are also wrong about beauty. We only think what we see is beautiful because the starship has told us what our ancestors considered beautiful. We must follow the guidelines set by our forebears because they're the only ones we have ...'

'Wrong,' interrupted Othman brusquely. 'It's beautiful because ... it makes me feel comfortable.'

They both smiled at this.

'We're lucky,' said Othman, looking at the forests once more. 'They need not have been guidelines – we could have been indoctrinated to accept everything, as we found it here, as perfect. But we were given the chance to decide. A narrow choice I'll grant, for those who sent us were indoctrinated by their own environments and influenced by their own ancestors – but they gave us as much of an unprejudiced choice of what is, or is not beautiful, as they had themselves.'

He moved away from her dark warm body then, for she was beginning to disturb him.

Othman roamed among the waking bodies, occasionally stumbling; like a new-born foal, he had no confidence in his legs. He paused by a man who was donning a blue robe.

'Where are the garments?' he asked the man.

The other pointed to a place where some canisters lay, their tops unclipped and folded cloth poking from their openings. Othman wondered, as he crossed to the canisters, whether some petty pilfering might now take place. Each person was surely entitled to at least two robes – one to wear and one to wash – but some might be tempted to take and hoard more. However, all the robes were blue and all were of the same cut and fabric. There would be no point in stealing. Soon they would be able to design and weave different styles – when the looms were available.

His eyes swung towards the starship which was in the process of carefully taking itself apart and manufacturing new equipment with the parts. The cannibalization units were neatly cutting the shell of the ship into panels which would later be used as tractor bodies and moulded into hollow girders for the necks of cranes. Wiring was stripped from the ship's circuitry for use in vehicles and to provide lighting until accommodation was built. Cannibalization was pre-programmed and the peculiar units with their cutting beams and multi-jointed arms would form part of the general assembly of vehicles and machines that would remain after the metamorphosis had been completed.

Othman watched an engine being craned from the ship's

interior where it had been nestling in its packing for thousands of Earthyears. That was another thing, thought Othman. They were going to have to devise their own system of measuring time.

He dismissed it from his mind – there were too many other aspects of their new world to think about.

Pulling on the robe he had acquired for himself, he moved amongst the crowd staring at the faces. Amongst them, somewhere, was his wife's. He would find her later. What he was looking for now was someone with bearing – someone in authority. Most of the faces belonged to tradesmen, who were distinguishable by their muscular frames and large hands. Othman was an engineer. He had no need for muscles.

Finally he came across a thickset man who was issuing orders and looked as though he had been out of his uterus for longer than most.

'Scouts, gather to me,' the man was calling. 'I am Said Rak, Master-at-Arms and leader of this party ...'

'What are you doing?' asked Othman.

'Are you a scout?' retorted the Master-at-Arms.

Othman snorted. 'Do I look like one?'

The other man began to scrutinize him so he added, 'I'm an engineer.'

'Time enough later for engineers,' said Said Rak. 'Now we must set up the defences. Post sentries and ensure that we are not taken by surprise by any natives.'

'Aren't you over-reacting?' suggested Othman gently. 'The ship would not have landed if there had been traces of technological development in the atmosphere ...'

It was the other's turn to regard Othman coolly. 'Spears can kill as surely as guns,' he replied. 'Listen to a leader's words.'

Othman remained silent. He was moving away from his own field of knowledge into one relatively unknown to him and he had to be careful of not making a fool of himself.

15

'Why do you regard yourself as the leader of this, what shall I call us, tribe?' he finally finished asking.

'Because I am,' replied Said Rak simply. 'It's in my mind. Is the suggestion in yours?'

Othman had to admit that it was not, but he was puzzled. Something was not quite right but he could not put his finger on the reason for his apprehension. There was something missing somewhere. He voiced his opinion to the so-called head of the group. The Master-at-Arms replied. 'You're right in that assumption. Look over there.' He pointed to the wheel of the uteri. Othman looked but could see only people, some of them evidently younger than himself, either lying or sitting around on the grass.

'Well?' he finally answered. 'I see nothing unusual.'

'Look at their faces. Hard.'

Othman stared, first at one, and then another, and finally he reached a conclusion. The distance between himself and the people he was regarding was considerable but the signs were, once the faces had been brought to his attention, unmistakable. The open mouths and the inarticulate limbs.

'They look ...' It was a horrible thought he had to voice and he naturally hesitated. 'Some of them look like morons.'

'Right,' said the Master-at-Arms emphatically. 'Idiots of the first degree. Not an ounce of brains among them – the young ones that is. We'll have to get a doctor to look at them later and then decide what's to be done with them.'

A newly-spawned tractor trundled to life and crossed the clearing to take its place as first in a line of vehicles. One of the young men in question rolled accidentally in its path and stared at it, uncomprehending. The tractor stopped obediently, then after a short wait cautiously circumnavigated the human. The idiot watched it go round him, then giggled and sat up and down hard, knocking all the wind out of his body and changing his expression immediately. Othman winced.

'How in God's name has this happened?' he said, more to himself than to Said Rak.

'I can answer that too,' replied Said Rak, 'though I can't answer why. You'll have to find that out, being an engineer. The reason we are blessed with these clowns is that the intelligence units ceased functioning at a certain stage in their development. For us there was no damage done – our education was completed. But the second batch of births, those whose embryos thawed later than our own, had nothing fed to their brains whatsoever. They're apparently stupid though I imagine we can teach them something – they're like fully-grown babies ...'

'This is terrible,' said Othman. 'You found this out from the ship, presumably?'

'Yes, I've been awake longer than most. Before the ship began its transformation I made a tour of inspection – there were red lights on the panels below the words *Intelligence Units*. They were the only red lights on the whole vast indicator board. All the others were green. I kept it in mind and later put two and two together ...'

Othman was dismayed. And everything, it had seemed, had been going so well! He informed the Master-at-Arms that he, Othman, would not be the one to diagnose the reason for the fault in the units as he was an engineer, not a technician – but he would certainly be interested in the cause of the fault. Would Said Rak keep him informed? The soldier promised he would.

Silandi was certain to be beautiful: both her parents had been so and there was a heritage of beauty throughout the history of both families. Her father had been a high-ranking Arab and had never been nearer to her Indian mother than a thousand miles, since one had once passed through Muscat while the other was in Bombay. As perversity would have it, it was the father who had lived in Bombay. He was the son of an army colonel who had settled in the east after the war. The mother was a member of one of those nomadic Asiatic families that distrusted the stability of a city life which, once the bombs began to fall, proved to be the most unstable of all.

In Silandi's simulated childhood on board the starship, however, her mother and father had lived and worked together, lavishing love on their growing daughter in a big white-walled house situated on the green shores of a large Arabian island.

Silandi was a trained architect. Her skin was a flawless dusty brown and her eyes the blue-black of a tropical mussel shell. She was the wife of Othman.

By the time Silandi had rested on the grass beside her uterus and had gained the strength to walk, cranes, tractors and bulldozers stood like a small army ready to move against the virgin countryside. She too noticed the large blossoms that Othman had seen, and her observations included large thread-like worms with wings but she had no fear of giant insects.

Once erect and with her hair tied tightly behind and falling like a thick black rope down her back to her buttocks, Silandi went in search of her husband. After several inquiries she was told he had last been seen walking down towards the sea. She went to join him after securing a robe.

Othman was staring out over a vast sea of bubbling silt towards a distant shore – a land barely visible from where they stood and distorted by heat waves rising from the mud.

'What is it?' a woman asked, moving to his side. Indo-Arabic from her colouring, he decided.

'What is what?' he replied, rather inanely, and then saw that the person who had intruded on his private thoughts was looking at the mud.

'Oh, that! It appears to be some sort of mineral disturbance – like lava from a volcano. Only this seems to be a more permanent activity. You'll notice later that our only river flows out onto the mud, over there, behind that peninsula' – he pointed towards the place, but the water was hidden from their view – 'and then I suppose it spreads out over the surface and evaporates to begin the cycle once again.'

The woman narrowed her eyes, trying to peer across the sea of bubbles that burst into sprays of sandy gelatinous fluid and left acrid smells weaving through the air.

'What interests you so much?' she finally asked.

Othman did not reply directly. Instead he asked, 'Is that a range of mountains over there? Can you see?'

She looked again.

'It could be hills, falling down towards the shoreline – but you need a distance viewer to see properly. Why don't you go and get one if you're so interested?'

He was mildly irritated by her lack of imagination.

'I shall later – but it won't help. The heat waves will distort the images – and then there's the steam ...'

Othman lapsed into silence for a while. Then when she did not leave him he asked, 'What's your name? It's not Silandi?'

She nodded, smiling up into his face.

'Then you're my wife?'

She nodded again but received no return smile. The sun was beginning to fall now, dragging its reluctant yellow sky behind it, and Silandi turned to go back towards the spot where the starship had landed and friendly company was to be found. Suddenly Othman moved forward and lifted her robe, staring at the body that held dark shadows close to its rounded contours. The sun fell quickly and the shadows glided like small beasts up and across the skin, alternately hiding and revealing what was Othman's.

She pulled the robe down sharply and Othman could see the anger blaze in her eyes in the dying light.

'You are my wife,' he said, indignantly.

'You've already said that once,' she snapped, 'and while I

am willing to acknowledge that fact, I'm not pleased at your display of ill manners and roughness.'

He blew heavily through his nose and he felt his lean face flushing. This female of his was quite a high-minded young woman. Young? Thirty? Well, it was not old and she was certainly beautiful.

'Sorry.' He was curt. 'Next time I'll ask your permission. I didn't realize we were carrying sacred goods – all that sort of thing was supposed to have been left on Earth. All the old religions and their trappings.'

He stressed the last word. This wife will have to be taught, he was thinking, that what appears ill-mannered in a stranger is merely appreciation from a husband.

Finally she laid her hands on his shoulders, for there was little difference in their respective heights, and reasoned with him.

'Please. We must go back. They will be concerned for us.'

Othman realized she was right, and by that time the equatorial darkness had closed around them and he was feeling somewhat afraid. The darkness of the womb had not been as *real* as this – albeit there were large clusters of stars that lit their path.

They climbed the slope towards the encampment and very soon they were able to see the lights. A warm breeze lifted their robes as they climbed, and the scents of the land drifted by, seemingly stronger now the night had fallen. Silandi stumbled, and reached out for his hand which he gave grudgingly, and helped her along. Her hand was smooth and silken. He liked its feel and was about to compliment her when something passed between their eyes and the lights ahead.

'What was that?' he cried, drawing up short. 'Who's there?' he shouted.

Silandi seemed bewildered.

'What is it? What's wrong?' she asked.

'Didn't you see it? Something up ahead – I don't think it was a man. It was hunched – like a beast ...'

'Stop it, you're frightening me,' Silandi whispered, gripping his hand. 'Perhaps it was one of our sentries?'

He said, 'What? Skulking about in the bushes? What for?'

She did not answer, but let go of his hand and ran towards the camp. He followed soon after, more afraid than he was prepared to admit to his wife.

Several large canopies had been erected inside a circle of vehicles and they were challenged as they ran towards them. Silandi called her own name and asked for entrance. Not waiting for an answer, she scrambled over a tractor and into the circle of light where several hundred people were preparing their beds. In the centre of the circle stood Said Rak with a thunderous expression on his face. For some reason Silandi felt compelled to go to him to explain her absence. The man, arms akimbo, clearly desired an explanation.

'Where in God's fire have you been? The roll call was an hour ago ...'

She opened her mouth, ready to deliver a humble apology when a cool though slightly breathless voice spoke from behind.

'Where she has been is my business only – she is my wife and she explains herself to no one but me.'

Said Rak faltered. 'You ... both of you. You are answerable to the community. I am the leader – you must observe the rules ...'

Othman was contemptuous. 'What makes you the leader? Soldiers are never leaders, they follow orders – the orders of the community ...'

A man of medium height climbed to his feet and in a quiet voice said, 'There's something very wrong here.'

Othman pivoted on his heel and stared hard at the smaller man.

21

'You are an oracle?' questioned Othman, meaning to insult the man. 'Or a philosopher perhaps?'

'I am a builder,' replied the other unwaveringly and still in the same quiet tone. 'That's one of the reasons why I think something is not right with our situation. We are all builders, or soldiers, or engineers – there are no philosophers ...'

Othman was calm now. He regarded the builder and saw a staid face. It was a lie. The man was obviously a deep thinker, though Othman knew that if he wished he could take the watchers with him and turn the builder's observation inside-out with mockery. Othman, however, was not a fool.

'Tell us your meaning.'

Said Rak nodded, looking eagerly towards the speaker.

'Just this,' the builder said. 'We don't know who is the leader of these people. We don't know why we are here ... does anyone know why we have been sent?' He addressed the crowd. There were murmurs but no definite answers.

The builder reasoned with Othman, who stood the tallest of the three.

'You have the bearing of a leader ... he, Said Rak, has the authority – but can either of you say that you, and not I, are the one to whom the starship has given the ultimate command?'

No one answered. In that moment Othman was prepared to lie. Something inside him was urging him to reach for the leadership – but that was not the way. Said Rak had opened his mouth and was about to speak. Othman beat his man to it by a split second.

'We none of us know who was chosen because the teacher units were destroyed before we were informed of the name of our leader and also our purpose, but one thing I do know,' he cried dramatically, 'is that we are surrounded by alien beasts and our diligent Master-at-Arms is one of the last to know about it.'

It was a superb stroke and a great babble of fear swept

through the camp. One of the morons screamed shrilly as she smelt the fear-sweat. Said Rak would be a long time recovering his lost credibility from the whimpering host.

Three

Othman was an opportunist and he pressed home his advantage. The following morning the quiet builder, whose name was Jessum, accused him of starting a panic: people had spent the night huddled together in fearful groups, afraid to look out into the night because of what they might see, and afraid not to look because of what might happen if they didn't. Othman took Jessum and Said Rak to the spot where he had seen the alien.

'It was here,' stated Othman, keenly searching the soil. But the ground was hard and showed no prints. Said Rak was dissatisfied.

'I would not call you a liar, Othman,' he said, 'but perhaps you would admit to a mistake?'

Othman's head was down when these words were spoken and he jerked it up to glower at the speaker.

'To accuse me of fantasizing is worse than calling me a liar,' he growled.

Said Rak shifted uncomfortably. Just then Jessum gave a shout from some near-by bushes and they ran to him. He was standing quite still with his back to them as they approached and he said over his shoulder, in the soft tones he usually employed, 'Be careful. Come slowly. There's one of them here.'

Said Rak began to lift a weapon which he invariably carried. Othman gripped the barrel and eased it gently from the soldier's grasp. He let it go but there was protest in his eyes. Cautiously then, they made their way forward to where Jessum was standing.

There was a small tree not far away, on its own among a cluster of rocks, and beneath this stood a stick-thin being, possibly a head taller than Othman. It backed away sharply when the other two humans came into view and when Said Rak smiled encouragingly to hold it there, it turned and ran, awkwardly, like a clown on stilts unused to fast movement.

'Did you see it?' said Jessum, unnecessarily.

Othman replied. 'Yes, of course. Peculiar-looking thing, wasn't it – and such soulful eyes. It would be quite captivating with that fur on if it wasn't so brittle-looking. Didn't seem much harm in it.'

'Can't tell that yet,' said Said Rak.

Nevertheless when they walked back into the encampment Othman called out in a loud clear voice, 'There's no cause for any further alarm – I and my two friends here' – he made the word 'friends' sound like 'assistants' – 'have investigated the possibility of this area being inhabited by hostiles and have made initial contact with what appears to be a harmless, sub-intelligent species of alien. Possibly a tribesman of a low order, but more than likely an animal. We'll let you know the full details as soon as we can ...'

The word was passed around with relief. Othman was dealing personally with the matter. His esteem rose rapidly amongst the people and Said Rak was disgusted at their gullibility.

'He'll lead us into trouble, that one,' he prophesied to Jessum. 'I could take over with my troops, now, but to what good? If we must have a political leader it might as well be a smooth-tongued lizard like Othman as any other ...'

Othman smiled when this was repeated to him later in the day. It meant he would have no more obstruction from Said Rak. His leadership had been accepted.

Othman, Silandi and Jessum were sitting in one of the bubbleskin tents which had been erected by a transformed piece of starship that seemed to have only one objective which it was carrying out with all the speed and relentlessness its motors would allow. Othman had been discussing their position with Jessum.

Silandi spoke then.

'We must consider Jessum's statement of last night with more seriousness than impressing a crowd requires. If you are to be the people's leader, Othman, then you must act like one.'

The engineer flashed her an angry look but acknowledged the point.

'That is taken for granted – you are of course referring to our lack of full knowledge? I have asked a technician to look at the intelligence units and his report is that he cannot see them ever being repaired. It appeared to him that the circuits had received a tremendous overloading of power which resulted in their present useless condition. That does not help us however – our plight is that we are here, wherever here is – let's call it Jessum?' he said with sudden generosity. The modest builder was about to demur when Silandi nodded her approval. He shrugged.

'Jessum,' he repeated.

Othman continued. '... we are here without knowledge of our purpose and seemingly leaderless. One of us *should* be the man – but no one knows who. That is now taken care of – I accept the challenge. The next problem then is – why are we here, on Jessum? We have tractors, but no ploughs. We have enough food for a few years. We have builders and building equipment – but no farm implements or farmers. We have the means to find and smelt metal and to cast implements, but I should have thought that a plough was one of the first priorities in a new colony. Are we a colony?'

Neither of the others answered. They knew no more than he did himself.

Othman pointed upwards.

'Somewhere, out there in space, is our purpose in life. It has been lost amongst the stars and we haven't the means to go looking for it. Our ship is now in useful pieces and the people not fit nor accustomed to space travel in their new state of awareness. We are stuck here, where we stand and we must devise our own purpose...'

'Allah will guide us,' said Silandi, suddenly very much afraid.

Othman's dark eyes stared at her lithe form.

'True, but he will guide fools into the chaos of confusion and wise men into cosmos. I am a wise man and I will lead you to order. Choose a fool at your peril.'

'I thought we had already chosen,' said Jessum drily.

Othman chuckled inwardly at this remark. Jessum was not as dull-witted as his face would have him be.

'What about the computer?' asked Silandi then. 'Won't that tell us what we wish to know?'

'The computer is not an answering service,' replied Othman. 'It is merely a triggering device for its units. The intelligence units needed a signal to begin our education and the main computer provided that – its memory store is part of those units that have been destroyed. There'll be no help from that quarter.'

'What do we do then – wait for divine aid?' said Jessum.

Othman stared out of the tinted bubbleskin at the outside activity. Someone had organized the morons into sitting in a large group. They were all about fifteen Earthyears of age and barely scraping manhood. Othman estimated that they constituted about half of the complement, which was more than he had first imagined. A head count would prove them to be a thousand strong. He judged that these would have been the non-skilled workers of the group since those of thirty years of age, the bright ones, were either tradesmen or professionals. The morons were never intended to be intelligent, but equally they were not meant to be completely and uselessly stupid.

How had this happened? Othman thought. Perhaps those who sent us had underestimated the power generated by two thousand minds and the feedback had created something – an excess of power? – which burned out the units? This seemed a plausible explanation. Who could know what motive force the human brain could conjure up under hothouse conditions?

Without answering Jessum's question Othman asked his wife, 'Are the animals ready yet?'

She nodded. 'We have livestock – goats, sheep and some cattle. Not really enough for ...'

He did not let her finish. 'I'm thirsty,' he said. 'Fetch me a cup of goat's milk.'

'Fetch it your ...' she started to say. But stopped when she saw his eyes. Without another word she rose and passed through the bubbleskin wall. It sealed behind her.

When she was gone Othman said to Jessum, 'You think the young morons were the farmers and the businessmen, don't you, Jessum? Arrested in age as well as intelligence? You believe we are a colony and that we should accept that idea?'

'What else is there to accept – can you think of anything?'

Othman replied. 'I think we should look for evidence of why we are here. Perhaps the planet will give us some clues – we could have been sent to find something. A rare useful mineral ...?'

'And how would we take it back to Earth? On a tractor? Several thousand years late before the journey begins? Be sensible, Othman.'

The other slapped his fist into his palm. 'But we don't know ... there are so many imponderables. It could be anything – you've obviously not got the imagination for leadership, Jessum. We must look. Tomorrow we'll send the one aircraft we've got for an inspection of the hinterland of those distant mountains ...'

'That could be dangerous – we don't know anything about the place.'

'No, and we want to. I say the aircraft goes, and it goes. Find the pilots – I hope to God that they're not among the morons, but it's unlikely.'

Jessum nodded curtly, aware that he had been dismissed, and Othman could see the man disliked himself for accepting such peremptory treatment. Too bad, thought Othman, he will have to learn the hard way.

The builder walked away from the tent with a fire inside his belly. Othman had no right to treat them all like children – he and Silandi were as wise, as old and as qualified in their own fields as Othman was in his. Yet he had this compelling air about him. A forcefulness difficult to resist.

Then he thought, did it matter who led and who followed? He sighed and began asking for the pilots of the aircraft.

Othman had been correct. They were not amongst the morons. He found the two men lounging against their cocooned machine and in easy conversation with one another. Men of action, thought Jessum. Such confidence in oneself was enviable. He instructed the two men to report to Othman early the next morning, asking them to ensure first that their vehicle was in good working order and ready for instant lift-off. They promised they would be there, and to Jessum's disgust their reply came unhesitatingly. Obviously *they* accepted Othman's leadership without question. Then, as he walked away from the men, Jessum realized that they also accepted him, Jessum, as a man of authority. It was a nice feeling to be able to wield power, even from a subordinate position. It also felt heavy, which was the responsibility catching up fast with his previous realizations. He shrugged irritably. Best go and look for his wife, she would be worried that her husband was not interested in her. What was her name? Niandi, or something like that. Pretty woman.

*

Silandi had found the goats and obtained the milk the hard way as the goatherd had been one of the younger passengers of the complement. She carried it carefully back to Othman, stood in front of him, and poured it just as carefully onto the ground at his feet. Then she waited for his anger.

Othman was not angry – he was amused.

'That was a foolish thing to do to your Imam,' he laughed. 'I might have had you beheaded.' He turned and darkened the tent's tint until the skin was opaque. 'Almost as black as your skin,' he smiled.

'You're not our religious leader,' she cried, horrified at the ancient title which he had bestowed upon himself.

'I'm *your* Imam – yours, Silandi's – no one else's. I'm also your lover, and I haven't yet tasted your flesh.' He bit lightly into her ribs through the cloth of her garment. In spite of her anger she felt herself growing excited.

'Don't you ever *ask* for anything? Why do you always *take*?'

'Because it's the way I like to do things,' he replied.

He pulled the garment up around her neck and seized her breasts in his hands. This time she really was angry and she attempted to push him away.

'No, thank you,' he laughed, and then he took her, rapidly, and it was only during the last few movements before his climax that her anger began to turn to passion. Kindly and wisely, he continued after his own needs had been satisfied.

'We have to sow the seeds for the new colony,' he said as they lay, side by side afterwards, and she bit her tongue. Was the man so unfeeling? Perhaps the ship had not given him the simple experience of love when it had endowed him with the various emotions necessary for a balanced individual?

He had said something to her and she had not been concentrating.

'What was that?' she asked.

'I must get a falcon,' he repeated, 'for hunting and for

company. They did send hawks and falcons with us, I hope?'

'I saw some cages full of birds while I was with the animals – why do you want one so badly? Do you think it will add to your impressive image? A hawk upon the wrist of our ruler, the Imam. See how proud they are, man and bird,' she mocked, 'see how they both defy the wind and stoop from a great height. The hawk-nosed Imam, Othman, and his tame predator – cold-eyed killers who fly the currents of power ...'

'That's enough,' he snapped, then in softer tones, 'I had a falcon as a boy – I know, not a real falcon for neither of us was flesh in that childhood – but as you are aware, the memory is real. I remember when that Saker died it broke my heart and I cursed God. A natural reaction from a boy whose world had exploded. He was fast, that falcon. He could catch a gazelle in full run and bring it down in clouds of sand. I loved him ...'

He was silent for some time after that. Then he rose and went out of the tent leaving Silandi alone.

So he could love, she thought bitterly. A *bird*.

She pulled her robe down over her smooth skin and tried not to feel sorry for herself. After all, she wanted Othman out of all the men she had seen, and no other. She supposed this was a result of the teachers artificially directing her feelings towards Othman. She could think of no alternative reason. He was not a beautiful man. Handsome perhaps, but then handsome men are, and should be, a shade away from ugliness. He was not a good lover – his mind was on hawks while his body played out its rhythms of passion. She had wanted it to be a tender experience her first real time, and one which she could look back on, identifying exactly her emotions at the time of the act. But were things ever that simple? Perhaps it was always a whirlpool of strange desires, anger, love and hate?

She stroked a sore breast with her hand. Perhaps the next

time it would be less of a maelstrom? It was too soon to judge. Much too soon. Perhaps he would even kiss her lips and whisper her name softly in her ear to let her know that he was not hunting in his mind, but making love to his wife in the flesh.

Four

They had been given the names of Allah and Mohammed, and they were told that this was the God and his prophet – all the other beauties of Islam were withheld from them, for the Moslem senders wisely realized that the activities that played such an important part in their own lives would have no meaning on another world.

Why tell them of the Caaba, the black stone itself from space, when they would never touch its smoothness?

Why tell them of a pilgrimage to Mecca which they could never make? And which direction they should face in prayer when Earth was lost to their eyes?

How could they give alms to a beggar when there were no poor? They were all as those that kissed the Caaba – robed alike and one man as simply dressed as another.

And what of the great book that guides men to their destinies? The book of *suras* of which all but one begin, 'In the name of Allah, the Merciful, the Compassionate'. Shall they be told of the Koran?

But the paradise of the Koran – the afterworld – is a promise of cool fountains, shade and high-breasted maidens. What if the ship finds a freezing waterworld? The delights promised by the Koran are for a desert-dwelling people. The Koran's hell is a place of boiling liquids and blazing fires. Who would work to avoid such a place where men froze or drowned in icy waters?

Those that sent them reluctantly decided that they should

be religiously unarmed save for the name and implications of Allah and his servant. They would have to find their own path to the Lord. The poetry of the Koran did not touch their ears. They did not hear of the Lord of the Ladders. The Night of Kadar would remain a mystery to them until their individual deaths, and he who created men from clots of blood would be as just, merciful and compassionate with them, as he was to the knowing ones.

The noise of the aircraft had frightened the moron. He had enjoyed the soothing hum of men and women in prayer, but shortly afterwards some of them had dragged a machine from its cocoon and shouting and bustle had begun around the shiny object. The moron had liked the shining of the monster but not its size. The machine was as large as a dozen men and soon it had started a squealing which hurt the moron's ears and made him back away with his heart beating fast in his breast. He had turned and tried to retreat and now he was lost in the forest.

His name, although he did not know it, Fdar, and had the teachers given him an education he would have been a messenger boy. As it was his mind was full of infant thoughts and infant dreams – a pretty alien bee with a toxic sting was an object of slowly-formed interest and beauty, and a harmless red beetle the manifestation of terror.

Fdar wandered through the trees, allowing the soft fronds to caress his skin with their dew-damp surfaces, and liking the touch of their fine, under-leaf hairs. Discovering a cave, he stumbled towards its entrance, then stopped and turned away because the darkness was like a solid wall before him. His mind swirled with transient thoughts, none of which let any of their clay stick upon its walls.

He saw the yellow sky streaked with the white of cloud and tried to touch it. He hurt his bare toes on the pieces of fallen branches and became angry and shouted nonsense sounds at the sticks. He was happy with the balls of fluff that floated between the flowers.

Then suddenly he came upon a clearing, in the middle of which stood a man. Only it was not a man. It was a tall brown animal which looked like a man except that it was very thin and had large, saucer eyes. For a few minutes alien and human regarded each other with fear in their faces – then somehow each of them knew that the other was harmless and the tenseness went out of their bodies, the moron's giving a small shudder. Still they stood without moving and did nothing. It was as if each were trying desperately to reach inside the other without the possibility of verbal communication. Then the alien bent down and picked up something from the floor, offering it to the human. It was a fruit – one of many that were scattered around. As the fruit was passed between hand and hand something happened in Fdar's mind that made him blink. A colour – a streak of brightness – had travelled through his idle brain circuitry. He reached out again and the alien put its fingertips on the backs of the moron's hands and the idiot's mind flowered with small explosions of colour. The colours became significant after a while and took form and rooted their meanings in his brain. And the alien spoke as it knew how, into a completely receptive mind – for the sponge it filled had been previously dry and was able to absorb all the language patterns it could offer.

The native and the immigrant stood for some while with their hands clasped, and though the moron could sense the alien's bewilderment at not receiving any response to his communication both instinctively knew that the other was a friend.

Fdar eventually broke away and found that when he thought of it he was no longer afraid of the noise and bustle of the encampment. He had no desire to return, but there was also no feeling of anxiety accompanying the consideration that he might be forced to go back, or come across the place accidentally. He was not suddenly charged with knowledge after coming into contact with the alien but he had gained a certain awareness which, before the meeting, had been missing. What was more important, he knew where to go for another infusion.

Once away from the native, Fdar wandered aimlessly, occasionally disturbing creatures small and large with his softfootedness, but although he did not know it at the time there were no dangerous beasts. His new home on the island was a haven for herbivores.

Eventually he reached the sea of quicksand which the planet chosen by their starship forced up through the fissures in its mantle and kept warm and live and in its present syrupy state with its hot gases from the core. There he followed the shoreline around until he came to a spot where two men stood under a shiny machine and moved their mouths making rhythmic sounds.

'Well, are you satisfied now that it's an island?' said the pilot. Then he added, 'What's this – one of our people so far from the camp?'

Othman turned and saw Fdar and noted the vacant expression on the moron's face as he stumbled along looking at the sky and treetops around him.

'It's one of our idiots,' replied Othman. 'He's obviously wandered away from the others. We'll take him back with us.'

Othman's attention then turned again to the view from the far side of the island. It was one of complete desolation as far as the horizon in the distance. Only the momentary domes of gas broke the monotony as they formed into blisters that were sometimes a kilometre in diameter, then either collapsed suddenly in folds of dark skin, or burst. It was a depressing scene and Othman's brow furrowed. Already he was beginning to feel the claustrophobic tension to which Earthmen had once given the nickname 'island madness'. Othman's childhood had been spent in the wide deserts of his mind. He understood the semi-liquid desert before him. He did not understand the mound of soil which held him prisoner.

'Let's go back,' he said to the pilot. 'Bring him with us,' he pointed to Fdar.

The pilot nodded and gently ushered Fdar towards the aircraft. The moron did as he was told, and when the engines whistled out their noises he did not cry out or struggle for release.

Back at the encampment which, as the day progressed, was gradually becoming a more permanent-looking place of residence, Othman announced to Jessum his intention of sending the aircraft over the sea to the mountains on the far side.

'We have to know what's over there,' he said. 'We came here to find a planet, not a tiny spit of soil in the middle of an uncrossable ocean.'

Jessum shook his head. 'Too dangerous,' he muttered. 'They ... we don't know what's over there. There could be anything at all.'

Othman stroked the feathers on the nape of his Saker falcon's neck and envied the bird its ability of natural flight. To be a bird was to be supreme above all things. Jesses and bells took away none of the predator's dignity. The invisible wires attached to human feet were far more enslaving than the tangible thongs dangling from the Saker's ankles.

'I say they go,' answered Othman, and began striding to where the pilot lounged heavily against his machine. Othman explained what he wanted and the man nodded. He was quite willing to find out what was behind the mountain ridge in the distance and he was confident of the machine's mechanical condition. If the co-pilot could be found they would start immediately. Othman was pleased but suggested the pilot wait until the following day to have as many light hours before him as possible.

*

The next morning the whole camp ceased working to watch the aircraft take off on its journey.

'Be sure to keep in constant touch,' said Othman.

'Don't worry, you'll be up there with us,' answered the pilot. Then the engines to the aircraft began their discordant whistling once again and the machine rose into the sun-washed sky.

The crowd watched it move out over the ocean and dwindle to a tiny speck of silver, but since they were not permitted to listen in on the conversation between Said Rak, who was handling the communications, and the crew of the aircraft they quickly lost interest and moved away to various tasks. There were cameras in the nose of the craft this time and Othman was able to follow the progress of the crew on the viewers.

Bumpy thermals hampered the aircraft as it flew out over the ocean and Othman had warned the men to keep a keen eye ready for the formation of giant gas bubbles. There was a danger that they would be robbed of their air as hot sub-surface gases forced their passage skywards after a bubble had burst. It had been evident to Othman earlier, however, that the island was the high point of a ridge that travelled out under the quicksand from the mainland and as long as the aircraft followed this ridge no bubbles would break directly beneath it.

As the craft approached the mainland on the far side it began climbing to meet the lip of the cliffs that fell sharply down towards the mud.

'By God, these are higher than they look from the island,' said the voice from the speaker. 'Not mountains – a plateau; kilometres high. We may have to use oxygen masks ... it's getting colder – can you see the snow?'

The three men on the island could indeed see the snow. Jessum was adamant that the aircraft should return immediately but Othman brushed away his fears.

'We have to know whether that plateau falls away down into a valley. Whether the land is hospitable.'

'Why?' questioned Said Rak. 'This island is big enough to contain our group. Admittedly it's narrow, but the length more than compensates for that.'

The leader said nothing. He merely urged the crew of the aircraft to continue their journey.

On the screen they watched the aircraft pass over the top of the cliffs into a white world of ice and snow. A blizzard was in progress and movement was slow. The aircraft's engines faltered in the thin, freezing atmosphere, and the pilot gave the first indication that he was alarmed.

'I think we'd better turn back now, Othman. As you can see, there's a slight slope to the surface under us – can you see it? – which might lead to lower ground eventually, but I would prefer to get back to the warm air below. There are some strong winds up here too – I don't like it very much ...'

'Come back then ...' Othman began in a tone which suggested contempt of the pilot's fears, but as he was speaking the aircraft tilted violently. On the speaker they heard the co-pilot scream loudly into his microphone. The aircraft was eventually righted but the screen was a mass of white and dark flecks which flashed in from all directions.

'Ice,' they heard a voice say. 'Pieces of ice as big as fists ...'

Then the screen went blank and all they could do was sit and listen to a noise resembling that of stones hitting the tin roof of a shack. The bombardment continued, growing louder by the minute, until finally a high-pitched cry of terror sounded above the battering on the aircraft's hull. Then came the short blast from the speaker which turned Said Rak's face the colour of the snow country they had just surveyed. The Master-at-Arms called again and again for the distant crew to answer. Jessum studied his feet, his arms folded tightly over his chest.

Othman said, 'I told them to return,' in a quiet, bitter tone. 'Now we've lost them ... and the aircraft.'

Five

Among the library of programming tapes Othman hoped he would be able to discover the plans for a large transport aircraft, but after weeks of running vast numbers of tapes through the monitor he could find little that would lift men off their feet and carry them skywards. There was a set of plans for a hovercraft and Othman had no doubt they could construct one, but it would be a dangerous business to cross the mud in a hovercraft. Such a machine would not only be subject to the hot gases which would, without a doubt, overturn it, but also to the side-winds the gases would create along the ridge. There was the problem too of constructing enough carriage space within the vehicle to carry animals as large as camels. They could not afford to leave any of the livestock behind. Besides, he convinced himself, the vehicle would need to be small since the materials they had would limit them, and even if they could carry four passengers per trip the thousand animals and two thousand people would take Earthyears to transport. Reluctantly he decided to discard the hovercraft plans. He wanted to move *all* his people. Not one or two.

There were also plenty of tapes for pilotless missiles available but none of them were practicable for use as an aircraft. They were in the main merely tubes fitted with explosive devices – not difficult to manufacture, for the giant ship had brought with it many chemicals and already the mining equipment had located a workable source of iron ore and cementite, and traces of nickel were also evident.

Why so many tapes for missiles? The senders had obviously wished them to be well-protected.

Somewhere on the planet Jessum he was sure he would find the key to their existence, their purpose, and he was prepared to expend all his energies in that direction – the energies of himself, his people and his machines.

An insect settled on his neck and he slapped at it irritably. They were extremely bothersome, the insects of Jessum, and had it not been for the tireless efforts of the ship's medical unit, probably dangerous. Othman's shoulders and the calves of his legs were covered in small red patches where the nerves in his skin had flared. Some were bleeding where he had scratched them during his sleep.

Rising, he went to the wall of the bubbleskin and walked through. It was a cold day and raining on the outside, but the water felt fresh on his face and it soothed the irritating insect weals.

He stood for a moment letting the rain soak into his hair and beard. Before him construction work continued in spite of the downpour and from beneath a canopy Jessum was busy directing operations on a tall, thin tower which was attached to the corner of a building. One of the stickmen – the planet's natives, so nicknamed by the ship's people – stood near by observing the tower, running his eyes up and down the length of the stone lance. Around him were six or seven of the morons. They were looking at the stickman, regarding him with a certain awe. Occasionally one of them would reach out and touch a brown limb. Othman made a mental note to put a stop to the casual way in which the stickmen wandered in and out of the area. It emphasized that security was weak, even if the natives had been found to be harmless. He would speak to Said Rak.

'What in God's name is that supposed to be?' called Othman above the hissing of the rain on the red clay ground.

Jessum looked in the direction of the voice and smiled nervously.

'Have you only just noticed it?' he called back. Othman felt the bite of a reprimand from a subordinate but suppressed his anger. Better to ignore the remark than to point out that he had been working too hard to notice anything these last two months.

'I asked you what it was, Jessum,' said Othman. 'You're a builder, not a Greek philosopher. I don't expect my questions to be answered in kind.'

The builder glowered.

'It was designed by your wife – I should have thought you could have guessed what it was. It seems obvious to everyone else – it's a gravity-feed water tower,' he ended hastily as Othman began stepping forward, his face dark with annoyance.

Othman reached the canopy and slowly raised his eyes from Jessum's flinching look to the thin, round tower which terminated in a blue cupola decorated with arabesque figurework.

'*That* is a water tower?'

Jessum said defensively, 'Utilitarian architecture can also be aesthetically pleasing to the eye without detriment to its function.'

'Did she teach you that?' snorted Othman. 'How much water does it hold?'

Jessum told him and Othman was surprised. She was obviously using the full height of the tower for storage and not just the cupola. He said to Jessum, 'You know I don't encourage the use of traditional structures unless they employ the only methods which will carry out the task. Our fathers and mothers used this design for religious buildings – it is mockery to adopt the same lines, which incidentally are not the best – operationally.'

'Silandi didn't ...'

'Don't start quoting my own wife to me, Jessum,' shouted Othman. He looked impatiently about him. 'What are we doing anyway? I gave no instructions to build a city ...'

On all sides the buildings were beginning to take shape and they were mostly of the traditional type associated with Othman's childhood. Othman had asked Silandi and Jessum to organize a semi-permanent residence but there was nothing in the nature of a transit camp in these buildings – they were built to last for ever.

'Where's Silandi?' he said softly.

'I'm here,' replied a voice behind him. 'I heard you shouting halfway across the encampment.'

Her face was defiant and she looked less willing to budge from her opinions than one of her buildings from their foundations.

'What's happening here, woman?' Othman rounded on her. 'I told you to start building an encampment, not a capital. You want your name to be architecturally immortalized? That chance will come later. Now we work towards another goal ...'

'What goal? We're here to build a colony, aren't we? Why else would we be sent?'

He hesitated, seeing her genuinely puzzled, and having nothing to offer her said rather lamely, 'I don't feel it's right – we should be doing something else – I know it, I feel it inside ...' he smashed a fist against his bare chest where the tunic split following the line of the sternum. Already the women were altering the robes – adding pieces and reshaping the cloth: Silandi had cut the split in Othman's robe to make it different from others.

She answered him, 'Well, the rest of us don't feel it – all we feel is the need to build homes and settle down and have children. That's our function in life.'

'Ha!' he spat scornfully. 'What are we? Cattle? Have we been put out to pasture by a disillusioned race? – or are we adventurers, seeking new experiences? Time later for founding cities – now is the time to satisfy the inner need. Stop work on these monuments to Earth – tomorrow we begin to find out where we are. I want surveys done of every inch of this island. I want the continental shelf mapped as far out into the quicksand as we can safely go.'

'But . . .' she began.

'But what?' he cried. 'But you want to sit down on your backside and grow fat? But you want to build brick insulations around families until they don't know each other any more? This is a tribe, not a population. We are Bedu, not gamin. You will do as I say, woman, and no more of your questions.'

He stormed away, his cheeks still quivering with anger, and roughly pushed aside a moron who was holding the hand of a stickman. Othman paused in mid-stride.

'That sort of thing has to stop too!' he thundered. 'All of our morons are turning into homosexuals . . . holding hands with the natives,' he said scornfully.

'How clever of you,' replied Silandi sweetly, 'to be able to tell us what sex the native is, when even our doctors cannot.'

Othman looked back at her, then at the native standing like a brown, brittle tree, unbending in the wind and rain. He shook his head quickly and continued striding to the shore below. On reaching it he threw himself to the ground and stared at the rain falling on the quicksand and instantly forming tiny streams. The air chilled his skin as he looked out into the rain which veiled the distant plateau from view. Even now, as he looked out into a wall of water, he felt a yearning to touch the solid rock of the distant cliffs. That morning, he had wandered down to the beach before anyone was awake in the camp and had found the air clear and sharp. The stegasaurus back of the distant land had been abnormally visible then, and he had stared hard at it, trying to find some meaning in his desire to reach it. What was it that pulled him? A cloud of birds came winding and wheeling toward the island, and then, on reaching it, fell on a bush like a shower of hand-thrown paper twists. There were many birds that flew over the quicksand from the mainland and Othman envied them all their wings.

Perhaps there was civilized life there? A race of intelligent stickmen perhaps? Not like the cretins of this island. Morons?

Yes, that was it. That was why they got on so well together, the human imbeciles and the natives. They were two of a kind. Well, what harm was there? Best leave them to it. The stickmen, funnily enough, were not herd creatures. They were content to be alone. They wandered in and out of the camp sometimes but bothered no one, and lately Othman had noticed that the morons had taken to wandering off by themselves into the forest. It was good that there was nothing in there that could really harm them. One or two annoying insects perhaps – but then they did not seem to bother the morons any more than they did the stickmen.

'It must be the insipid blood,' he said aloud to himself. 'Too watery for their taste ...'

Suddenly, as he stared at the quicksand, he saw a movement, a horizontal movement – not a bubble. The spot upon which his gaze was transfixed was about a metre from the edge of the shore. Resting his head on his hand he held the point with his stare, trying to discern a shape. Something had surely stirred the mud – but what? After about two minutes of keen study he was startled to make out a circle of small black pebbles which looked back at him with what seemed to Othman to be alien malevolence.

'Wha ...' he jerked backwards, in fright. The eyes remained balanced on the mud and he recovered his breath, searching for a rock as he did so. His groping fingers finally found a sizeable stone and he heaved it at the creature in the artless manner of someone unused to throwing missiles. It landed half a metre to the left of the ring of eyes but that was close enough, for the animal was broad and flat. It slid away at a tremendous rate over the top of the quicksand, its body a full two metres in breadth. Othman pulled in his stomach in revulsion. If it had touched him he would have fainted. He loathed smooth creatures.

His loathing soon fired his frustration for he realized that the creature was heading in the direction of the mainland. Why was it that a low, despicable mudskate was permitted to cross the ocean of quicksand when Othman had to sit helplessly on the firm ground of the island?

As he was sitting in miserable contemplation one of the morons, a girl, came to join him, squatting quickly by his side and staring out across the simmering wastes. Two people, far away from each other intellectually, yet both human and warm-blooded. An engineer and an idiot from the same world, thought Othman, both as helpless as each other. One obviously happier than her contemporary: the result of her ignorance. Othman quoted, 'See the happy moron, she doesn't give a damn. I wish I were a moron – my God, perhaps I am?' Instead of an engineer, he added bitterly to himself. The moron smiled at this gentle treatment from Othman. Then Othman cried 'Engineer! Of course!'

He jumped to his feet and ran back to the camp. On reaching the edge he slowed to a walking pace and regained his breath before striding along its puddled streets. He saw his wife and lieutenant still by their water tower.

'Jessum, Silandi – I have our purpose. It came to me as I sat on the shore. We are going to build a bridge to the mainland – a causeway. We begin tomorrow.' His eyes showed none of the fire of enthusiasm for the project which he felt inside. It was the stern delivery of an order.

'A ... causeway?' Jessum faltered, '... but the distance?' Rain dripped from their faces as they stared at him.

'So it will take us a year – or two – or a hundred. What else have we to do?' Othman said.

'But our work ... the town ...' said Silandi.

'Damn the town. This is real work – this is our purpose! I'm going to draw up the plans. Tomorrow we cut wood.' He strode away, leaving them standing like statues.

The word tumbled from mouth to mouth, swiftly. They were to build a causeway to the mainland – Othman had decided. They would begin tomorrow.

Six

To tell if a woman is truly beautiful you need to study her face while she lies sleeping, when all the animation has fled her features and her personality is buried deep within the brain; her bewitching eyes hidden beneath twitching lids and the curving of the mouth slackened to an open noose; when the cosmetics, be they the natural effect of wind or sun on skin, or artificial additives, enhancing where nature was not quite as deft as a woman's skill, are absent. This is the time to study closely and at leisure, as Othman did Silandi, while the sunlight fell yellow upon her dark skin, spotlighting imperfections, and emotion was missing from her proud face. Any woman can be vivacious, eye-catching, insipidly pretty, magnetically attractive, and can mesmerize her audience with the hypnotic tricks of movement passed from Eve downwards through all her female descendants, while she is full of life and vigour, but it is a rare beauty that can withstand such an inspection and have her husband say, 'You must truly be the most perfect of Allah's creations.'

She opened her eyes.

'That is blasphemy – but it does me good to hear it.'

Othman, caught out, hastily pulled away.

'We start today,' he said in a tone which implied that efficiency was to be the key-word throughout the exercise. 'The causeway begins its life. I want Jessum to inspect the local timber for its suitability for use as piles. Also I want to test the depth of the quicksand at the point that the natural ridge begins ...' He reached for his robe but her hand grasped his wrist.

'You cannot wake me in that manner, and then turn and run. A wife has some rights – do I have to demand them?'

He stared into the eyes, no longer heavy with sleep. Slowly he let the robe fall loosely to the floor.

Silandi was born from the starship a sexually-aware virgin. That is to say, the awareness was gathered during her simulated childhood: a dream that had been reality to her, but being a dream it had been uncontrollable, forming her personality with its unexpected twists and turns. A dream of reality, if that will define it, stimulated by the ship, but allowed to gather momentum by feeding itself from the vast store of edited memories in the banks of tapes.

Her teenage years had been spent on a large island immediately off the Eastern coast of Arabia which was then known as Qalala. From the outset she had not been one of those girls content to look and be looked at. She wanted to compete, especially with the men, and her happiest moments were spent on horseback. She once rode in the Qalala races. This in itself is a feat which attracts admiration, for the horses are all half-broken Arab stallions, more interested in fighting each other for the supremacy of a non-existent herd of mares than in winning a race. They are also ridden bareback.

Silandi owns a horse called Sham-san, a sturdy, thick-limbed animal with iron-hard neck muscles. The very first time she rides him she is taken out into the desert and spends all her energy battling for control. Finally her young arms, aching with the constant effort of holding in Sham-san's head, relax, and the beast snorts triumphantly before taking off on its powerful legs over the hot sand and deep into the wastes. In the beginning her wet-clothed body delights in the coolness of the rushing wind but when the stallion shows no signs of tiring she begins to become anxious.

Sprigs of steam hiss from the beast's nostrils and his unshod hooves make multiple explosions in the soft sand. The muscles move like hard shells beneath his sweat-smooth coat with the rhythm of his run, and his eyes stare at his destination point a thousand miles away. Beneath Silandi the desert flows like an unending river of brown water.

For two hours the stallion drums the hollow world with his hard hooves, awakening the quick creatures of the desert and sending these scuttling to their hiding places away from the thunder. At ground level the earth vibrates and the tremors are felt for miles around the points of impact. This is probably the greatest single event in the existence of many of these lowly forms, and afterwards the peace that descends somehow seems more than the quiet with which the day began.

Finally they come to the foot of a range of hills and still the stallion beats upon the floor below, but the pounding becomes less musical and without warning he slows to a walking pace, his chest and lungs creaking like old leather.

Silandi considers: there is little point in turning back. Evening is coming on, the sky is red above the folded hills and the desert air begins to chill as all the heat of the day dissipates quickly into the atmosphere. Not far away is a group of caves she once visited when a schoolgirl. She decides to spend the night in one of them.

The caves look dark from the outside, and frightening, but around the entrances and on the slopes are scattered sheep, for the hills are the hinterland of the cultivated coast on the far side of the narrow desert over which she has just ridden. The shepherds could not be far away. She calls, twice. On the second cry she receives a response and heads towards the sound which comes from above her.

The short climb takes her, pulling the now submissive horse behind, to the entrance of another cave in which a fire glows warmly. Over it and almost within its flames sits a man. He is old to Silandi, perhaps forty-five, with dark skin roasting in the flaring wood. He wears a hide jacket, cracked and worn with use, over a sheepskin vest and his body bears the bulky, heavy frame of a fighter. One of the short sleeves of the sheepskin is empty. On his head is a ragged headcloth of a Bedu.

Sham-san allows himself to be hitched to a gnarled stump of what used to be a bush and suffers a pinch, tempered with affection, on his wet nostrils, for taking his mistress far from safety.

'May I share your fire, shepherd?' She receives a nod and sits down. His eyes remain upon the flames. The wood spurts blue and orange light.

He says, 'I am no shepherd. I am a soldier.' He points the stick he holds at the sky, aiming it at a star.

Silandi gestures. 'Then whose are all these beautiful animals?'

She notices for the first time his bandolier, empty of cartridges and stained with berry-juice spit.

'I am a soldier who must keep sheep. What year is this?'

'If you are of the Islamic faith then it is 1358,' she replies. He turns his face towards her.

'Do I look like an unbeliever? I am one of the fighters of the Imam of Yemen. A royalist and a patriot,' he stares moodily into the fire. 'We lived in the hills and swooped down like hawks upon our enemies. I was young then and I did not care that flour was scarce and my belly groaned in hunger. All I cared for was glory – the glory of myself in the eyes of the Imam. The revolutionaries held the cities and because of that they won, pushing out the old order and installing the new, but the Yemen remained – beautiful and green, its rivers running towards the sea, but never quite completing the journey ...'

His head snaps up. 'And you ask me my faith – it is here, in the soil of Arabia!' He points to the grime in the creases of his unwashed skin.

She shrugs. 'Shepherds are a raceless breed. They wander the world with one face, sunburnt, starburnt – ruggedly mapped like their outdoor home.'

His eyes remain on her face – they are still, and she wonders if they are unseeing.

'A poet,' he replies at last. 'Girl poet with a young girl poet's body ...' He is not blind. 'Perhaps you are here in search of physical adventure with an ageing soldier who keeps sheep?'

She half-rises, frightened now, but he waves her down and turns his attention to the fire.

'Don't worry. I'm not interested in the bodies of young women. If I was I would be living in the city like everyone else. I would be clean and smell sweetly of false odours – there are softer women than you in those places, I know. I lived there once, for a while. But I soon grew tired of moving from box to box. Did you know that men and women no longer need to make children together? They can even make babies in bottles ...'

'I know,' Silandi replied quietly. 'I am one of those children. I am Silandi, as I am, and this is a dream I am living. I know this, that at this moment my body lies in a box, tens of thousands of years from now, light-years away in space, and you are not really here and I am not really here ... we are ghosts, you and I.'

'In that case' – the shepherd's eyes crinkle – 'it would not matter if we made love, here in the firelight, for ghosts cannot feel the melting of hot flesh ...'

She says hastily, 'But it would matter, for everything is real to me – and you know that you are no ghost to yourself.'

'I am the spirit of what was once a soldier.' He spits a bullet-like globule into the flames, making them hiss. 'That is what I am ...'

'You live all alone,' she says sadly. 'No one does that any more – at least, so very few of us. Why, you don't even know the year in which you live. Have you stopped counting your age? You don't look ancient enough to be a sage.'

He turns and at last he smiles. 'I know the year – I wanted to see if you did ...'

Later, lying by the fire, she hears him whispering a *salaam* to the moon – in the traditional manner that Arab Moslems use

49

when greeting one another. She answers him softly, '*Alaikum as salam*,' and for a moment he is puzzled, then he says, 'Ah yes, you are the daughter of the moon. You travel the night in your little black box ...'

Then they both fall into a silence that is occasionally broken by the sheep disturbing loose rocks, or the horse releasing a bored-sounding and drawn-out snort. Silandi dislikes the night. It is the time when she is unable to rationalize her fears. The sounds come to her from all the corners of the Earth and in those sounds are the irrational fears of her fellow creatures: the shuffling of the kite on its perch; the pi-dog with its ears full of ticks, always running from something – even as it advances to one place it is retreating from another; the shepherd, stiffening at the snuffling of his own gentle sheep. The real enemies are so few, she thinks, yet their shadows all join with darkness to fall over the whole world. One in a thousand noises at which we start is the sound of the enemy's coming. Only the cat seems to know which is the one discordant click in the thousand. He hears and knows.

Throughout the night she listens to the shepherd and smells the thick tea he stirs in an old tin can. She knows she is safe, for though he was once a soldier, he is now a shepherd. She reads it in his face. There are some faces as uncomplicated and roughly drawn as cave-wall frescoes: faces of shepherds that were never as young as the minute-old lambs that they wear like scarves; faces that eternally rest on wooden staves, hawking and spitting, and splitting scrublands of beard with grins; faces as raceless as their trade, shouting the soundless greetings of men who work alone.

Seven

The first pile was hammered into place at about noon five days later. Othman was afraid that the ridge might be formed of solid rock and the wooden pile would split or fray uselessly. He had had a metal collar placed around the neck of the pile to prevent fraying at that end but he was impatient to get the first supports in place and was reluctant to spend time in fixing a metal tip to the other end. The pile went in with effort but it did not split.

Felling the trees then began in earnest and the forest became a bedlam of cries and shrieking timber as machines cut down hardwood giants and dragged them towards the shore of the quicksand under the supervision of the men.

'This is real work,' said one man to another. 'Building houses is too slow to give satisfaction. The trees come down quickly and easily, and for a good purpose. Othman says there is a better land for founding a city on the far side – I was never one for islands myself. It's too claustrophobic for my tastes ...'

Man is an artist at destruction, even though his intentions may seem pure. Ten, a hundred, a thousand years to grow a tree, and ten minutes to bring it to the ground. The longer it has been standing, the more satisfaction as it falls. Not always, for man is not devoid of a feeling of guilt – only when it can be justified by need. But the trees of Jessum were not quick to die, as Othman was to find out later.

Jessum, the builder, also threw himself into the work, for brave ventures capture even the dullest imagination, and excitement and enthusiasm are their own generators. Silandi remained aloof from the project because there was no place for an architect. She did not seem disapproving however. Said Rak continued his own work of protecting the encampment that was now a township, at the same time as loaning some of his soldiers to Othman for use as labourers. Because Othman did not wish to strip Said Rak of his position, he allowed the Master-at-Arms to keep up the pretence of posting sentries and making patrols into the interior of the island. To have demanded all the men under Said Rak's command would have destroyed the soldier's spirit, and Othman needed the support of the faithful, doglike Said Rak as an insurance against future troubles. Othman knew that the first flush of enthusiasm would melt when the hard work was no longer viewed as invigorating, and the boredom of repetitive tasks outweighed the desire to complete a long-distance project. Said Rak was not the brightest of companions, but as long as he felt needed and had no reason to doubt his importance he would stand by his leader, an immovable rock.

A month after work on the causeway had begun, Said Rak was speaking to Othman concerning the natives.

'They don't like us cutting down the trees,' he said. 'They hinder the men and they seem to be encouraging the morons to do the same.'

Othman was standing at the end of the causeway, which now extended some considerable distance out into the quicksand. Faintly, on the horizon, the distant cliffs of the mainland glittered. Around the two men the work continued unhampered by the heat of the midday sun.

'It's difficult,' Othman replied, 'to see how morons can be encouraged to do *anything*. They do not, after all, have any minds to respond to encouragement ... are you now telling me that they're gaining in intelligence?'

There was a puzzled expression on Said Rak's face as he considered these words.

'Well, I hadn't thought about that – they seem to club together, the morons and the sticks. I haven't heard any of them speak yet. If they were becoming more intelligent wouldn't they be saying one or two words?'

'Possibly,' replied Othman. 'I suspect that they are mimicking the natives – I can't believe the natives have persuaded them to help their cause, even though it is a right and a just one ...'

Said Rak looked dumbfounded, and Othman smiled down at him.

'You find that surprising? That I should recognize that without the forest the natives will be homeless, and might possibly starve, since they live off the fruit that grows on the trees?'

'Frankly, yes,' replied the soldier with a stubbornly defiant set to his jaw. Othman knew that Said Rak enjoyed being what the soldier considered *slightly insubordinate*. He was aware that it gave the man a feeling of satisfaction to be in the privileged position of Othman's trusted general and *being frank* with his leader was one of those privileges which Said Rak would quickly stamp on if the words had come from any mouth but his own. Only he, as the right hand (and perhaps Jessum as the advisor) was allowed to speak his mind to the Great Man.

'Well, it surprises me too,' Othman remarked.

This went beyond Said Rak, who at that moment stepped aside to allow a workman access to the crane that was lowering the ten-metre-long cable that would span two piles and form a bent.

'I don't understand you,' he said at last.

'I mean,' grunted Othman, 'that it was my wife who brought the fact to my attention.'

Said Rak indulged in a smile at this.

Othman continued, 'However, I am aware of my duty and we shall endeavour to persuade all the idiots on this island to trail in our wake. No doubt they will find a reasonable substitute on the mainland for what this island offers them.'

Just at that moment a shriek of terror tore the air and all work ceased abruptly as the man who delivered the cry was seen to be about a metre from the end of the causeway and up to his armpits in the quicksand.

'Quickly,' shouted Said Rak. 'The crane ...' Someone began manually directing the crane's cable down to the swiftly disappearing workman. The man who was drowning was the one who had passed Othman and Said Rak a few moments earlier.

'Help me,' cried the white, disc-like shape of the face – which was all that was now visible of the body.

'Don't struggle – reach up,' urged Othman.

The cable with its loops of rope dangled just above the drowning man's head. All he had to do was lift his arm carefully and grasp the proffered loops and he would be saved. The arm came up, black and crab-like, and fingers snapped at the rope. The action was too jerky to enable the terror-stricken face to remain above the surface and for an instant it disappeared. The claw fingers brushed by the rope, making it sway, and then plunged down into the quicksand again. Every person watching knew that panic had overtaken the sinking man. He had struggled below the surface, trying to push his head above the quicksand, and had forgotten about the life-line now centimetres above the mud.

'Get a grab crane quickly,' shouted Othman.

No one moved. After all, the man was dead.

'Now!' screamed Othman, and someone broke from his trance and climbed into the cabin of a grab crane, running it out onto the causeway. Said Rak had his eyes fixed to the spot where the man had disappeared and directed the open grab down slowly. They might kill the man with the heavy jaws of the grab but he was a corpse without the attempt. The grab went down into quicksand to the solid ridge and the moment the driver felt the jaws touch the bottom he closed them and raised the grab quickly, swung it out over the causeway, and with a hundred pairs of eyes on him, opened the jaws. Mud oozed out and was suddenly alive with a wriggling that came from within it. As the sand spread away and over the edge of the causeway, a yellow-black lava, the hopefuls moved in on the active centre of the mess, only to retreat rapidly as a grotesque-looking bulbous creature that was nearer to a limbless octopus in shape than the human form, shuffled its ungainly body to the edge of the causeway, dropped into the quicksand and sank from sight. There was to be no rescue. Yussof, a private soldier, was dead.

Othman was aware of intense annoyance deep within him as Silandi fired the questions at him.

'How did it happen? Someone should have been watching and ready to throw a rope.'

Othman replied patiently. 'You can't prevent accidents by saying what should have been done. Of course in the future we will have someone standing by with a life-line but no one had considered the possibility of a slip, if that's what it was, and anyway' – he was on the defensive again – 'we had the line there as quickly as we could. He was gone within seconds ...'

'It was your responsibility. Now we not only have a dead man, we also have a widow.'

Othman ground his teeth, and Said Rak who was standing nervously by backed away in embarrassment.

'Don't keep this up, Silandi. I am not responsible for the fact that we have a widow – I didn't ask for the man to be married. If she's a tramp, marry her to one of the morons, then she can't cause trouble. A woman who beds husbands yet has one of her own is not such an evil to the other wives – a widow is considered to have an unfair advantage and causes trouble, as you imply.'

He was conscious of having scored deeply here and Silandi came back, not viciously, as he expected but with a hurt expression in her voice.

'You know I didn't mean it that way,' she said.

'I know,' he spat back at her. 'You wanted me to feel guilty – to bear the weight of a widow on my shoulders. Well, I won't do that – personally I accept that, as leader of this community, everything is ultimately my responsibility, but I don't accept personal responsibility. I shall appoint an officer in charge of safety and there ends my defence. You have no real function with regard to the project – good, I put you in complete charge of safety. If anyone dies in future it will be *your* responsibility. Now don't bother me further – get on with your job.'

He could see she was fighting back the tears – frustration probably – but he felt no sympathy. She had brought that on herself. If she had not attacked him there would have been no counter-attack.

Finally she said to him in a quiet voice, 'I shall need some people – to help me discharge my duties.'

'Approach Said Rak about that,' he replied brusquely. 'I'm putting him in charge of all matters dealing with personnel. The more I delegate, the easier it becomes to do so.'

The man in question, who had been standing apart amongst the trees, stepped eagerly forward on hearing his name and began discussing details with Silandi immediately. Without realizing it and possibly intending the opposite, Said Rak was widening the rift between the two. Had he allowed for a few moments of calmness to settle before coming physically between them one or the other might have softened in attitude. The two bodies might then have embraced and an understanding developed. Now they could not melt, with a barrier between them. It was the beginning of a long, drawn-out feud.

Jessum was studying the slopes to the highest piece of ground on the island – a mountain standing a thousand metres above the level of the quicksand. The slopes were heavily wooded and the timber would make good supports for the causeway. Stickmen had gathered there in numbers, however, and stood too close to a tree for their own safety. The tree was about to be felled. Jessum had no desire to hurt any of them and he was going to suggest to Othman that they build some sort of reservation, with high, wire fences on the panhandle of the island to contain the natives and the morons. It was not possible to work efficiently while they stood in knots around the felling area. They moved away when inveigled, but it all took so much time and Othman was impatient for timber.

The large tree was about to come down, and several morons and natives began milling around the trunk.

'Okay,' sighed Jessum to Hinna, his number two, 'move them away.'

Just then he received a call on the communicator. It was from Othman.

'Come down to the shoreline, Jessum. We may have something.' The voice was excited.

Jessum jumped into a tractor immediately, calling over his shoulder that Hinna was to carry on working. He would be back later. The tractor hummed to life and he threw it down the slopes.

When he reached the quicksand he found what appeared to be the whole town lining the shore. They were staring out into the ocean, towards the distant mainland.

Jessum joined Othman.

'What is it?' he asked, trying to see what it was that the others had in view. 'Is there a craft or something?'

Othman replied, 'I don't know. Someone reported seeing an object out there a while ago. We're not sure what, but it could be a craft from the mainland. It keeps surfacing every so often, apparently.'

'How many times has it been seen?'

'Twice. Each time it's been closer but it's difficult to ascertain size or distance because it's only above the surface for a few moments – there!' he shouted, and his actions and words were duplicated all along the shore. Out in the quicksand a black shape had appeared for a split second.

'I saw it – did you? Did you see it, Jessum?'

Jessum was less enthusiastic.

'Yes, I saw it, but it didn't appear to be very large. There are animals out there as you know – creatures of the planet. Perhaps we should prepare something – not a reception but a display of weaponry.'

Othman nodded. 'I've thought of that. Said Rak has his soldiers all along the shore. They'll open fire at my signal, but it's just possible, isn't it – that this may be some sort of an envoy from the mainland?'

'Of course it's possible, but the more likely of the two ...'

'Let's wait and see,' said Othman firmly.

They stood and waited for many long minutes for the reappearance of the object and just as they were tiring of watching gas bubbles burst out in the ocean, one smallish bubble rose about fifty metres from the island. When it exploded there was a scream from one of the women in the crowd. What had appeared from its centre was the silt-blackened corpse of Yussof, his loose arms rising and the hands meeting above his head as he sank again. Yussof was being taught to dance in death by the currents and gaseous streams and channels that continually stirred the quicksand, keeping it alive.

'God help us,' whispered Jessum, white-faced, as a wail broke from the people.

'Damn the man,' whispered Othman in a flat tone. 'Haven't I enough trouble without his coming back to haunt us? Now they'll begin inventing superstitions about the quicksand.'

He left Jessum standing staring at the spot where the grotesque form had surfaced and went to find Said Rak; the soldier was where Othman had left him.

'You saw it?' he said to Said Rak softly.

'Yes.'

'Well, *next* time you or any of your men see it, I want it blasted to pieces. Destroy it, do you understand?'

'But the body? The widow might ...'

'Do it,' ordered Othman. 'If she sees, then she'll under-

58

stand. I'll get Silandi to talk to her. The man's supposed to be dead and I don't want him bobbing up and down like some ghastly apparition from a nightmare, scaring people out of their minds. It wouldn't be so bad if he didn't wave to everyone, as if he was having a good time ...'

Said Rak did not smile. He merely nodded and swallowed hard.

Eight

It was becoming warmer. Fdar could feel each morning pulling itself into the sky sluggishly – like this hot, sultry morning that made the air hang as heavy as a damp cloth on his skin. He was lying in the grasses of a hillock, staring down at the busy ants below. The ants were building a bridge out into the quicksand which would eventually link the island with the mainland. The natives considered this to be a bad thing, and since he was now one of them, so did Fdar. Somehow his friends knew what was on the far side and wanted no part of it.

He himself knew, for instance, from the patterns of a bird that had sipped the waters of a river deep in the hinterland, that there were heads without bodies which the carnivorous insects had picked clean. These heads, human skulls, were planted in the fields according to the bird's patterns, and they sang death songs, morning, noon and night, never pausing, only changing in volume from time to time. Sometimes the songs were high, shrill and insistently loud. Others hummed low and melancholy, staring sadly into the mists of the river. Fdar did not want to see such things.

He was mildly angry at the ship's people. They did nothing but work towards the destruction of the natives and themselves. They were cutting down the tall trees which in turn protected the smaller plants from the fierce frosts in the winter and also from the hot sun in the summer. Soon there would be no more plants to feed from, especially when the summer came and dried out the ground. There would be no shade for the berry and fruit bushes. It was all very bad.

The moron rose and left his sleeping-nest to walk in the undergrowth. He knew of a spot where some melliferous insects had built *their* nest and he was looking forward to a breakfast of honey. The way to the hive was through the streets of the new town.

He walked towards the various buildings, most of them machined out of cool hillside stone by the rock-cutting instruments brought by the ship. Multi-armed building machines had followed the directions of architects and master-builders to form a hotchpotch of both traditional and modern structures. There were the dove's wing eaves of the post-oil era of plastiglas, when the East was running out of money but not ideas. There was a half-completed copy of the Court of Lions from an eleventh-century palace, and the stucco decorations of a later era in a small private house. Nothing was completed – all structures had stopped at a point in time when the bridge had begun and, since the builders and machines had been flitting from one job to another as demands from each quarter for a fair distribution of their labour changed in intensity, not one building was completely ready for habitation, although most were lived in. Fdar was sad for the occupants of the town – there was no harmony amongst them, nor inside them. They showed it in the way they fought with each other and in their outward culture. Noise and wild actions – that was what filled the streets of the town.

He walked through at an unhurried pace, to be patted and smiled upon by some of the women. Others scowled. Truly a mixture.

At the end of the town he met another moron and exchanged thoughts. She was a girl, heavy-breasted, with beautiful curling hair that hung to her waist. He ran his fingers through the hair and felt the patterns. They excited him. But he stopped because the girl was in late pregnancy – they could not make love with safety. Soon she would produce one of the second generation of humans on the planet.

On finding the hive Fdar thrust his hand in amongst the effervescent insects, making them spill over like liquid from a pot. They settled on his wrist, but only for an instant, even when the fingers scooped honey from their precious hoard.

Fdar examined the sticky substance before offering it to the girl. She filled her mouth, smiling.

'What have they got in their mouths?' Jessum demanded of Said Rak. Said Rak shook his head. 'I'm afraid they've obtained some kind of weed which they chew. They say it makes them feel good – it clears the brain I'm told.'

Jessum stared at the workers with their bulging cheeks and doubted the truth of this statement. They had heavy, drooping eyelids and were lethargic in their movements.

'Find me an expert,' rapped Jessum. 'Someone who can tell me what it is these fools are killing themselves with.'

Said Rak duly dispatched one of his men to find a doctor by the name of Malek, who was also a keen biologist.

He answered Jessum's call to the builder's presence with a dignified stroll, implying that he, as a doctor, was unused to being summoned for purposes other than medical, especially by a man whose job it was to put bricks together. Malek was a physician, a builder of bodies, and he still liked to maintain the idea that the chemical machines which housed men's souls required a certain mystical touch above the understanding of the ordinary man. He had little real work to do because his medical instruments were, in the main, capable of diagnosing and treating complaints without his help. He was merely the backup in case of mechanical failure, but no one would have dared to suggest this to him. After all, if the automatics did happen to fail, you had to rely on this man's help, and showering him with insults was no way to prepare the path to a sympathetic reception.

'Yes?' he inquired loftily of Jessum.

A tree crashed to the ground before Jessum could answer, but when he was sure he could be heard he said, 'Doctor, we need your help – your expertise in identifying this plant.' Jessum showed him some small, toothed leaves. It was the right approach. The doctor's interest was visibly awakened.

'Of course, of course,' he replied, 'but I'll have to take it away with me. I'll let you have my opinion later today, once I have studied my manuals. It needn't be listed of course. However, some of the flora on this island has a similar counterpart on Earth. There are many differences, but basically wood is wood, and grass is grass. I'll analyse these leaves for their chemical content and try to offer you some terrestrial equivalent.'

The man's pompous attitude irritated Jessum but he smiled and thanked the doctor, who took his overweight form down towards the town.

Jessum then turned to one of the men near by.

'You, could you come here please?' The man did as he was asked.

'What's your name?' demanded Jessum.

'Abdulla.'

'Well now, Abdulla, I want you to tell me how you came to be eating the leaves of trees.'

The man looked abashed and turned around for help in answering the question but none of his friends offered any. They wisely kept their heads to their tasks.

'I don't know,' he said at last.

Said Rak snapped, 'Don't be stupid man – you must know. What if the leaves were poisonous?'

Abdulla brightened.

'Ah, the light!' murmured Jessum.

The man replied, 'I saw another man chewing it.'

'Fetch him,' ordered Jessum, feeling that it was going to be a long and onerous task.

Eventually it was found that the morons had been seen chewing the weed and since it had not hurt them, and they seemed to know what tasted good in the plant world of the planet, the townspeople had followed suit.

'At least we've discovered how it came to be in their mouths,' Jessum told Othman later in his house. 'Perhaps our doctor can give us an idea what it is later – although, despite his optimism, I very much doubt it. There is no reason why this planet cannot produce a totally alien chemistry in its plants.'

Othman was frowning as he sat in his high wooden chair which enabled him to look out, through the window of the house, and observe the progress of the causeway below.

'It sounds familiar somehow,' he told Jessum. 'Something from my childhood – it'll come back to me. How's the work going today?'

'Well enough.' Jessum looked around the untidy room and then at the dark figure brooding in the chair, the black beard with its twin points lying like a fish's tail on Othman's chest. A falcon perched on the back of the sturdy seat, as silent as if it was asleep. Its eyes regarded Jessum without expression. There were droppings slpattered here and there upon the floor and furniture.

'Where's Silandi today?' he asked.

Othman blew noisily through his nostrils.

'Gone.'

'Gone? Where?'

'Anywhere that I am not, to put it in her own words. We had another argument about felling the trees. She's left me, she says for good. In fact I believe I told her to go – it's difficult to remember what I say later, after one of those blistering quarrels we seem to have. I'm glad she's gone anyway. It will give me more time to concentrate on the causeway ...'

Jessum was quiet for a moment, then he said, 'This will not look good to the people.'

The leader appeared to be turning this over in his mind and Jessum wisely remained silent. Finally Othman replied, 'They need not know – so long as she doesn't take a lover they can only guess what her situation is. I won't divorce her – that would attract attention and it might also start a trend. I need a settled camp ...'

He still called it a *camp*, thought Jessum, when the town had been established for some eighteen months according to the computer's Earth-time clock. The man was truly a Bedu, with the blood of the curious traveller in his veins. What would happen once the causeway reached the mainland? It was almost halfway across now. An expedition into the interior of the mainland? Doubtful, thought Jessum. If Othman had anything to do with it, they would all evacuate the town – camels, horses, dogs and ducks. Jessum was proud of the town – much of it had been built by himself. Well, half-built, he amended regretfully.

'By the way, Jessum,' said the leader from the depths of his chair, 'I've decided we are going to have a feast. We're about at the halfway mark now and I want the people to be refired with some enthusiasm for the project – of late they've been flagging ...'

The builder protected his workers.

'Yes, true, but the heat – you know it's getting hotter? And that soft wood we used held us up for weeks – I still have to keep three men going full-time on the pruning.'

In the beginning they had not worried too much about the type of timber they used, so long as the pith was solid. Unfortunately for the project the quicksand was extremely fertile and the freshly cut wood, unseasoned, began to throw out new roots almost immediately. Then it sprouted green fingers – new branches began to show and the necessary replacing of the faster-growing species almost halted the main work for several months. It was a body-blow for Othman who had counted on the earthwork causeway being completed within a few months. Now, what had at first promised to be an arrow-straight work of art linking the island with the mainland, had been transformed into a comical switchback as some piles grew faster than others.

'What kind of feast anyway?' asked Jessum, who was eager to get off the subject of work as quickly as possible.

Othman said, without comprehension in his voice, 'A Ramadan feast – whatever that is. I remember them from a boy but I can't recall what their purpose was ...'

'Ramadan?'

'Yes, the ninth month. I've thought hard about it, and I can only conclude that it has some religious significance about which we are meant to remain ignorant.' This remark opened another avenue for discussion. 'Has it crossed your mind at all how little we know about Allah? We know he is the one God, and we know of the prophet, but when I try to look deeper it's as if I'm looking directly into a blinding light – a light as bright as a sun only nearer than one would ever get to a star, almost within touching distance. I can feel that there must be something else there, besides the light, but it is blotted out by whiteness and the harder I try to see what it is, the blinder I become.

'We have a religion you see, Jessum, we believe in God, but we have none of the trappings that a belief needs to keep it burning hotly within the soul. If I believed that trees were gods and had immortal souls, as the natives appear to believe, then I would have an image, a shape, to revere. I would have the deity's component parts, the bark, the branch, the leaf, to study and hold holy. I would have a place to worship – the copse on the hill perhaps which forms a perfect circle ...'

'We cut it down last month,' interrupted Jessum in a practical, if irreverent, tone.

Othman went on, ignoring this remark designed to bring him down from his tower.

'I have the small quiet mosque which Silandi tried to disguise as a water tower, it is true, but where are the other embellishments of a religion – where is the art, Jessum? – that's what I mean.'

He slapped his hand hard on the arm of the chair making the falcon's head bob in fright.

'The *art*, Jessum? Where are the ancient carpets, the wonderful leather-bound books with such intricate designs on their jackets, the mosaics, the golden trappings of a beautiful religion? I knew them in my youth – I saw them. Yet they are misty in my memory – they have no solid form. Are they those things I sense hidden in the light, Jessum? Could we reproduce them? Or should we design a new religious art around our old God and his prophet? A new religion?

'But art is a consequence of tradition, and as yet we have no tradition – everything we have is formed of a newness. We were robbed of something before this trip, Jessum. Before our embryos were stowed in their stainless steel pockets the senders took something from us which might have ensured a certain stability – they took our art.'

Jessum said nothing. Othman occasionally went into these deep moods of reflection on what should, or should not, be. The musty, bare, stone room in which the leader lived did not improve these moods – more probably it engendered them.

'Shall I ask Silandi to see that the women weave some carpets?' said Jessum at last.

Othman sat up quickly, as if waking from a deep trance.

'Enough of this,' he said. 'You should be back at the felling site. Why are you here anyway?'

Jessum said, surprised, 'I came to tell you about the weed the workers are chewing.' There was a sound from the doorway and Malek the doctor coughed apologetically before stepping inside uninvited. He had the smile of success upon his round face.

'Outside,' ordered Othman. 'Wait until I ask you to enter.'

The doctor's smile disappeared and he turned to go.

'Wait,' said Jessum quickly. 'I called him here, Othman. He has something to tell us. Doctor?' He gave the man an ingratiating smile and a hand pressed encouragingly on the doctor's shoulder.

'Well ...' Malek hesitated, then it tumbled out.

'We have something remarkable here.' He offered the crumpled leaves of the offending plant back to Jessum and the builder took them.

'See the serrated edges to the leaves? And, if you remember, the flowers are small and white. This is almost certainly a member of the staff tree family – evergreens growing to a height of around three metres. In fact I would stake my reputation' – he puffed out his chest – 'that this plant is *catha edulis*.'

'What?'

'Qat weed. It makes a nice beverage – tea.'

'Tea?' The other two men looked at each other as if to say, who let this imbecile into the room?

'Then why are they chewing it?' Jessum asked of the doctor. Then he suddenly cried, 'Qat! Of course – the drug that reduces wakefulness and alertness of mind in the addict.' He was quoting a sentence from his scholastic youth.

The doctor nodded eagerly.

Jessum was disgusted. 'What did they send that along with us for? If I remember rightly, excessive use is harmful, makes the addict listless besides being bad for his health. Camel driver's ruin,' he added, with a sudden flash of humour.

'What?' chorused the other two.

'I mean,' said Jessum, 'it destroys the sexual urge.'

'Give me some quickly,' said Othman wryly.

Jessum smiled, glad that his humour was infectious enough for Othman to catch a dose. The leader was of course thinking of his recently departed wife.

'But,' stammered the doctor, as he dared to interrupt Othman. 'The whole point is, sir, we didn't bring any qat seeds with us. I checked the stores lists. There's nothing on them about qat ...'

'Duplication of plant life?' Jessum suggested. To a builder the idea was not as fantastic as it apparently appeared to the doctor. Malek shook his head.

'I would hesitate to accept that as an answer. The similarity to the Earth qat is too close – it would be a miracle. Not that there aren't such things in nature as miracles, but ...' he shook his head.

Othman interrupted. 'Then we must look for a simple answer, like the qat seed was amongst the stores but not listed, or there were qat seeds amongst some of the other types of grain that were brought with us ...'

Jessum laughed. 'Exactly – too obvious. Seeds in the linings of garments – why seeds? One seed would do it. I think we're trying to invent mysteries where there are none. The qat was brought with us – inadvertently, it seems, but even that need not necessarily be so. Our senders were only human too – they could have forgotten to list this particular item, as Othman said.'

Malek's face was impassive.

'As you please,' he replied. 'But I suggest we forbid the people to chew on the leaves – let them make tea by all means, but employing the plant's properties to stimulate the senses can only end in the users becoming hard addicts and there will be a gradual breakdown in their health.'

'I agree,' Othman terminated the meeting. 'See to it, Jessum.'

Nine

The Saker falcon was no longer any use as a hunter. One morning, early in their relationship, Othman had taken him out on his wrist and walked along the shores of the quicksand sea. There had been some previous practice flights and a strong bond had developed between the two fellow creatures – as was necessary if the predator was to be any good as a man's hunting companion.

It was an unusually fresh start to a day and the grasses sparkled under the new sun with fragments of overnight raindrops still clinging to their blades. It was a morning that sharpened the hunters' minds towards the promise of a kill – a morning of spearpoints; the thrusting leaves of the broad-bladed plants, the hanging-crystal spikes of water, their points buried in branches, and the long scything flexure of the sun's rays. This was a morning that honed animal senses on its bright edges, and man and beast felt that they themselves could slice into the enemy at full speed and cut to the thickness of a shadow.

Talons sank into the man's wrist as the falcon impatiently flexed its muscles, but Othman seemed to delight in the pain. It was as if he could share the falcon's excitement this way. Both of them would be up on those sheets of high wind. The hood was removed and the falcon spread its wings and began the climb up into its natural domain. Once up, it balanced its body on the back of the wind and moved slowly in circles, eyes on the floor of the world below.

Creatures were there, darting in and out of bushes and sprinting vertically up the trunks of trees, but much of the wildlife of the island was too small for the Saker. Once, his kind had been trained to hunt gazelle at full speed.

The island was a scimitar-shaped patchwork of green and brown below, and around it oozed the ever-fermenting ocean of viscous alluvium, watered by the rivers of the island and mainland and stirred by subterranean gases; it was too thick to float upon and too thin to walk over. Scanning the yellow-black loess the bird noticed a movement over its surface, a nervous flickering such as an animal would make: though the creature's camouflage was virtually perfect and the falcon had no idea of size, it had been pinpointed. The bird felt the ancient stirrings of a desire for aerial combat deep in its breast, and it waited to see if the creature was able to become airborne like itself.

The man had noticed the prey too, and was standing, rock-still, on the shoreline below.

After a long time the quarry moved again – a short distance, but enough for the predator to see it was a fish-like creature that was under its observation. A prickle of disappointment ran through its poised frame as it searched for a decision in its small brain. Should it, or should it not, attack? The master was not moving, which indicated that he approved of the target. If he did not, he would have recalled the bird with the lure, for he was aware of the interest his bird was showing in the beast below.

But the man was still!

Another slow circle on a thermal and then the decision was taken.

Strike!

The prehensile talons were bunched stilettos as the body dipped and fell groundwards.

Wind tore through feathers. The world grew rapidly larger and rushed upwards towards the killer, offering the prey on its broad, expansive belly.

Hit!

The talons were deep in rubbery flesh. Man laughed and swung a fist at the air in his excitement.

But as the falcon's legs sank with the impact, a white light seared through the bird's brain and it was flung violently away from the alien creature, as a man is sometimes thrown by coming into contact with high-voltage electricity. The falcon was unhurt, but less willing to meet again with the strange fish.

It recovered and stooped, but only to receive a blood-red transmission which blotted out the sun with its intensity. Again the bird was thrown aside with great force. This time it did not go back. There was no desire to fight with a creature that used weapons like a man. Weapons hidden within its breast.

The man had been puzzled when the falcon began to wing back to the sanctuary which was his wrist. Thereafter the falcon had become disinclined to hunt and had turned into a housepet, much to the disgust of the master who had no real interest in animals that did not have a positive function in his life.

Neither the falcon nor the master had known that physical contact in hunting, on Jessum, almost always ensured the failure of the hunt. Those carnivores that hunted creatures their own size for food almost always killed from a distance. That way the mind-patterns of their prey were forced into impotence and it became possible for the killers to touch their kill without the polarity suddenly being reversed.

Othman has been allowed by his father to leave home for the first time and is travelling the Shanghai-Asyût mono-rail which passes high above the Arabian peninsula. He is heading for Al Jawf, the junction of Eastern Irrigation Wadis, where he is to study the engineering principles that are behind that great project. Below him the land blooms like a garden, the greenery broken only by the occasional town or rockland bulge of a national park.

'What's your name, boy?'

Othman, already sixteen, does not like to be addressed as 'boy' by a complete stranger. He turns, however, and sees a youth perhaps two years older than himself – like Othman he wears the traditional white *jalabiyah* and a *kuffiyah* headcloth, also white with a black rope *agal* to keep it in place. He realizes the youth is only trying to be friendly and says his own name. The other replies.

'I am Hassan. My family was once royal – but that's no longer in fashion. I'm told that we used to cut off the heads of offensive commoners and display them on stakes – the heads, not the commoners ...' He smiles at Othman, knowing that he has shocked the youth.

'What does your family do, Othman?'

'My family are commoners – we're an offensive bunch of people really. I imagine that once upon a time we were always getting our heads cut off.' His face is blank.

The other youth laughs, showing a set of long, horse-like teeth. After this they become friends, talking animatedly to one another, sharing experiences, hinting broadly at the less moral activities.

'I will show you something of life,' promises Hassan. 'My family live in Al Jawf – we run a textile business there.'

'How low the royal stoop in these democratic times,' remarks Othman, and they both laugh again.

The world changes slowly. Men can reach the inner planets, have scooped out bases beneath the surface of the moon and have caused the evolution of engines, from Steam Age monsters, the dinosaurs of machine life, to the silent laser-circuited brains performing the multifarious tasks of the day. Yet other men have seemingly been on the Earth for two thousand years, their life-styles remaining unchanged from those of people who lived in the time before the prophet found the path.

The human race is like a snake trailing its body, from the

active head, back through history to the tail. A snake whose length is completely present at one moment in time.

As the train enters the station tube with the soft bumper of air hissing by the segmented carriages, the two young men see the reservoirs dotted with boats, from modern wave-hopping spheres that barely touch the water, to ancient dhows, dirty white lateen sails moving bloated in the sunshine.

They descend by way of the elevators to the town below where the crowds are white dots that move slowly in and out of each other. (Silandi could never become part of those dots – her simulated childhood takes place in a different age, a younger era where women are gentle, inhibited creatures who still have a certain amount of naïveté and respect of social morality, and still retain a certain mystery.)

'Have you any hawks?' asks Othman hopefully, as they wend their way through the people to a coffee shop.

'Ah, you enjoy seeing the blood?' says his new friend. 'I can show you blood closer to home than that while you are here.'

Othman does not understand, but the words chill him at the same time as creating excitement in his young breast. Until now, life has been hard schoolwork with infrequent visits home. He feels that a window has been thrown open and the hot airless study has a breeze racing around its walls bearing in its hands the smell of blossoms, grasses and – something faintly sinister underlying all else.

The coffee shop is on the old wharf where the dhows come in, up the canals from the sea. The water is salty at this stage, and the ozone-laden air soon makes the young men sleepy and listless. Irrigation ditches radiate from the main lake, with filters to remove the harmful chemicals before the water is sprayed into beautiful rainbow umbrella shapes out in the fields.

An ancient craft floats near by, dropping its sail when it turns into the wind, as a reptile sheds its skin, revealing the narrow wooden mast. The gunwales have been rubbed smooth and have soft dips where ropes have worn a valley for their lengths. Old, salt-white boards creak and groan with each movement of the broad craft. Every piece of the ship testifies to its age – each part is worn and cracked like a driftwood log found on the shore.

At the tiller stands a brown skeleton rattling orders to Somali sailors on the deck. The Master's cheek bulges with a quid of qat and suddenly he launches the juice towards the wharf. Instinctively the young men scrape their chairs backwards, even though the globule of green liquid drops metres away, between the boat and the wharf. The Master sees, and grins.

The boat runs alongside, wood squealing against wood, and Hassan watches through narrowed eyes.

'Remember his face,' he says.

An air of seriousness pervades the scene for a few minutes, then Othman tries to revive the earlier joviality that existed between them.

'How could you forget a face that ugly?' he laughs. 'Skin stretched over a skull!' He stares more keenly and notes the wrinkles. 'And not stretched very tightly either.'

Hassan laughs too, and soon the pair roll in the creaking chairs, making the Master and his mariners turn and stare for an instant. Then the men are bent-backed again, over bales of rags soiled white with sea-water stains.

After the young men have drunk the hot bitter coffee they part with a promise to meet the following day, and Othman goes to find his lodgings which are in the terraced quarter on the cool side of the city.

Leaving the old precincts, behind the wharf, where the heat collects in heavy, almost solid clouds at the bases of skyrisers, Othman makes his way through to the whitewashed alleys and to the house of his father's friend in the old quarter. There will be concern because of his lateness, the old friend being responsible for the young man, but Othman decides to say he was lost in the wonders of the city and walked slowly on that account.

He will not say anything of Hassan because there is something unsavoury about the royalist – it is, at this stage, only a feeling but he does not wish to be warned off because his new friend excites him and promises to make his stay less dull than anticipated.

(Like Silandi, and all the other ship people, Othman is aware that he lives with a dream. It is a dream with stability and has none of the time-telescoping tricks, the supernatural elements or the sudden scene transformations of a normal dream. It is abnormal in that it is lived like an ordinary life. Othman knows that *whatever happens to him, he will not die,* but he might suffer the agonies to the point of death, and there is fear enough in that. Still, he would like an escapade – what boy of sixteen can resist one?)

He passes a mosque as the call to prayer floats lyrically over the city. He hears but does not pay heed, for most of the religious side of life has been edited from the tapes – this in itself leaves very little material for a Moslem brain to feed upon. Islam is so tightly woven into an adherent's life that it is one and the same garment. Othman prays in his room, but reads no poetry, no fiction. He loves Allah when he sees him in the birds and the waves of the sea, but understands him not. He knows that others have something he cannot have, cannot participate in: for a devout Moslem, religion, law, commerce, education, the arts and social policies are inseparable, and this must continue to flow around Othman, but the young man cannot be touched by it for he must find a new way to Allah in a new world. His learnings must be levelled to the mere induction of unembellished raw material and he can never know the mountains and peaks of beauty to which Islam can pull a few simple words or a mathematical formula.

His father's friend is pleased to see him and they exchange

salaams before sitting down to coffee. After being shown his quarters he spends the evening in the company of the old man, talking and listening to the nasal songs issuing from the flower-decked roofs of houses that, between them, the walls and the street, leave not one piece of soil exposed to the air and are thus one large multi-blocked building that sprawls below the stars. Through the stillness there are calls from wives to husbands, and from husbands to wives. There are laughing children and there are some that cry. The dogs croon to one another, and the city is more alive during the cool evening than it ever was during the day. The young man looks forward to meeting Hassan and wonders what the other youth is doing on such a pleasant night in the dream of Othman.

Ten

The next morning Othman goes with his father's friend to be shown the city before the heat of the day drives even the insects into the shade. He sees the newest part of the city where the overhead wind machines create their artificial breezes for the tourists and businessmen. The market and *suq* are still fashionable, as they have been for several thousand years. Their general appearance varies little from age to age: only the coinage changes face, and the wares their shape. Black-market money-changers still ply their illicit trade in the adjoining alleys, faceless and urgent. ('Here, quickly.' The sound of money. 'I must not be seen. I have been fined twice already this month.')

The stalls are left behind and the marina where the yachts and power-boats are lined like sleek white sharks along the quays, is the next point of old pride and young interest. Then the animal mart, now underground because of the smell, and the joy of finding hawks and falcons, not for sale, but accompanying their tourist-seeking masters. The offers are from those who have trained their creatures with patience, for time and kindness are the only true methods (although some look on the denial of sleep to the birds, necessary in the initial period of training, as a cruelty), to those with neither time nor patience to participate as observers in the hunt. Some will pay a fortune to watch a feathered express train hurtle over the sands of a national park, towards a fast, frightened target telemarking and using the ground as a trampoline, the air for acrobatic bids in escapology, in a vain effort to escape the talons.

Lastly Othman sees the great aerial race-track for which the city is famed, which glints in the sun; a twisting, curving strip of adhesive steel without crash bars along its edges. The old man is not himself proud of this particular construction but wishes to impress Othman with a local engineering feat. Othman makes the necessary acknowledgements, and they return to the house to talk over what has been seen.

Later, when the twilight comes in, and is gone with the speed of an athlete, Othman tells his father's friend that he is meeting someone he befriended on the train and the old man nods, unsure if the youth means a girl or not, but too polite to ask. Othman leaves quickly.

He makes his way to the café where Hassan suggested they meet and as he approaches he sees his new-found friend sitting at a pavement table with two others. They are all talking animatedly. Othman pauses before advancing towards them for there is something about the group that worries him. The city's overhead beams are on and the streets are as light as if the sun is shining. The figures before him are bent over steaming cups, their faces conspiratorially close in the centre of the white Parisian-style table. The scene appears very Arabian but Othman cannot help but realize that, even in his day and age when national identities are ostensibly so dear, the characters and cultures of the individual nations are merging swiftly. Looking at Hassan he can see in him the same gestures and actions used by other boys he has known – boys from all parts of the world when a world shrinks to the point where two hours are ample time to encircle it, when, he thinks, all peoples live under the same roof and, people being impressionable, constant contact makes them follow fashionable examples.

Hassan's features are narrow and drawn, with shadows beneath them that give him a haunted look. His long, narrow fingers are expressing something with delicate movements and as he reaches an important point, he glances up and sees Othman standing on the corner of the street. Their eyes lock for an instant. Hassan says something quickly to his companions and then smiles and gestures. Othman joins them at the table.

'Why were you standing watching us like that? Are we so obvious when we brag about our conquests?'

'Conquests?'

One of the youths laughs at the way Othman squeaks the word. He turns on the boy in fury.

'It was a reasonable question – I assume you mean amorous conquests, for you don't look like fighters to me ...' His fists are bunched in his sleeves as he waits for retaliation.

'Easy, easy,' says Hassan soothingly. 'We're all friends here – a little jesting is acceptable among friends, surely?'

Othman is calmed but not mollified. He is irritated by Hassan assuming a conciliatory role.

'I don't even know their names – how can I call them friends?'

Hassan smiles. 'That's easily rectified. This grotesque excuse for an idiot is Ali.' Hassan indicates the boy with whom Othman is at loggerheads. Hassan is still smoothing the wrinkles out of the atmosphere by calling his companion names, and Othman decides to accept the situation for what it is. He smiles and nods at the short, skinny youth who sits before him.

The third youth looks older than Hassan but there is no

strength in his face. He wears a soft, pallid expression and under the overhead lights his jowl is an overfull pouch. His name is Amelik and he nods quickly, making his cheeks quiver, as he is introduced. Othman judges him to be the tallest of the three but it is difficult to see by how much since none of them is standing.

Othman pulls a chair from a near-by table and sits down; at the same time Hassan signals for another cup of coffee.

The conversation returns to women again, and Othman listens to the tales of three youths loose in a town fed by European tourists.

'There was this girl,' says Ali, 'with skin like ...' he looks around wildly for an object to fit a vague simile he has in mind, 'like coffee,' he says finally. 'She was a British girl, third or fourth generation from somewhere else – a place called Lucia or something – my soul in Allah's hands, but she was beautiful. I was sixteen at the time ...'

'Yesterday,' winks Hassan.

Ali ignores this remark, apparently enraptured by the picture he is creating for the others. It is difficult for Othman to tell whether this creation is fictitious or is recalled memory. The faces of the other two give nothing away.

'I am walking along the lakeside just after dawn looking for seashells – it is a hobby of mine – when I almost have a heart attack. Out in the water is a swimmer, thrashing around for all she's worth. Now, we not only get plenty of gastropods and bivalves dragging themselves up the canals to the lakes from the Red Sea, we are also honoured with much heavier marine life ...'

'Sharks,' interrupts Hassan.

'Precisely,' says Ali, his eyes shining. 'Well, this young person – for I could see amongst the clothes on the beach some very feminine and foreign articles – was a tourist. It was ten to one that the reason she was swimming so early in the morning was because she wished to avoid the crowds. Why would anyone wish to do that? Because, because,' he licked his thin lips, 'she wanted to swim naked.'

'So you thought,' Hassan says seriously, 'that this tourist ... person, ought to be made aware of the local dangers.'

'Exactly,' Al-Ali spread his hands. 'It's necessary to protect these people – they are so vulnerable – such soft, warm bodies for the sharks to sink their teeth into.

'Well, I stood on the lakeside for a short while wondering what I should do, and finally took a well-planned course of action. Firstly, I wrapped the clothes in a stone and threw them into the water. They sank, of course. Then I called to the girl – rather I screamed at her, my face distorted with terror – "Shark!"

'She stopped swimming and looked towards me. I waded up to my ankles and repeated my warning, pointed in a certain direction at the same time. Her face changed and she swam rapidly towards the beach. I stayed ankle-deep, encouraging her all the way and frantically reaching with my hand.'

Ali pauses for a sip of coffee and Othman notices how silent they have all become. The youth is certainly a story-teller, truth or not. Ali continues. 'Finally the slim, coffee-coloured hand was in mine and I pulled her ashore. She was exhausted with her swim, of course, so I carried her to a near-by dune that had been planted with tall grasses. Yes, she was naked and her soft brown breast burned through my wet *jalabiyah* as I ran with her. All over her body, she glistened with drops of salt water, and where the sand flicked up from my sandals it stuck to her thighs and buttocks.

'I let her recapture her breath, for I am no rapist gentleman, and then I told her about the tide. How it must have taken her clothes away and yes, there was a fragment of cloth out there on the blue water, floating. She was distraught and it took me a full hour to comfort her, hidden in the grasses – then I left her ...'

'To fetch her clothes?' says Othman.

Ali looks at him strangely.

'What for? I had finished with her.'

A lump comes into Othman's throat as he realizes the story is true, and all he can see in his mind for a moment is the distressed look on the face of the girl whose oral picture Ali had drawn. He feels a sudden loathing for the boy sitting opposite. This is not allowed to mature into anything evident to the others, however, for Hassan has suddenly stood up and is looking hard at a man who has just arrived at the café.

'He's here,' he murmurs to the others. 'I told you. They all come to this place sometime during their stay ...'

Othman looks across the tables and recognizes the Somali sea-master who docked the dhow the day before.

'Let him take a sip of coffee,' says Ali softly, 'then he will have to leave the money for it. How those sailors hate to spend their hard-earned money.'

'What do you mean ...?' Othman begins, but by this time the others are on their feet and walking towards the Somali, whose face is bent over his cup. Othman follows them.

The Somali looks up as they spread themselves around his table, his lips drawing back from his stained teeth in nervousness. He looks around quickly, but there is no one to whom he can turn for support.

Hassan leans over the table and stares into the master's coffee.

'You have two hours,' he says to the black man. 'The canal is narrow where it enters the lake and widens as it moves seaward. We shall wave to you from the banks, you understand? The nearer you are to the banks, the more chance we have of recognizing you. Two hours.'

They leave him sitting there and guide Othman back to the table. He is confused by what is going on around him. Hassan's voice had been low and full of menace. The sea-master has been threatened, obviously, and from the way he has gulped two more sips of coffee down and then fled, leaving his chair on its back, he also knows with what. But Othman does not.

'Why is he in so much of a hurry?' he asks Hassan.

'Because he's the quarry, Othman,' comes the reply, 'and you, as a hawker, should know that the quarry is always in a great deal of hurry – and panic – when he has, at last, spotted the hunter in the sky above him ...'

The lump in Othman's throat is still there, but as he stares back at the faces of his three companions there is also a heavy weight in his stomach. The faces are hard and that of Amelik is crossed with a sneer.

Ali says, 'Have we a fourth weapon for this new member, or has he the power to skim pebbles over a quarter of a kilometre?'

'There's a spare rifle in the vehicle,' replies Ali, sitting down again. 'Now we'll drink some more coffee before the hunt ... Coffee!' he yells the last word. The waiter comes at a run.

The hummer slides along the bank of the canal like a stunted snake. Hassan is at the controls. Othman is glancing at him from the adjacent seat. Ali and Amelik are on the far bank, half a kilometre distant, in a second vehicle. Both hummers have caught up with the dhow, which wisely maintains a course in the centre of the canal.

'Why not modern weapons?' asks Othman, balancing the rifle in his hands. The old brown butt is worn and polished.

Hassan shakes his head. 'Too easy – there would be no sport in it. They enjoy this as much as we do – they're of the old school. It's great sport.'

Othman says nothing. He watches the dhow, a fat grey ghost in the moonlight gliding over the still canal. It is a strange sensation being out under the stars – strange for a sixteen-year-old boy who has not strayed into unpopulated regions except in public transport. He wonders what induced him to come with these three unsavoury characters. Having no previous experience of teenage wantonness it was easy for the persuasive Hassan to convince Othman that no harm was intended to the Somali. That this was all a game which, though not entirely approved of, was looked upon indulgently by the authorities. Now Othman is not so sure, sitting beside the intent older youth and seeing in his stance a suppressed, unnatural excitement – an excitement Othman knows to be tinged with fear. And why should Hassan be afraid if this is just a boys' prank? There is also Ali to consider. The boy is plainly malicious, if the picture he painted of himself is a true one.

The noises of the night pass over the hummer, clearly audible above the soft whisper of the motor – even the creaking of the stays and the flapping of the dhow's sail carries to them over the black water, flat and smooth as slate. Men's voices sound to Othman as if their owners are within touching distance, yet they are out there, on the water, accompanying the discordant joints of wood that moan and cry out with every movement of the ancient craft. It seems as if everything in the world is in a conspiratorial mood, conferring in low tones against other, equally menacing groups. A shiver passes through Othman's body and he wonders for the fifth time how he came to be persuaded to join this idiotic venture.

They reach an outcrop of rock and Hassan stops the vehicle and jumps out with a rifle in his hand. Othman follows reluctantly. They have passed the dhow and now they wait until it draws alongside them before opening fire.

'Where do we aim for?' asks Othman, hoping they will merely attempt to bring down the sail or smash the boat's rudder. Men are visible on the deck amongst the bales of rags. Othman wonders what those rags hide. Contraband of some kind? Unlikely. Perhaps something exotic? – there were still those people who liked to believe in the magical properties of powdered rhinoceros horns. Or possibly the rags disguised riches? These were the romantic thoughts of the adolescent as his companion said, 'We aim for the men!'

'Don't be stupid!' Othman's voice is harsh with fear.

'Don't call me stupid,' replies Hassan in a pleasant tone, which is at variance with his next action. He lifts the rifle, works the bolt and takes aim at the craft. There is a long, agonizing moment, as long as a man's lifetime for Othman who sees the Somali master at the helm, a black silhouette against a grey backdrop waiting for death – then the shot crashes out over the water and almost with relief he hears the round splintering through wood. The shape at the helm bobs down after an instant and others jump up.

'Stop this,' shouts Othman at Hassan. He climbs to his feet.

'*Mafishmuk,*' growls Hassan. 'Get down, you brainless fool, before you get hurt. They may have weapons too – I'd be surprised if they didn't.'

'What kind of stupid game is this?' yells Othman. 'Men killing each other – over nothing?'

'It adds a little spice,' smiles Hassan from his position behind the rock. '*Now* will you get down!'

'I will ...' begins Othman but the sentence is unfinished, for he is flung violently backward from his perch and he sprawls on his back in the sand. As he lies there, his lower right ribs splintered, front and back, he hears the sound of the shot drifting to him from over the water, and in that second he wonders whether it came from the far bank and he was an unintended recipient of the round, or whether it was deliberate marksmanship from the master with the crooked teeth, from his dhow.

'I will not die,' he says, to comfort himself. Then as Hassan bends over him, a yellow gaunt face, at last full of concern, the pain that calls for death floods his young body, and he screams long and loud for the night to release him. For then he *wants* to die, would give anything for death to take him. Even as he does so the messengers of his pain increase their urgent demands for the release that cannot come.

Eleven

Jessum stood waiting for his wife as she admired herself before the long wall mirror. She was not a beautiful woman, her prettiness was elfin-like, but he was very proud of her. She rarely complained and was constantly ready to lift her husband out of one of his own despondent moods with gentle cheerfulness. The builder could not imagine life without her. Of course he admired other women – he was even willing to admit to himself that he desired certain of the other wives – but he was fairly confident that he would not need to stray: Niandi satisfied his needs. He wondered what he would do if one of the women he knew was ever brazen enough to invite him openly – he could parry hints quite successfully, but a direct approach was something very different. It was not very likely, however, for Jessum was well aware that his own inadequacies were only too evident in his stolid features and equally square frame. He was not a sensuous, skilful lover. Niandi was good with him – patient. He would be lost without her, which was why he could not understand Othman. Why the leader had let his own wife live alone (or not alone?) and had allowed her to oppose him overtly, was beyond Jessum's comprehension. There was a time, long ago on Earth, before the periods chosen for simulated childhoods, when women were not equal to their men. A time when they shared their households with several other wives, and wore masks in public, and showed certain deferences to their husbands that Silandi would now consider servile and base.

Jessum wondered why the senders had not revived those times for the starship's people. Possibly having numerous wives was impracticable – the space in the starship being limited and the need for men on the new planet being paramount. Also, polygamy would introduce in-breeding within the colonials too early – too many half-brothers and half-sisters would be marrying each other if the ratio was in favour of the wives at the outset.

He sighed. It would have been pleasant though, having several dutiful wives running his house for him.

'Why the long sigh, dear?' asked Niandi as she tried, unsuccessfully, to clip on her own copper amulet. He moved over to her, to help her, thinking that he was wrong to wish for old traditions. All wives were not like Niandi – he imagined that he would have ended up with three or four shrews. Instead he had one devoted woman whom he loved to distraction.

'You haven't answered me,' she said, mildly reproving.

'What? Oh, nothing really.' He could not even remember the question now.

By way of conversation, she too began to speak of Silandi.

'I don't like that man Silandi has with her now, Jessum, shouldn't someone speak to her about him? He's very uncouth.'

Jessum was taken aback. This was the first he had heard of a man.

'You mean she has a lover?' he said, horrified.

Niandi laughed. 'Not necessarily. Don't go all prudish on me. I just mean he's seen with her sometimes. He's one of the weapon-makers – the one called Zayid – but he's a coarse-mouthed, aggressive individual with a chip on his shoulder.'

'What has he got to be aggressive about?'

Niandi sat on one of the stools near her small trinket table and began selecting a copper ring. Copper was plentiful on the island and the machines made easy work of mining it, because the ore was found close to the surface – it made reasonably attractive jewellery.

'He says,' she replied, 'that Othman has it all wrong – our purpose here. This Zayid considers that there are too many weapon-handlers and weapon-makers for us to be either a colony or a group of nomads. He thinks we are a warship that has been sent to destroy this planet because the inhabitants are threatening Earth in some way ...' Jessum laughed out loud. A thing he seldom did normally.

'Yes, like the stickmen! A really terrifying bunch of warriors they are. Highly technological, with a huge fleet of warships, noses pointed towards Earth ...'

'No,' said Niandi, 'but what if our senders can see something that we cannot? What if the *real* intelligence on this planet lives underground – or under the quicksand? Or perhaps they are on the mainland that Othman is so anxious for us to reach? What then?'

Jessum stood for a moment and seriously considered this. Then he replied, 'No, I'm sorry Niandi. If what you are saying has any truth in it anywhere we should not be here now. Do you honestly think they would allow us to work our way to the mainland? We should have been splattered over the ground long before this – and don't tell me they don't know we're here, because that would mean they were blind. Come on – let's go to the feast – with any luck Silandi won't be there and Othman will be in a good mood.'

Jessum's hopes were not to be fulfilled on the first count. Arrangements had been made to cover the few trees left near the town with lanterns and the food to be spread on the ground below. As Jessum and Niandi approached the spot, the darkness was just beginning to fall and the lights swung gently in the trees.

Odours of cooked food flowed in rivers over the brown grass: spices, meats and bread baked by slapping pancake shapes onto the walls of an earthen oven and then allowing them to brown before peeling them away. A lot of eating is going to be done tonight, thought Jessum with satisfaction. Then, as he approached the ring of people who were awaiting the arrival of Othman, he saw Silandi standing beneath a tree, arms folded and eyes running over the scene with what looked like contempt. A man stood beside her, hidden in the grouping shadows. Jessum touched Niandi's arm and went over to Silandi.

'Are you here to cause trouble?' he asked, without even greeting her.

The man, whom Jessum took to be Zayid, answered for her.

'We are here because there is a feast – if trouble comes, however, it will not be before time.'

'You are Zayid?' questioned Jessum. Silandi remained silent, regarding the interchange with a bleak expression.

The man spat. 'Aren't you even sure of the names of the people you share your town with? There are only a thousand or so – is that too many for your small brain, builder?'

Jessum stiffened as he stared into the face of the other man, twisted as it was with contempt and dislike. The nose was crooked, the tip pointing to the left side of the thin-lipped mouth – the result of a fall, Jessum knew. Oh yes, he had seen the man around of course, but to learn and remember everyone's name, why, that was not possible.

'I know you,' he said.

'Yet you question my name? You don't know me – you are not interested in me. Only those things which gain your interest remain in your memory, builder. I know everyone's name. So does Silandi. Most people do. Except you and Othman. You are the men who lock yourselves in your ivory towers. Aloof, disdainful of the rest of us . . .'

While that might have been so in Othman's case, it was not true with Jessum. With him it was simply a narrowness of memory. He could not retain as many facts, not all at once, as other people. He was ashamed of the limitation but there was little he could do about it. He had many details of his work to contain in his small memory and these just seemed to crowd out the unimportant matters.

'I came to speak to Silandi ...' he tried to parry the fierceness of Zayid's argument.

'You spoke to *me*!' snapped Zayid. 'You asked me who I was ...'

'I asked you whether you were the person I believed you to be,' said Jessum, aroused to anger at last, 'which is entirely different to what you are suggesting. Now please let me alone to speak with the wife of our leader.'

'*Your* leader, not ours,' came the rejoinder.

Silandi at last stepped between them. Jessum was aware of her fondness for him and seconds earlier he was hoping she would do something of the sort. Now he was not so sure he would not rather land a few blows on the crooked face before him. It would have been a fairly even fight for height and weight, but it was doubtful, Jessum realized, whether he could have matched the viciousness of his opponent. He was not going to get the chance to find out.

'Please, Zayid, let us talk. I'll join you again in a moment.' The weapon-maker nodded reluctantly to Silandi and then turned to melt into the darkness beyond the lights.

'I won't thank you – I wanted to fight him,' Jessum said quickly.

Silandi replied, 'I'm sure of that – but the result would not have pleased me whichever way it went. What did you want to ask me?' Her dark eyes regarded him with at least receptive affection in them, and as always Jessum felt like a small boy in her presence.

The people around them were beginning to settle by the dishes of food, and there was a great deal of chatter and excitement going on which was effectively drowning the conversation of the two of them to outside listeners.

'I wanted to ask if you were his lover,' said Jessum. The builder was conscious of at least one pair of eyes upon him; although he knew the owner could not hear the conversation from her position by a clump of tall grasses, away from the milling festivities, Niandi was watching them talk. Jessum knew the scene looked intimate.

Silandi said, 'I hope you don't ask me such a question, Jessum, because I should have to tell you that it is none of your affair.'

Jessum retorted, 'It is my affair – it is everyone's affair when it concerns the leader of the group.'

Silandi grew impatient with him.

'God's eyes, Jessum, he's not that precious. We could do without him you know – probably we would all be far better off if he did die tomorrow ...'

'You don't really mean that,' said Jessum, aghast at her display of contempt.

'I mean it!' flared Silandi and strode off in the direction taken by Zayid. Jessum contemplated following her, but decided against it. He had no desire to find his leader's wife in the arms of her lover. Guessing was one thing – knowing was something entirely different.

He looked across to Niandi and noticed she was trying to attract his attention. She was pointing to a tall man moving through the people that had now begun the feast: Othman had arrived. He looked awkward and out of place amongst the others – almost inaccessible. He still wore the same simple garment that had come from the canisters on arrival. Nothing had been done to alter the style or colour from the original except for the slit cut by Silandi down the breast. It had faded somewhat as well. On Othman, amongst those who had sewn all kinds of embellishments on their robes, embroidered the necks and sleeves, had even woven new styles of garment, the faded blue robe appeared regal. Jessum would have gone so far as to say it almost looked holy.

He saw Othman frowning and looked to where his leader's gaze was falling. Please God, not Silandi and Zayid, he thought. But it was only the morons and stickmen, drawn by the noise and excitement to the area of the lights. He knew that Othman did not approve of the stickmen – they bothered him in that there seemed to be some sort of rapport between them and the morons which none of the other ship's people could share.

Jessum's mind went back to the time when he saw a moron and stickman running their hands over each other. At first, like many others, Jessum was revolted by what he was witnessing but he gradually came to realize that something was passing between the two – some kind of understanding. Partly hidden by the undergrowth, that dripped green around him and ran its rivulets down the giant trees of the jungle forest, he had studied the pair who stood shafted by a pillar of sunlight which had forced its way through a gap high above their heads.

The native's hair, tawny in the golden light, was dry and fluffed and contrasted sharply against the smooth skin of the human. The pair of them traced each other's features with their fingers, obviously gaining something from the exchange. After a while Jessum had stepped out of the shadows and purposefully walked towards the alien. The moron, a young boy, was startled and stepped aside quickly. Jessum could see his heart racing in his chest. However, he ignored the boy and confronted the alien putting forward his hands in invitation, hoping that no one would see them and report his strange behaviour to Othman.

The native reached forward and touched the proffered fingertips. They had stood in the same position for several minutes before Jessum returned his hands to his sides. He had felt nothing and was disappointed. He had thought at the time that perhaps his previous deductions had been misguided.

He wondered now, though, what sort of reception he would have received if his hands had not been offered in friendship. Since that time he had heard of one or two instances where men had struck or pushed the natives and had received some sort of shock, not unlike an electrical discharge. Certainly the attackers had landed on their backs, having been repulsed without any physical movement on the part of the native. According to observers the attackers had merely been winded, but when questioned they were unsure of exactly what had happened to them at the time of contact. Since these incidents the stickmen had been left well alone and had gained a certain amount of respect in people's eyes. The ship's people found that the natives were harmless if left untouched and could be intimidated anyway by a mere waving of the hands in front of their faces.

Jessum moved amongst the squatting guests towards Othman after signalling his intention to Niandi. She arrived with Jessum at Othman's side and they exchanged greetings with the leader, who then said, 'These people move around like ghosts – why don't they ever make a noise? – it's weird and unnatural the way they never speak...'

Jessum turned his attention away from the natives and morons.

'Let's not brood tonight, Othman, the people want to be happy. Tonight you must inspire us to go on with the work. You must tell us of our future – we need a purpose, Othman. If we are to be nomads, to have the Bedu strain injected into our systems, then you must be the one to do it – now, while they are pleased with you.'

Niandi nodded vigorously. Othman looked down at their faces and he too nodded, but slowly and with dignity. 'I shall do it,' he promised loftily.

His dark eyes swept over the sprawling hundreds, some of the women now with infants: small children or red-faced babies. Some of them were merely pregnant. The expansion of his tribe was well in progress. A smile stretched his curved, sensuous lips to a crescent and he raised his hands.

'My people ...' he called over the bobbing heads, and a cheering began, which swelled in volume as he waited, smiling, hands raised, smiling, smiling. 'My *fortunate* people ...'

Twelve

A canister throbbed with the beat of drums long since reduced to dust or ashes, and the moron woman moved slowly to the rhythm, her abdomen rolling and subsiding with the same undulating movements as a deep-sea swell. Someone had switched the music on because Othman's bloated guests were falling asleep after the heavy meal. There is always one that hates to see the party die on its feet. One of the morons, the girl now dancing, had begun by swaying in time to the music and was now pulsating heavily, the perspiration running from her naked torso to her hips, as she weaved in and out of the guests. Not a single man's eyes was on anything but the moon-like abdomen at that time. Even the obvious displeasure of the wives was no deterrent. Feast the eyes now, thought Othman, pay with the ears later.

The drums stopped suddenly and the mood was broken. An eclipse, as the girl fell to the ground and two moron males moved forward to lift her to her feet. Othman was suddenly quite conscious of the fact that the morons were self-assured, confident people and in no way the gangling idiots they had been on arrival. They still did not speak, he thought, yet they understood. Was it possible to have understanding without language? The question was asked of himself but he was distracted by a new event: the people were stirring, shuffling to their feet as the mellow-voiced confident ones amongst them began a nasal humming or sang and danced to their own music. The canisters were forgotten and memories were searched for the tunes of their adolescence, the natural feel for the roots of rhythmic music in greater evidence than the cognizance of the craftsmanship of singing. The songs came out as blurred and haunting melodies – the music of the seas and deserts – that they would never touch. Songs that had formed in the salty throats of seafaring Arabs and had been moaned into the night; songs that had cracked the lips of hooded Bedu, skins like papyrus, as they waited out a wind full of stinging grit; songs of raiders, songs of the raided.

Othman, too, was singing lustily from a prone position on the ground and Jessum and Said Rak (who had returned from one of his numerous inspections of the perimeter sentries) were on their feet, swaying in time to sounds. More surprising were the natives who had suddenly come alive and were leaping and cavorting like gazelle, shuddering as they jumped, and even *their* throats were emitting some harsh staccato noises which added to the rhythm of the songs. It was obvious to Othman that the humans had awakened something from the depths of the stickmen. This was evidently not the first time they had danced and sung. He stopped singing himself and watched them curiously. The more he studied them the more he became convinced that they were re-enacting some kind of event.

Fascinated, he began to read the drama in their movements and gradually, as he understood, the hair on the back of his neck and on his arms began to lift. He looked around quickly to see if anyone else was aware of what was happening. The rest of the people were intent on their own enjoyment of the intoxicating music they were producing, or upon their own dancing. His eyes went back to the natives again, on the edge of the area, and the more he watched the more he was convinced of what he was witnessing: the awakening of the starship occupants after their flight in space. There were other actions being depicted which he did not fully understand – animal-like gestures, the movements of elephantine creatures slithering and sliding over the grass. There was something uncanny in the way they reproduced these scenes. There was nothing clumsy or maladroit about their movements, as he would have expected: the bodies no longer seemed angular and awkward, but performed their separate parts with a liquidity of motion which was beautiful to watch.

Interrupting Jessum's singing, he drew his lieutenant's attention to the natives and asked him what he considered was happening.

Jessum studied them through narrowed eyes – it was difficult to see every movement they made because they were often half in, and half out, of the perimeter lights. Eventually Jessum said, 'They're dancing, obviously, but I can't make out exactly what the dance consists of. Proves they've got a culture of some kind anyway – no harm there.'

Othman was about to put forward his own views and had actually opened his mouth to do so, but on thinking further he decided to remain silent. Jessum was a good man when it came to carrying out orders – he performed his precisely blueprinted instructions with thoroughness and diligence, but he was lacking in imagination. He would strain to 'see' what his leader was attempting to put across to him but Othman knew that any opinion forthcoming from Jessum would be preplanted by himself. What the engineer needed was uninfluenced confirmation not helpful agreement.

Jessum went back to the song, which was now a single tune over the whole of the party, and Othman continued to study the movements of the indigenes. He saw a dramatization of the first piles being driven into the floor below the quicksand and the hauling of freshly cut trees from the high slopes. The long arms of the natives swung up and down in time to the music, mimicking the motions of the mechanical trimmers as they cut away the branches from the main trunk. He saw the cranes at work, lifting piles, and people running to and fro with messages – the women, bringing the lunch to those who could not leave their work.

The song had stopped, but the natives continued their mime, centering the act on one of their number: this tall, long-haired creature was obviously the star of the group and although its motions were more exaggerated than those of its contemporaries, a love for dramatic movement was evident in its dance and its mime was highly credible. Othman was only vaguely aware that the singing and dancing amongst his own group had ceased and that everyone was now following his lead in giving audience to the stickmen, so engrossed was he in the scene on the edge of the darkness.

The arms of the main dancer suddenly lost their coordination and were flung into the air as it stumbled into the full glare of a lamp, the white circle spotlighting the flailing action. The alien fell to the floor and its fellow dancers moved backward with hesitant steps to the brink of night. It was as if the light was a deep pool of water and they were anxious not to fall inside it from out of the solid darkness, although one or two made half-hearted but evidently anxious attempts to rescue the main character from its position under the glare.

This one was soon back on its feet, in a crouched position, clearly floundering, all pretence of smooth motion gone. What was this? thought Othman. Was the alien ill? Or was this part of its act?

The native rose slowly from the crouched position and stretched as far as possible to its full height, the arms in the shape of a 'V' above its head. Its face registered pain and terror, and suddenly Othman and several others comprehended what was happening. A gasp came from one or two mouths as the memory of that day on the causeway came back to them. Only those who had seen the actual accident were aware of how vividly the scene was being replayed in front of them. Othman was unsure of what he should do. Stop the dance and cause an incident, or allow it to continue until it carried over into more pleasant recollections of their time on the planet? He decided on the latter. If he spoke now it would confirm what could only be suspicions at this time. His people were already very prejudiced against the stickmen.

The dancer went down again, and its cheeks bulged, the

low-fingered hands clawing at the light around it. Punctuated grunts were coming rhythmically from the morons and stickmen, hidden in the darkness around the camp, and the sound was increasing in volume.

Move on, thought Othman, move on!

The body rose again, painfully slowly in a serpentine movement, towards the imaginary surface of the quicksand, and broke through with another waving of the arms, but this time the mouth was no longer open and round with fear – it was slack and lifeless, and the whole facial expression told of loose muscles and death.

'My God,' said a white-faced Jessum quickly from beside him. Othman clenched his fists but still said nothing.

Several times the body went down – and always it came up to haunt them with its horrific expression, and as it came up for the last time, Othman realized he should have stopped the dance. Several of the stickmen stepped into the light at the edge of the circle and aimed their arms like weapons as the main dancer waved its own arms loosely in front of them. There was a hissing, clacking noise from the alien's lips and the body in the centre jerked and leapt as the imaginary missiles blew it to pieces – and then followed the high nasal whine from the audience. It was not the sound of fear, it was the sound of hate being released from within a woman, and one of her hands reached out towards Othman. The face above the accusing arm was twisted in anguish.

'The widow,' said Said Rak.

Othman nodded. 'Get her out of here,' he said softly to Said Rak. Then to Jessum, 'Move those creatures – get them well out of our way for a few days. I'll handle this side of it.'

Jessum motioned for a couple of men to follow him. Niandi was shouting to the widow. 'Don't worry' – she turned to the crowd – 'that lady is ill, having recently lost her husband. The soldiers will look after her – take her back to her room where she can rest. I'll come with you ...' she called to the widow.

Niandi forced her way through the throng towards the woman. All eyes were still turned in the direction of the scream.

'I don't want to come with you,' the woman screeched at Niandi, who took no notice and began in soothing tones by saying she was overwrought and needed help. One or two murmurs of dissent began to creep into the crowd as the soldiers, brought by Said Rak, gently but firmly grasped an arm each. A voice was heard clearly over the others as she was pulled away.

'So this is how our great leader handles delicate situations? He stamps all over them, trying to pound them to nothingness in the dust – not happy with desecrating the dead, he bullies the mourners when they object ...'

It was Zayid. Othman found his face in the crowd. This was a situation he could handle, crossing verbal swords with the weapon-maker. Hopefully it would steal the attention from the woman – the opposite, no doubt, of what Zayid had intended should occur.

'Do I hear a crooked voice from the crowd?' boomed Othman. 'Who is it that speaks through his nose at me?'

Pro-Othmanites, taking the cue, laughed softly.

'Stop trying to change the subject, Othman,' said Zayid, 'you played that woman false.'

Othman's voice was suddenly full of anger.

'You dare to accuse me of that? The woman herself will swear that I have not been near her since her husband's unfortunate death. Nor have I ever been. Your mind is a pit of filth, Zayid – you are a lazy, indolent man with nothing better to do than dream of lies in order that you can warp the goodness in our lives here.'

Someone shouted, 'Yes, he does no work, all he does is talk ...'

'Revolution, no doubt,' called Said Rak, who had returned. 'We know how to deal with those who incite others, innocent but gullible men, to revolution ...'

The crowd began to murmur, jostling Zayid.

Zayid growled angrily, something about warping what *he* was saying. Othman spoke rapidly.

'There'll be no need for that, Said Rak – we'll not have any hangings here – not tonight ...'

Silandi's voice was heard then. A frightened tone.

'Who spoke of hanging? No one even considered it ...'

'Of course not,' interrupted Othman. 'I would not allow it. I do not believe in hanging men until it has been proved, beyond doubt, that they *are* guilty of treason. I don't consider Zayid guilty of any crime, merely because he feels it is his duty to speak out against me instead of participating, like his comrades, in the necessary hard work associated with building a new life here ...'

'You sound as if you regard yourself as a king,' snarled Zayid.

'Only in that I am concerned for the welfare of these people, which includes yourself. I don't regard myself as *above* them – I am one of them. But someone must bear the responsibility for their guidance, their well-being, and this task has fallen upon me. With that task go certain tools – one cannot carry out one's work without the proper tools.' Othman's voice was hard. 'Those implements of which I speak are necessarily only used when the welfare of the group, or one of the group, is threatened. As I have said, I am one of the group, and you threaten me, Zayid, with your talk of revolution. The punishment I am entitled to use in order to protect the individual rights of the group are only used in the extreme. I do not wish to use the law against you, Zayid – do not make me. Never,' he paused, 'give me cause to hang you, for I should be bound to do so, however much it grieved me.'

'What terrible words you use, Othman – do you consider hanging proper?' cried Silandi.

'Only in extreme cases,' said Othman, 'rape, murder, treason ...'

'Adultery?' she added quickly.

There was silence. Zayid wisely began moving back into the shadows while all eyes were on Silandi.

'Adultery?' Othman laughed, 'Why, I should have to hang all the morons then.' This broke the tension and the crowd laughed with him. He shook his head. 'No, I can't believe anyone here would want to commit such a moronic act. Husbands and wives are too attached to each other and it is only the idle who have time to look for such silly games to play ...'

He paused. 'Now. How shall we complete the evening? A fine feast's been eaten, we've all rested after our meal and enjoyed our own entertainment. The natives attempted, childish creatures that they are, to spoil any celebrations but they could not succeed.' He clicked his fingers. 'I have it! A horse race! The dawn isn't far away – we shall have a horse race the length of the shoreline and I for one plan to bet heavily. I have only a few possessions, but by God I intend to increase them today – or lose them, every one then ...'

The people cheered and there was an uncontrolled rush towards the stables.

Silandi was left standing in the centre of the lights, looking very lost and alone. Said Rak grasped Othman's arm and began to walk him away, talking quickly. There was a surge of anger in Othman's heart as he looked towards his wife: he even went to raise his hand, but her eyes remained elsewhere and very soon he allowed his attention to be diverted by something Said Rak was mentioning in the course of his prattle. Inside, however, his heart felt as if it had been twisted like a wet cloth, forcing out like water all the fondness he had ever felt for Silandi. Adultery! She had admitted – practically admitted at any rate – her infidelity in public.

What worried him more was the reports from his adherents that Zayid was plotting against him. Othman could do nothing until the man made a wrong move but it might be too late then. It was rumoured that Zayid had two targets – the causeway and Othman himself. Possibly political assassination – or perhaps the pair of them even sought his death? They would not need to destroy the causeway then, for he was the only true supporter of his own plans. Even Jessum was for the man, Othman, rather than the idea.

Thirteen

The horses had, like the camels and falcons, been included among the starship's births purely for their recreational value. The community needed certain outlets and the horses and stables were an integral part of the unit which supplied the leisure pursuits. The camels could be raced too – they were dromedaries – but they were not as popular as the horses simply because they did not have the romantic impetuosity of the young stallions. (None of the horses were gelded, as those that did ride saw no necessity to remove the ginger from their mounts.) The mares were also ridden but not often and then only by women. Traditionally the horses were ridden without saddles, though reins were used, and the participants fought with their favourite mounts in the early dawn, as legs and hooves flashed backwards and sideways, to maintain some sort of distance between the stallions. Bloodstock joined animals with less than perfect pedigrees in scooping clods at the crowd. Kings of speed nodded noble heads heavily in the humid atmospheres of dew-steam, and trim ankles crossed and re-crossed in a variety of nervous dances. Horses rise quickly to meet the *ad hoc* fevers their masters produce and are swift to add their own brand of excitement to unusual gatherings.

Onlookers shouted encouragement to the riders and the betting was brisk considering the limited possessions with which the punters bargained.

'The new set of stools I had made by one of the carpenters, what will you offer against them?'

'The tapestry which my wife is weaving – I'll lay it on the grey ...'

'But that tapestry is unfinished –'

'It's all I have apart from my wife.'

'In that case I accept – my stools are on the small palomino. Whichever one of those two horses comes in first, agreed?'

'Agreed. But I also want to bet on the blue roan ...'

'I'm sorry, one wife is enough for me. I might win ...'

The stallions lashed at each other viciously, occasionally curling back lips and revealing rows of long teeth with which they snapped at their opponents' rumps. There is only one stallion that counts in the herd, the leader, and, being well fed and strong beasts, they all wanted to be leaders. There was a breeze that lifted their manes and tails and as Silandi, accompanied by the truculent Zayid, watched in envy, she often thought of Sham-san, her own magnificent stallion. Was he a ghost? Just a dream? – or had there been a real Sham-san on Earth? She knew these questions could only remain questions. Earth could only be the somewhere of her simulated childhood – a place she had never physically touched. If Sham-san had lived, he was not her Sham-san. Even if they had taken a model from a real Earth-born stallion, to form the picture they had placed in her mind, they could not have reproduced the same odours, the same feel. She could smell the aromatic muscles of her stallion now, the sweat-stink was heavy in her nostrils, and her hands yearned to stroke a finely-planed nose. She looked around her sharply – was it possible that Sham-san was one of the stallions? She had only ridden twice since they had landed on Jessum, and then with only half a mind on the pleasure. There had been too many other, more serious, considerations with which to concern herself. Perhaps all horses smell the same? Nevertheless she felt the old excitement stirring in her breast and her thighs began to long for the pressing of wide flanks beneath them.

'I'm going to ride,' she said to Zayid.

He looked at her quickly.

'Why?'

'Because I want to – not because of these fools, but because I need to prove something to myself.'

She walked over to a stallion that was close to Sham-san in its markings and looks – it was a tall bay. The rider was an overweight man and he was sucking a ball of qat. His name was Mahmond. Othman had forbidden the use of the drug but the law was not strictly enforced and no punishment for any infringement of Othman's so-called laws had ever yet been issued.

'Can I ride instead of you?' she asked of him.

He laughed at the joke, spitting green liquid at her feet.

'I've got the horse, why should I give him to you? Besides, a woman would be slaughtered in a race of stallions and men. Find yourself a quiet mare and trot along behind.'

Silandi held back her anger but was adamant. 'I wish to ride this stallion – you know who my husband is?'

Mahmond laughed again.

'I don't think you'll get any help from that quarter tonight – you can't turn your back on your army and run, then expect it to fight for you when your running leads you into trouble . . .'

'All right, Silandi,' said a voice behind her. 'I'll deal with Mahmond.'

It was Zayid. She had half hoped it would be Othman. The horse began to get restless and was side-stepping. Mahmond, trying to keep control, said, 'What business is this of yours, bent nose?'

Zayid smiled wickedly.

'Off the horse, you fat oaf, or I'll bend more than your nose for you.' He took hold of the rein. 'I'll start with your neck.'

Less indignantly, and with a little less confidence in his voice, Mahmond repeated his previous sentence, leaving out the insulting epithet this time.

Zayid gave the rein a little flick and the stallion reared,

making Mahmond clutch at the mane for support. His face was growing pale.

'It would be an interesting experiment to stick the point of my dagger into this twitching flesh,' said Zayid, staring at the stallion's rump, still retaining his grip on the reins.

'You would no doubt win the race with very little effort then ...'

'You're only trying to frighten me, Zayid – I'll call to Othman. He'll soon show ...' But he didn't have time to finish what he was saying, for Zayid had reached up and dragged him to the ground by his robe front. Mahmond lay stunned on the grass and several onlookers gasped as Silandi leapt on to the stallion's back and moved off to join the starters. It was one thing to witness an argument between two men – that was not unusual. But it was quite another thing to see violence displayed so openly. Most of those who saw the deed were obviously deeply shocked.

The chosen starting point for the race was at the delta of the island's one small river, and there was great confusion over who was judging and as to the precise details of the course because there were places where the shoreline was inaccessible and could not be followed. However, several men had been dispatched on camels to act as umpires and to keep the less orientated among them on the right path.

Silandi chose a spot amongst the milling hordes which would give her a clear run along the shore without having to circumnavigate rocks or trees. If she could manage to get out in front in the first few hundred metres she had a chance of staying there. Around the second bend, a kilometre ahead, the ground level rose sharply from the quicksand to a small overhang. Silandi envisaged that there would be trouble in that bottleneck and she wanted to be well clear of any packs that might be rolled together at that point. The old feeling of excitement was beginning to affect her now and, looking round at the other riders, she appeared to be the only woman in the race. That, too, was consistent with her childhood memories and gave her a feeling of superiority over the other females of the town, who she knew were making her a focal point for their gossip. This will give them something to spear with their sharp little tongues, she thought. Suddenly the crowd had gone silent and she was aware that the self-styled officials had ceased bickering and were about to start the race.

At the last moment, before the raised hand fell, Silandi caught the eyes of Niandi and read in them sympathy, not envy or awe, and she realized that her real reason for riding in the race must be altogether too evident. Then her horse heaved forward, instinctively, as the other mounts were at last allowed to give vent to their frustrated nervous desire to be free from restraint.

Silandi broke clear of the cluster quickly and fought hard to keep her horse ahead at this early stage. Two other stallions remained with her, one so close that flecks of spittle hit her cheeks as she leaned forward to clear a fallen log which lay in her path. As her mount hit the soft earth on the other side it kicked out savagely with its near hind leg, catching the accompanying roan on its flank with a crack, and she heard a cry of pain – then the roan's rider slipped from view. The cracking sound must have been a bone in the rider's body.

While this difference of opinion was going on, the third horse, a grey, had gained a few metres and was now rounding the first bend. The horseman on its back was tall and dark-skinned, and he knew how to ride. Wearing only a loincloth, he worked his mount with the minimum of effort, using his knees to guide the animal, leaving his hands free to signal other instructions through the medium of the reins. A flick for more speed. Gentle pressure on the mouth for an easing of pace. Warning signals for objects ahead. In this man Silandi had a worthy contender and she increased her own stallion's gallop to keep within striking distance.

Behind her, as she had forecast, was a tight knot of riders

shouldering each other for space. Already the shoreline was beginning to narrow as they approached the second bend. Silandi took the curve leaning against the slope. Once or twice the stallion, which she had now renamed Sham-san, whatever his previous name had been, lost his footing, but Silandi's gentle encouragement persuaded him to maintain full gallop and with a lot of snorting and heavy wheezing he continued to pound the soft rocks to powder beneath his hooves.

As she pulled out of the bend the riders and horses behind entered it, and there were shouts of anger and fear filling the air. She spurred on Sham-san with her heels. In the near distance, through some trees, she could see the front rider forcing a path through the foliage. She had not planned this particular aspect but her strategy had been wise – not only could she slip-stream the grey, she could let it do the work of cutting the course for them. Below her, Sham-san the second worked his thick legs and the sweat from his flanks ran down her thighs and calves. She could feel the hood of her robe billowing to its cornet shape behind her head, probably adding to Sham-san's work, but there was little she could do about it.

A man on a stationary camel, a marshal, suddenly appeared in front and she turned Sham-san inland as indicated by his arm. There were about eight metres between her and the leader now, and he was gradually increasing the gap. The next pair were some twenty-five metres behind Silandi.

'Come on boy! Come on!' she urged softly. The fatigue of heavy exercise after a night without sleep was beginning to hit her and her shoulders were starting to ache.

Two more course umpires were passed and still she had gained no more ground on the leader – in fact the rider behind had closed up on her. Sham-san was still moving strongly. She gave him a flick of the reins and received a rewarding surge of speed.

The pain from her shoulders gradually spread throughout

her entire body and soon she found herself battling to reject it instead of channelling her concentration into getting the best out of the horse. The home stretch was in sight and she could see the people, some of them squatting high in the crooked trees that had been scorned by the cutters.

The front rider was a silhouette against the intense glare of the new yellow day – and then, quite suddenly, he was gone and his mount was over.

He had fallen!

Eagerly she pushed Sham-san with her knees.

'Move, damn you, move!' she said.

But the leader, though down, was a determined, seasoned rider and he quickly remounted before she could pass him. Once back on his mount he was again in strong contention and the man, with only a metre between him and Silandi, his loincloth rippling in the winds created by the power of his beast, bore down on the finish line.

'God's eyes, just a little more speed,' cried Silandi, and at the very moment when the realization that she was not going to win began to enter her brain, a moron stepped out of the crowd and into the path of her horse, whose sweat-sore eyes were firmly fixed on the distant horizon.

Desperately she sawed at the horse's mouth in an attempt to halt him. Had she swerved either way, she would have ploughed through the people who had formed a channel to the finish line. Sham-san, weary with expended effort and entranced by the sheer length of the race he had run to the thudding rhythm of his own blood, would not have stopped running even if his heart had ceased to function.

Fourteen

Othman walked beneath the rows of missile tubes and wondered at the intelligence of those who had sent him to this place. The high banks of the launcher's blow-hole black nozzles pointed at clouds, and external casings glinted silver-blue in the sun. Behind them dull black canisters, each the height of two men, stood on the shoulders of others in covered trenches twenty metres deep. This was the ammunition for the tubes and it was kept cool from the heat of the day by the sunpowered refrigeration system that ran around the storage area. Guarding the trenches and the missile-launching banks were conventional fireball catapults. These could throw a compact bolt of energy, in the form of heat, up to fifty kilometres. Said Rak had once told Othman that the missiles themselves, each one of them, were capable of destroying around thirty spaceships the size of the one that had brought them to Jessum, provided the ships were no more than one hundred kilometres apart. Apparently the missile was segmented and jumped from one object to another like a jumping jack with a perfect sense of direction.

There were eight such missile sites around the island. The ship's machines had placed them in strategic points on arrival.

Othman had come to the site for privacy. His own house was used as a politician's forum and all those who wished to air their views (or curry favour with Othman and his officers) could call there when they had a mind to. Normally Othman enjoyed this communication with his people, and encouraged it, but today he wanted to sort out the events of the previous evening in his mind.

His wife, God curse her beauty, had struck the first blow with the oral attack in front of the guests at the feast. To admit adultery with that unspeakable foul-mouthed son-of-a bastard – but what was he thinking! They were all bastards, spawned by a machine. Bastards of metal tubes like these, that spat flashes of light at him as he walked by them. He sighed. Even that was not true, for their parents *were* human and the ship had merely cosseted the embroys, like an incubator, until they were ready to flower. Until the ship had *allowed* them to flower? No. The ship had been programmed by the senders – the parents, who were not legally married – which led Othman back again to his original thought. Zayid *was* a bastard. They were all illegitimate children of long-dead parents who had lived in some other time, some other universe.

Who are we? thought Othman. When were we born? Were we born on Earth? – the cycle had begun there. Who is to set the stage of growth at which a person is born? When is life truly life? Not surely when the ovum and sperm are in their separate carriers, the male and female. How about the instant when the spermatozoon enters the ovum? Is that birth? Certainly it is the beginning of life.

Or is birth the conventional time when the baby appears, fully formed, and is divested of the umbilical cord? The point at which freedom from the host is reached? But the freedom is purely physical, for the child is still dependent upon its parents, or at least one of them, for life. Without its mother or father the child dies.

Then birth must be when he or she is also spiritually, as well as physically, independent of the parent. When the child becomes an adult? That statement in itself proves that birth at that point is not true birth for to become an adult the person must have been an adolescent, a child, a baby – and before the baby the birth must take place.

Which leads us back to the embryo again, thought Othman. Us. We, the ship's people. Born of a machine; an engine. But what is a planet, the planet Earth, if not an engine, a large, beautiful engine that turns in space, thought Othman, and manufactures life? And the metal that made the ship, and the machines in the ship, and the computer, and even the parents that never met or married were all born of Earth, a life machine. All those worlds in space, created by God, are the engines of birth, he told himself. From the intricate insect to the ungainly camel the spherical engines produce their life forms, churning out plants for them to eat; sucking water from the seas with hot breath and coughing it back as spray over the fields and mountains. Perhaps, he added the final touch, just perhaps, all planets in the universe came from one cloud of gas and the world Jessum and their parent Earth were both from one and the same source. Then he would be standing on the twin of the engine of his birth. The idea made him feel more secure.

He leaned against one of the launching tubes and found it surprisingly cool. There must have been an ingredient in the metal that acted as a thermostat, preventing the expansion or contraction of the tubes whose gauge possibly needed to be accurate to a micrometre. He stared up at the rows of open, silent mouths and considered Said Rak's statement that they should have deployed these weapons and made them ready for action. The machines had merely dumped the tubes and ammunition in lots. It was up to the humans to have emplacements built and manned and the weapons in war condition. Those snouts should have been swivelling now – penetrating the several layers of atmosphere into the black outside; living, breathing metal beasts with eyes and ears, and a quick, destructive blowing of the nose – like the explosive sneeze of a dog sniffing an ants' nest.

Othman sighed. All the preparation of the senders and still things were going wrong. He had walked out to this place to be alone and consider his friend's plight. Even now no one was quite sure what had happened. Had the horse trampled him? Or was it as the crowd had afterward insisted – that the moron had used some kind of martial art to throw Jessum from him, believing himself to be under attack?

The moron had walked out, according to reports (given in the heat of excitement and possibly unreliable) in front of Silandi's horse as it sped full-gallop down a channel of cheering punters. His wife had obviously not been fully attentive and had failed to rein in her stallion. The moron would have been killed, or at least seriously injured had Jessum not dived from the crowd and carried him out from under the falling hooves. Unfortunately, even as his life was being saved, the moron had no realization of the danger, and onlookers saw Jessum thrown violently backwards to a distance of about five metres, where he landed on his back and lay still. Malek had said that Jessum's right arm and part of his right side were paralysed.

'The nerves are completely dead,' he confirmed later, when Jessum had undergone an inspection by the machinations of the medical unit from the ship. 'Nothing can be done.'

So Jessum was a cripple. This morning he had been a man, and now he was – what? Still a man? God, yes. Jessum was not the type of person to allow an infirmity to lay him permanently low. He would soon be on his feet. He had to be. Othman needed him.

'He's beginning to recover. He's a lot better now.'

Othman looked up from his hang-head position in the shade of the tubes. He had been so deep in thought that he had not been aware of Niandi's approach. She stood before him, small and petite – a strong will belied by her finely-cut features.

'I'm glad,' he replied. 'Has he asked for me?'

'All the time,' she said. 'You know you're his main concern – even above me.'

Othman felt uncomfortable beneath her cool, calm gaze.

'I'm sorry,' he said quickly.

She tossed her hair.

'Don't be. It's the way he's made. I don't doubt that if it came to a choice he would pick me anyway, out of a sense of loyalty, but it need never come to that. You understand me, don't you, Othman?' She stared at him coolly.

God, no, he groaned inwardly. A wayward wife was enough to worry about. He had no need for a mistress – least of all one like this, who would cling to him as a hawk holds a precarious rock perch – hard and tenaciously.

'I mean,' she continued as if his thought had penetrated her delicate skull, 'that as long as you retain him as your second man, he and I are your people. You could have no one more loyal than Jessum. Many leaders have spent their lives looking over their shoulders at their subordinates – you need have no fear. But Jessum must stay, despite this ...'

Othman interrupted, relieved. 'I need Jessum as much as he needs me, Niandi – tell him that. I have no fears ...' She was determined to push it home with all her force. 'He is simple in his principles ...'

'I know, I know,' Othman reassured.

'Good. Now I must tell you that the bridge has been damaged. I wanted to be sure of Jessum's position first, as he is in charge of your project ...'

Othman's eyes opened very wide and he took her hard by the shoulders.

'Is it very bad?'

'You're hurting me – no, not bad. A gap, that is all. A gap of some twenty metres ...'

'The morons!' he snarled. 'And those natives ...'

'No. It must have been someone who could work a digger. It was done during the feast – half the sentries sneaked away to join the party that night and the other half were dozy with the heat. Someone took a digger and dug out a good chunk ... will you let me go now, please? I don't know why you're so wrought up. The damage is only slight – a gesture, that's all.'

'Or perhaps whoever did it had no more time – but plans to do more serious damage later?'

Niandi shrugged him off finally.

'In that case, we'll make sure the guards are wide awake. I'll attend to it, don't worry. Said Rak will soon tire of the sharp edge of my tongue and he'll have his men in better fettle even before night-fall. You leave this to me.'

He looked hard at the woman and his mind rejected a wild thought that formed in its putty-grey mass. Women were only women. Sometimes a woman could be part falcon – but she could never replace a man. Jessum might need a crutch, perhaps had always needed one, but it was Jessum who stood for Othman's authority. And Said Rak, bumbling man that he was, he was still a man.

'Thank you,' he replied. 'I accept your offer to help until Jessum is back on his feet.'

'I was ...' she began, but he interrupted her, touching her lips with his fingertips and looking upwards. Coloured shapes arrowed above them and then grouped before dropping to the grasses below.

'See how magnificent those birds with the green plumage are? And strong-looking, compared to the duller, smaller mates? – they are the cocks, the male of the species. Beautiful, aren't they?' He locked with her eyes, and slowly the protest left them, and she nodded, comprehending.

'We must be getting back,' she said at last.

When they arrived back at the bedside of Jessum the injured man was awake and managed a smile. His face was the hue of graveyard clay. His right arm lay still alongside him: a giant, subsurface, slug-like creature, gassed in its own dirt tunnels and forced to the surface to die, half in and half out of the dark armhole of the robe. The dull shades of grey-white left no doubt in Othman's mind that the ugly limb would never again function as a completely live thing, and the revulsion he felt for it made him consider asking Malek to remove it – to amputate the paralysed flesh. It was not his arm to have cut away however, and all he could do was avoid looking at its dull, heavy form on the white sheet.

'How are you?' he asked Jessum.

Niandi was hovering in the background and before he could answer she screeched and pointed to the corner of the room. Malek came waddling in to see what was the matter and saw where she was pointing. He nodded. 'The moron – yes, well I've had him thrown out three times but he keeps coming back in. Sits in that corner with his head touching his toes and only looks up when Jessum speaks. I think he's sorry for what he's done and wants to make amends – but he doesn't know how.'

Othman turned to Jessum.

'Do you mind him being here? They're quite clean now – something I've always found strange about them. When we first came they urinated and dropped their faeces where they stood ...'

'I don't mind him,' said Jessum.

Niandi snapped, 'I do.'

'Please,' Jessum said, 'I don't want any more disturbance – just leave him there till he gets tired. He'll go away in his own time ...' As he was speaking Jessum's grey face seemed to swell slightly, and suddenly he was vomiting again. Othman and Niandi moved to the doorway, and Malek reluctantly stayed to offer his patient his ministrations and best bedside sympathy. The moron rose from his couch and began to clean up the mess. After a while Malek left him to it and joined the others at the door.

Fifteen

Fdar was bound, as surely as if he was a slave, to the man with the one arm, and he tried not to feel bitterness towards the woman who had caused the accident – the wife of the leader of the town people. The moron could not even say he knew he was being attacked at the time. The man had jumped on him from the crowd and Fdar had used the repulse pattern instinctively – the involuntary regions of his brain had used it, as it would on an unwelcome insect that settled on his flesh, and now he was responsible for damaging the body of the man who had saved his life. It was right that Fdar should replace that arm.

But it made him unhappy because his people, his real people, were not staying with the town people for very much longer. They were going away, when the time was right, to find a new place where the trees still grew strong and plants were not torn from the ground with no thought of replacing them. Already the sky was hotter, the mornings yellow as the mouth of a fire machine.

He was watching from the windows of one-arm's house the machines repairing the hole in the bridge. The men who worked the machines were burned black by the sun and their headcloths were wrapped around their faces and showed only their eyes. On the sill of the house was a small plant, and Fdar touched its petals. If he concentrated very hard he might be able to feel the patterns but today was a bad time and concentration did not come easily. He was not patient enough to put in the effort. One-arm was asleep beside him and stirred only occasionally. The man's wife had not approved of Fdar's presence until she had seen him clean up the vomit. Then she knew why he was there. The wife had left them alone a short while ago and was now on the bridge, talking to the men who carried the weapons. Fdar sighed. He was dead now. His life was in the man who slept by his hip. A man with no patterns.

Why?

Why were the town people empty? And their animals? Because they were not born of the planet? The ship's plants had patterns, but then they had been seeds and had sprung from the planet's soil. Fdar knew why he could send and receive the patterns through his own nerve ends – because he had only

115

been a shell on arrival, whereas the creatures that were human already had the animal of themselves within their minds when they opened their eyes. They had a sad way of life. To see colours was not enough. One had to *feel* them to know their true worth.

To touch a reptile and experience the slow, lazy rivers flowing through the mind! Liquid malachite in the young. Sludge green from the mature amphibians. Or the short, sharp electric flash of an insect. A dull brown from a flying mammal, dozing in the thick of a tree's branches. Sudden lines of bright thread weaving a tapestry in one of the quick forest creatures, stationary only a nervous second before dancing with the trees again. These were valuable. These were denied the town people.

And the most beautiful sensation of all – those strong patterns, the planet's core, comet-tailed, cloud light, sun white ecstasies of a man and girl locked together, fast as tree roots around a rock, making love: the crisp salt of their bodies mingling as the wetness flows from their skin, the iron in their blood forming tight wires to jerking muscles, the smell of oxygen burning, circuit fusing in their veins as they reach out to touch the innumerable corners of the universe.

Othman was on the causeway, supervising the repairs. With Jessum ill he could no longer maintain his Periclesian aloofness.

He knew, of course, that it was Silandi and Zayid who had sabotaged the causeway even before they had disappeared – before Othman had had the chance to prove himself a rational politician. He would not have had them punished – he had been prepared to forgive them this indiscretion in return for their attention. Once he had them listening he would have explained to them just how necessary the causeway was to the survival of the group. The problem was one of food. Since they had been living on the island, some four years by ship time, they had been delving into their stores, supplementing the rations with local forest creatures and the livestock they bred for themselves, rather than the other way around. Although the stores would last some while yet there was not enough grazing on the island for the livestock and soon the herds the women had built up would be dying for lack of grass.

The fault lay with themselves: with Othman, since he was the leader. No crops had been planted. No ground had been cleared and tilled to receive the seed. The stumps were still hard in the soil where the trunks had been severed. The machines had been fully employed on the causeway and there had been none available to plough and prepare the soil for sowing. There were small patches planted by the women but these amounted to very little.

He still considered he was right, however, to build the bridge. There was something indefinably wrong with settling down in one place. The group was meant to be on the move, he was convinced of that. Othman's main argument to support his decision was that there were only a few farmers amongst them. Surely if they were intended to settle, they would be formed of a majority of agricultural experts, with certain associated tradesmen? God, their only real expert in plant life was the doctor, Malek.

Malek. In his mind he went over a conversation he had had with the doctor only a few days previously. They had been standing on a high point, overlooking the raw side of the island.

'The qat trees are few and far between – wild plants,' Malek had said, 'but qat is not the only Earth-type vegetation that grows on our island. There is also wild corn and one or two domestic fruits – date palms.'

'What are you trying to say? Surely we've planted some of these ourselves?'

'Yes, but I've found the plants in places where we have not considered settling – on the mountainside and towards the crescent point at the far end of the island. I think the natives are stealing the seeds and scattering them – trying to replace what we have taken from them. In which case it cannot really be considered stealing.'

Othman thought for a moment, then said, 'But doctor – does it matter?'

'It matters because when we do eventually settle we're going to need all the seeds we can find. My advice is to put some guards on the seed canisters ...'

Othman nodded. 'I'll consider it. But at the moment we need guards on so many things.'

'Like the causeway?' said the easily perturbable Malek.

'Like the causeway,' confirmed Othman with finality in his voice.

Malek was a fussy man, thought Othman. But his knowledge was useful.

A woman was at Othman's elbow, businesslike.

'Daydreaming again?' It was Niandi.

Othman took her arm and gently pulled her aside as a bulldozer rumbled past. It was nowhere near them but Othman had inexplicably felt the need to touch her. He needed the physical contact with another human being occasionally, to pull himself back into the world.

'Yes, I'm afraid so.'

'Thinking about Silandi?'

'Not in the way you mean. All I want is for them to be found so that they cannot damage the causeway again. It won't take long. There can't be many places to hide.'

Niandi shook her head doubtfully.

'There are the caves on the mountain, and the swamplands near the crescent point ...'

'They'll be back,' said Othman, 'when they get hungry.'

Not wishing to continue the conversation, he shouted a command to a man further along the causeway. The man acknowledged the order with a wave of his arm, but glanced towards his foreman before carrying it out. Othman gave himself a mental kick. If he was to maintain his detached authority he would have to learn to go through the line of authority. He had left it all to Jessum before. He looked at the woman beside him. Niandi? Why not? She was a female and it would be grudgingly accepted, but if they knew it was only a stop-gap until Jessum was well again they would not mind so much. So far as Niandi was concerned it would prevent another man usurping her husband's position, and Othman, for his part, trusted her implicitly. He needed to trust someone.

The next morning Othman accompanied a party of soldiers, led by Said Rak, up the mountainside. They were heading for the natural caves which fly-specked the south face.

The temperature was high and the men were sweating freely as they moved despondently towards their objective. They met one or two of the natives who stood watching the group as they struggled past, more like children on their way to school than well-trained soldiers. Heat knocks a lot of alertness out of a man, saps his energy and instils listlessness into his limbs. The clouds of insects moved in and out around their heads, feeding on the sweat, not biting but an irritant all the same.

There were no well-worn goat tracks to follow, no paths of any kind. The natives had no reason to venture up the mountain as there was little vegetation on its sides. Trail-blazing is a very different thing to treading in the steps of others and progress was slow.

'I think we had better follow the stream until we're on the right level for the caves,' said Othman to Said Rak.

The soldier nodded. 'Yes, it wouldn't do to lose our way, would it? One of my men is drawing a rough map as we go but I agree we should play it safe.'

It took most of the morning to reach the level of the caves.

When they did so Othman turned to look down on his work, and seeing the dark, straight line of the causeway streaking out into the quicksand below, all its faults lost in the distance, he felt the same sort of arrogant, magnified pride that the words of Ozymandias express in Shelley's poem. These were *his* words. Othman, the engineer. Then, almost immediately, he felt depressed, for who would ever witness his achievement save a few natives and his own motley band of workers?

'Let's start on these caves,' he said sharply to Said Rak.

The man raised his eyebrows at the sudden change of mood in his leader, but being a good commander he did not question, he acted.

'On your feet, men!' he ordered, and the grumbling soldiers stirred from their sitting or prone positions, slung their weapons untidily over their shoulders and began to move along the ridge which led past the caves at a shuffling gait. Othman thought: I must speak to Said Rak about his training programme. These men should be the group's most fit and able – instead they look like shambling zombies. One day, possibly soon, they would be needed.

There were many caves and each one was deep and dark and took a great deal of courage to enter. Towards evening they had covered only a third of those they could see, and Said Rak expressed concern that the sun would leave them stranded for the night. They had torches but it would be dangerous to descend by the poor light of a hand torch, especially since there were no proper paths to follow.

Othman was on the point of agreeing when a shout came from one of the caves and a soldier came bounding out of its entrance. Immediately every man, including Othman, fell to the ground, and those with weapons hastily covered the entrance to the cave, wondering what grotesque form would follow their comrade out into the light of day.

'No, no,' shouted the man when he saw all weapons poking from behind rocks. 'It's not that. I've found something – a boat. Come and see!' He re-entered the cave, offering reassurance to those pounding hearts behind the rocks, and after a moment or two they followed. They were not to be blamed for their cowardly reactions for they considered that if the natives did not come to the mountain there must be something up there to keep them away.

The cave walls reflected the light of a dozen torches as Othman entered, and the men clustering around him spoke unnaturally in conspiratorial whispers as they moved forwards. The cave opened into a large cavern and in one corner, on the dirt floor, was the shape of an upturned boat with the torch lights flickering over its surface. Othman moved forward to inspect the find, cautiously since he had no desire to trip and break a bone in the near darkness.

The boat was approximately the size of a long, single-storied building, and appeared to be constructed of overlapping sheets of a blue-black metal, though it was difficult to tell its true colour in the dark. Othman tapped on it with his torch and found it thick, though it sounded quite hollow.

'Strange-looking boat,' Said Rak remarked. His voice echoed in a normal tone throughout the cavern and his men looked nervously around them. It was as if they were desecrating a holy tomb: they were afraid of something but did not really understand what it was.

'Why do you say that?' asked Othman.

The Master-at-Arms replied, 'There doesn't appear to be a keel of any kind, and the stern is almost the same shape as the bows – if I've got the ends right. Almost like a large, narrow canoe.'

'But this is a different place to Earth,' one of the men said. 'They may have aliens here who build their boats in a different manner.'

'Said Rak is right,' said Othman to the man. 'The laws of hydrodynamics don't change, even though we are on another world. This boat would be most unstable on the water and besides' – he pointed with his torch beam at what he had found on the 'bows' – 'those three holes up there are too evenly spaced and too circular to be accidental. I don't think this is a boat at all.' He inspected the object more closely as the men watched and chipped at it with a knife he had taken from one of the soldiers. It powdered white beneath the jabs.

Left with just the object itself Othman would have been as perplexed as his men, but there was something about that shape – it had been described to him before, visually. Yet there was more to it. Not just an upturned boat but frills and feelers. God, those native dancers could communicate as well with gestures and fluid movement as any human could with his tongue. At the feast the dance had meant little to him, but faced with this shape he recalled it vividly and could see the beast moving: sliding and rippling over open countryside, its antennae waving like young saplings.

'What is it?' asked Said Rak.

Othman stepped back for one last look at the object before answering, 'It could be a shell.'

'A shell?' repeated one of the men. The word sounded ominous in the dark cavern and several soldiers took an involuntary backward step.

'An exo-skeleton – the shell of a mollusc or something of that nature. I really don't know what sort of creature it belongs to, I can only guess. This is one thing that could and does change from world to world.'

They all stood watching it for a time and then one man voiced their thoughts.

'But it's so big,' he said. 'What do you think it lives on?'

No one answered, because nobody knew, but they all had their own ideas, some of them less pleasant than others.

When they eventually decided to leave it was dark outside and Othman told them they would have to stay the night. It would give them another day to search for the two rebels.

Not a man slept inside the cave, however. They preferred to be out under the thick, tight clutches of stars, where they could also draw some comfort from the lights of their town below them.

Part Two

Out of the spent and unconsidered Earth
The cities rise again ...

Rudyard Kipling, 'Cities, Thrones and Powers'

Sixteen

The natives had known it was coming. They knew the cycle of the seasons, even if they did not know that the planet was on its inward flight into the sun and was reaching the perihelion of its ellipse now that it was free from the influence of the two outer planets.

There had been no rain for a long period and the depleted stream that bubbled out of the foot of the mountain no longer reached the quicksand sea. It died short of its journey's end in the parched soil of the island that sucked it down swiftly into its dusty throat. So it must have been for all the rivers that had once run down to the shores of the alluvium. They came forth from their holes in porous rock, from their impervious watersheds, from their limestone fissures, out into the relentless heat and turned to steam during their descent to the ocean. They came from the atmosphere and rejoined it without ever becoming more than rivers.

It was summer.

The quicksand creatures, the flatfish and others, had all left for cooler parts of the world – the annual migration. Over the place where they normally skated was a crust of sand, hard enough for a man to walk upon, pinpricked with dry vents which allowed the subsurface gases to puff out clouds of dust whenever the pressures suited. It was a lumpy desert of pockets of gas which stretched between the island and the mainland now – a blistered pancake of bread, always fresh from the oven.

The natives were preparing to cross these new wastes, but

not to the mainland. They had gathered on the far side of the island with their stretchers of fruit and roots and sapglued water bags of thick leaves. They were looking for a new island, somewhere beyond the horizon. The morons were going with them. It was fair to say they were not very organized, but then they had never undertaken such a journey before. They had not needed to consider it, previous to Othman's systematic destruction of the vegetation of their island. And if Othman was leading his people to the mainland, the natives were going in the opposite direction. They had had their fill of the company from Earth. The morons they regarded as people of their own tribe, born of their planet and formed of its environment. Othman could go to the sun in a bucket for all they cared.

The causeway was two-thirds finished and Othman cursed his people for their slowness, for not completing his monument to the ingenuity of Earth before it became a useless, superfluous strip of dirt. He even tried to make them continue with the work – hopelessly frustrated, he had ordered them back to the machines, but they had refused (kindly, for they were still fond of him and valued his leadership), and now even the maintenance had ceased. The live piles were allowed to burst into leaf and were greener than those trees which still stood on the island, for they found moisture below the crust. What a beautiful avenue would run between the island and the mainland, Niandi pointed out to Othman, as she and Jessum attempted to console him. An avenue lined with trees and surely a greater mark to his efforts than a mere causeway. Future generations would see, and know of Othman.

'Almost,' he had murmured in answer.

Niandi had given a puzzled smile.

'Almost what?'

'Almost!' he shouted slamming his fist down on a table. '*Almost* an avenue running *almost* to the mainland – but not quite either, you fools! Can't you see? – like it is, it's something to be patronizing about, not a work to admire. They'll look at it, our children's children, and say, "Not a bad attempt – pity the simple pioneers didn't consider the seasons. They *almost* made a bridge out there!"'

Niandi and Jessum left him to sulk, hoping it would not be long before he would pull himself together and start to give them some direction once more.

For weeks Othman sat in his house overlooking the causeway and stared at it. There was still a bite out of its side which had been caused by Silandi's and Zayid's latest attempt to thwart the project. Even *their* cause had been in vain. Now they had been confined to their separate quarters, captured running away from the explosion they had engineered. Zayid was the worse off of the two since his wife was allowed access to him and her visiting time was spent in constant beration.

The world grew hotter and expanded. The lethargic natives, wise in the ways of such a life, used only those movements necessary to carry out their individual tasks. Their preparations were simple but they took their time, while Othman's people looked anxiously towards their leader and feverishly prepared for their own expedition, frightened that the summer would wane before they could reach the mainland. Othman himself watched the natives. When they left, the time would be right. They would not allow themselves to be caught with their road turning to liquid beneath their feet.

He also thought about the giant three-horned mollusc. He would like to think that the creature was extinct and that what they had found on the mountain amounted to a fossil, but he knew that was wrong. The natives had seen one of these creatures alive and he was reluctantly inclined to the belief that they lived on the mainland and occasionally walked, or rather slid, over the solidified seas to the islands. Still, their size did not make them dangerous, and perhaps, though the thought revolted him, they might make good food. With creatures that size his people need never go hungry.

Their preparations were completed – all he was waiting for

now was the natives. Today he had promised Jessum that he would make his peace with Silandi. His people would look on such a move with favour. They might even forget the folly of the causeway. He had also lost a lot of prestige when he had told them that they could not take their machines with them. The cliffs at the far side looked formidable and he could see no way of dragging tractors and cranes with them. It was best they went on foot, using the camels and horses as pack animals and driving the livestock before them. A caravan. It was a romantic necessity that they should return to the old ways.

Silandi had been told by Niandi, that hard-headed pixie, that Othman would be coming to see her that morning with the idea of patching things up between them. Towards Niandi, Silandi had been non-committal.

'Don't expect too much,' Silandi had told her.

Niandi had raised her excessively arched eyebrows at this.

'I don't expect anything,' she had replied. 'In fact, it is in my interest to keep you here – or at least in confinement. While you are under guard I'm the most powerful woman in the group – when Othman lets you free, you might change that.'

Silandi had bristled at this frankness.

'You can be sure I will. I'll change quite a few things around here.'

Niandi had smiled.

'Well, you'd better be quick about it – we're not staying *here* for very much longer.'

'What does that mean? Where are we going?'

Niandi had terminated the conversation by saying that Othman would tell her, when he got around to it.

Silandi sat in front of her mirror and brushed her long black hair in preparation for Othman. She wanted to be beautiful in order that he could see what he had been missing. If he was sincere enough, she might even consider returning to his bed. A tremor ran through her body at the thought. She knew she was too tall for a woman and that men preferred small, large-busted women like Niandi, but she liked to think there was something of the leopard in her – something slightly wild and untamable which attracted reserved and highly-civilized men like Othman. Her full lips were pale as she stared at them in the image-holding metal and for the first time in years she considered using make-up – but then shrugged off this thought. It would not be in keeping with her picture of herself as the casual gold-black beast. She was a natural animal; the elements – the wind, sun and rain – were her cosmetics. She needed nothing that was artificial. Before Othman entered, however, she deliberately tore the front of her embroidered gown so that it revealed more of her breasts. The gown had been a gift from a nimble-fingered wife of one of the workers and had been given to her in the days when she had stood beside her husband.

The metal threw back the perfection of her skin and as she admired herself she remembered Jessum and the limb she had indirectly taken from him. Imperfection! Oh yes, many had said that it had been unavoidable on her part, but she realized that she was partly to blame. She had begged Jessum for forgiveness through Niandi and true to his character that gentle man had sent the reply that no forgiveness was necessary – it had been an accident. But the imperfection was there, beneath her skin, and it marred her external beauty, she was sure. How could you rob a man of part of his body and show nothing on your own? There had to be a mark, a scar, a furrow, a blemish. Was there? She searched for something, to ease her guilt, but found the skin flawless.

She heard Othman speak to the guard in that quiet, assured tone of his as he entered, and she stood up in the middle of the simply-furnished room awaiting his scrutiny. How long had it been since they had last seen each other? A quarter of a year?

He seemed taller than she remembered, and his beard, though black and glistening as a panther's coat, was wild and unruly. He was the beast, she thought, not her. His eyes regarded her solemnly and her heart raced as she lifted her chin and said,

'Yes?'

Othman cleared his throat and looked away from her.

'I've come – that is, I find it in myself to forgive you.' His stiff formality, she was sure, was indicative of his shyness, not of his true feelings, but she could not accept those words. They were wrong.

'You'll have to rephrase that,' she said bluntly. 'I don't require forgiveness – I'm not sorry for anything.'

His face changed and his bitterness showed through the previously inscrutable mask.

'You bitch,' he said, 'you sleep with another man and expect me to come crawling? I come willing to accept you back – used. But on my terms.'

So that was it? She had forgotten about Zayid. No wonder her husband stood like a metal rod before her, unbending. The situation made her melt towards him.

'I didn't think you cared about that – I thought it was only the bridge – because I had damaged your precious causeway, which you know I never believed in. What a fool's work that has turned out to be, hasn't it?' she said in an amused tone.

It was a fatal mistake to make, to think that Othman could ever laugh at himself. Especially about the causeway.

'You stupid woman,' he shouted, and turned abruptly on his heel and began to leave the room.

'Wait!' she said quickly.

He stopped in the doorway and his emotion was evident in the rise and fall of his shoulders as he breathed heavily. Then he was gone, before she could explain to him that there had never been anything between herself and Zayid, nothing sexual that is, and that she was returning to him, Othman, as chaste as she had left him. As chaste as a married woman can be, who had only known one man.

She sank to her knees in the centre of the room.

'God curse his face,' she said in frustration, her fists clenched. She even considered calling the guard and offering him her body – not as a bribe to let her escape for she had nowhere to go now, especially if, as Niandi had hinted, they were to move soon – but because she wanted relief for her sexual needs and also to revenge herself on Othman. At least if she gave herself away she could allow Othman to forgive her and all would be sweet between them. It was ironic that the thing that stood between them was her fidelity. If she *had* been unfaithful they would be crying in each other's arms now and he would be feeling noble, as he loved to do, and she would be feeling cherished and wanted – accepted, not *in spite* of her infidelity, but because of it. What a cruel way fate had of ordering her life. God's will had her marked for a loser, no matter which way she turned.

She lay, full length, on the floor, and pressed her breasts to the cool stone, but she did not call the guard. She wept instead.

Seventeen

Was there a caravan moving in the first grey years of Man on Earth? Some pack animals, and a man and woman setting forth in the half-light across the wastes outside a garden? There must have been, for ever since man has drawn dust and air into his lungs he has wanted to seek out new places, to travel beyond the empty sections of the globe.

Othman had heard stories of caravans where overhead the sun was a molten ball that beat men's brains to pulp and, pulsating, planted its blindness in unwary eyes. Those old caravans sailed tawny waves, pausing at liquid islands where hooded men lubricated their tongues and told tales of nights upon the ocean of powder. Nights of studying the worn brass astrolabes, plates that mirror the heavens: the pins, the horses, the mater, the retes, the alidades, fitted together with precision by an expert for men to find their way in the empty quarters of the world. Nights of perfume, vaporous veils and copper-coloured skin, and raiding nights of stallion, steel and scarlet death. These were Othman's caravans.

His caravan, the sight he had long waited to see, was crawling with monkeys, busying themselves with fussy tasks, and donkeys, horses and camels, some overladen, some (the known vicious biters and kickers) with no packs at all. Organization seemed to have been trodden underfoot, and while, on the far side of the island, the natives left quietly, carrying their stretchers, the hullabaloo of Othman's caravan roared out, ran in circles, and had the appearance of a demon's holiday.

At least, he thought, we are doing something – it *is* happening.

'Jessum,' he bawled above the furore. Jessum did not hear, but the faithful Fdar, ever at his elbow, touched him and pointed to Othman. Othman waved him up to the high point above the beach where he was standing. Leaving the strap on the donkey which he had been engaged in trying to tighten, awkwardly one-handed, but insistently by himself, Jessum climbed to where Othman was standing.

'Some kind of order is necessary here,' said Othman, with a trace of irritation in his voice. 'If this motley gathering is any indication of what it will be like later on then we will be in trouble from the beginning. Move all the people back – separate them from the animals – get Said Rak to help you – then allocate one animal to every two families. If they argue tell them ...' he paused, then 'tell them that during the march martial law is imposed. The penalty for infringement is ...' he paused again '... once, hobbling, twice, being cast out alone – yes, banishment. I have to be harsh, you understand?'

There was no answer.

'Well, do you, Jessum?'

The reply was hesitant. Jessum looked upwards, shielding his eyes from the huge sun with his good hand.

'Why?'

Othman's eyes regarded him steadily.

'Because later on they will need to be in fear of me. A benign, respected man can control, to a certain degree, well-fed and amiable people. Only a feared man can control starving, thirsty animals with aching bodies, nowhere to rest without being burnt black by the sun and with nothing to face but despair. While they are still people, they will listen to a soft voice. When they become animals they will only respect a man who can prevent them from killing each other for water.'

'Will it be as bad as that?' Jessum was wide-eyed.

'It might be – probably will be if those mountains don't lead into a river valley quite quickly. We must prepare for the worst – not the best – of what is to come. Later I can return to my benign leadership. Where's Said Rak?'

Jessum sat down on the parched earth and fingered a clump of dry, yellow grass. It crumbled to dust in his fingers. Othman could see he was wondering where their water was going to come from. They were used to drinking all they needed – and more. Jessum suddenly became aware that he was still awaiting an answer.

'Said Rak? Oh, he's taking a last look at the ship's skeleton – and the old computer. I think he's sad at leaving the computer, possibly because it's part of the defence system he's also got to leave behind. He has a theory you know ... his own idea of why we're here.'

Othman stared down at Jessum. Everyone had a theory.

'And that theory is?'

Jessum shrugged lopsidedly.

'That we were sent here to destroy something ... or someone.'

Othman snorted and flicked his foot at a chicken that looked as though it was about to dash back to its old scratching patch by some tree stumps. At the threatening gesture it retreated back to its fellows.

'All this way? Thousands of light years – to blow up a city? Then what? We set off for home? Rubbish!'

'What if we are a suicide mission? One ship sent to destroy a world that had damaged our own in some way – revenge. It's one of the strongest motives, Othman – there's no denying that,' said Jessum.

'I'm not denying anything – I'm saying that I find it hard to believe. But, yes, it's possible.'

'You mean there *might* be enemies over those mountains? People – *things* – that are at war with us?'

Othman nodded his shaggy, black hair.

'Might be – yes. But I wouldn't worry too much about them. They know we're here, unless those teacher units were destroyed by a freak storm in space, and they're watching us. We'll be peaceful enough – hand weapons, okay – but the heavy stuff we'll leave behind.'

Jessum's eyes narrowed as he took in Othman's words. Fdar watched his master's features, concerned.

'You've thought all this through quite thoroughly, haven't you, Othman? Said Rak's theory is not new to your mind by any means. In which case I suppose you've got an answer for me when I say I think it's foolish to leave the "heavy stuff" behind when we might need it to protect ourselves. Perhaps it's the only thing that has prevented our aliens from attacking?'

'You're becoming insubordinate, Jessum,' said Othman. He paused and toyed with the idea of leaving Jessum without an answer, but in the end his pride in his own skills of deduction would not allow him this luxury.

'I'll tell you why,' he said. 'It might have escaped your attention that we're concentrated on an island small enough to be blown to grains of sand by a few ground-to-ground missiles. Most of *our* weaponry is surface-to-space – but that is not important. What *is* important is that we're in an extremely vulnerable position and if anyone was anxious enough to destroy us they'd have done so years ago.' He was cold in his delivery and he disliked being so patronizing with Jessum but he thought it necessary. He had to keep everyone, even his trusted aides, in place – and that place was under his unquestionable command. If they *did* meet anything beyond those mountains – not sophisticated aliens, for Othman's people would stand no chance against high-level technology, but possibly wild beasts or savages – then there could be no debate on the sanctity of life or whatever. His orders must be the only words before the troops open fire.

The disorder around him was still rife and he spoke sharply to Jessum.

'I asked you to find Said Rak and create some fusion in that rabble out there. Please do so.'

Some soldiers were at that moment leading two captives down the slope to the shoreline. The prisoners were manacled with the wide magnetic bracelets that Othman knew took tremendous strength to separate. If one attempted to do so the bracelets slammed back together again. There was no way a man could keep them apart, for his efforts in drawing them away from each other sapped his strength and even should he hold his arms stretched out wide, a slight deviation in position would have them smashing together, in front or behind the body. Sometimes with injurious results.

As they passed Othman, the woman, Silandi, averted her eyes, but Zayid stared indolently up at the leader's face.

Othman said, 'Have a long look. You will be seeing much more of me.'

Zayid spat out towards the crust.

'I see nothing but a pig's bladder,' he said.

Othman's eyes blazed and he felt a lump in his throat. He would kill this excuse for a man before long. Moving forward, he intended to speak into Zayid's face but Jessum and his moron, both fearing the worst, quickly jumped between them. Othman checked himself.

Zayid sniffed contemptuously.

'Let him go,' he said. 'If it gives him satisfaction to strike a man held prisoner, why stop him? – we might all feel the benefit of the relief of his frustrations. Yes, let him work out all those inhibitions upon my face ...'

Silandi said, 'Stop it. Leave him alone.'

Zayid and Othman stared at her. The tone of her voice had surprised them both. She refused to return the stares, pointedly looking out over the crust.

'Well, well!' said Zayid, but wisely left it at that. The soldier, who had been standing all this time expecting an order to cuff the prisoner, and not really sure in himself whether he could bring himself to do so, for Zayid was a hard character, ushered the pair along to await the beginning of the march. They both went quietly now.

'Find Said Rak,' said Othman to Jessum for the third time. 'We must get this menagerie moving.'

Jessum left him and Othman folded his arms and looked towards the distant cliffs that rose to mountains almost immediately behind their top edges. The caravan might need oxygen to pass by those peaks, which they had in unused cylinders from the workshops. They would have to carry the oxygen on the pack animals. It was going to be a hard struggle but he had hopes of finding passes through the mountains. They could not possibly go over them. Some would die, no matter how easy it was, that was inevitable. Perhaps they would all perish? Why, then, was he making them do this thing? They were comfortable here – or would have been if the crops had been planted, the farms begun. He did not even understand himself, so how could he explain to his wife, who was plainly desperate for an insight into her husband's mind on the matter? It was an unease – more than an unease. It was a compelling urge that moved his muscles and organs in that one direction, away from where the people were now. Away from the island. He was probably not leading his people to salvation, but he was sure he was taking them away from danger. If only he *knew*! But that was wishing for the unobtainable. He would never know the answer. That was lost in a blob of melted wires and blocked circuits.

'I've found him – he was at the ship, as I said.'

It was Jessum, his naked companion, and a heavily-dressed Said Rak. It was sweltering under the morning sun but Said Rak sweated beneath an animal-skin overcoat worn over a gown! Othman wondered at the man's sensibility but he had ceased to comment on the eccentricities of Said Rak. It was a useless pastime. The coat had something to do with his position as Master-at-Arms. A badge of office or something. Perhaps he needed to feel important more than he needed to feel cool. It would certainly be of use in the mountains.

'Well, get to it then. We want to be on the move by nightfall. We'll sleep during the day.'

They did as they were asked and very soon, with the help of the soldiers, had a semblance of order, simply by separating the people from the animals. Othman watched them work with satisfaction, the Master-at-Arms, expert on the defence of towns, and the builder, footsteps dogged by his slave (for what else was the moron, who would take nothing but food in return for his services?).

It was interesting to watch the development of the relationship between Jessum and his moron. At first Jessum had been embarrassed by the boy's attentions and had tried to send him away. When this had not worked he pretended to ignore him, but when he did have to acknowledge the moron's presence, he treated the boy with extravagant kindness. Now familiarity was beginning to breed contempt and the would-be slave was truly becoming what he wished to be. Jessum treated him in an offhand manner and became mildly irritated if the moron did not understand what was required of him.

For Jessum this was a strong reaction – he very seldom

became annoyed with anyone and would often go out of his way to be pleasant, even to continual complainants whom Othman would have banged over the head were *he* confronted with them. It remained to be seen if this stage of the master/slave relationship could be overcome and true friendship set in.

Othman was slightly envious of Jessum's slave. He wished he had one. Not because he wanted the constant attention but because he would have someone in whom he could place his trust implicitly. Raise any free man to the exalted secondary position and there is always the fear that he might one day be persuaded to try to climb the last stair, and push his king down to the floor below. Raise a slave to that position and there need be no fear, for he is the buffer between the ambitious ones and the throne. He cannot be persuaded to take the last step for he knows that as a slave the people will never allow him to hold it. He has all the power he will ever command and no one is going to make him risk that on certain failure. While the king is in command, the slave is safe, and he keeps the king safe to stay in power himself. Roman Emperors realized this and used it well. Powerful slaves make vicious masters for they visit their grudges on those below. Othman could do with such a slave, for he believed in fear as a human propellant.

Eighteen

By noon of the first day the excitement had died to a whisper and if it was there at all it was suppressed. The caravan moved quietly forward as a long line with many knots. Occasionally individuals groaned with the heat or exchanged a few laboured words with a neighbour, but for the most part they stared resolutely ahead, towards the swimming, heat-warped cliffs, damning silently the oven under their feet and the fire above their heads. Their bodies were unused to such harsh treatment and already many were regretting the actions that had led to the march. Othman may have believed in his ancestral Bedu blood, but his people knew that what ran through their veins was nothing more than townsfolk water.

They arrived at the foot of the cliffs on the evening of the third day, exhausted and far from at peace with their souls.

The cliffs themselves stretched as far as the eye could see on either side. Upwards, they almost reached the stars. Only one thing could be said in their favour: they were not as sheer as they had looked from the island. There was a backward slope to them, which had been grooved by streams now dry, the silt dust between the banks.

When the tents had been erected Othman sent for Said Rak and Jessum and asked them if they knew of anyone who had had climbing experience during their simulated childhoods.

'Mountain climbing?' queried Jessum.

Othman replied, 'Any kind of climbing. Trees, buildings, mountains, I don't care. All I want is someone who is competent and not afraid of heights.'

Said Rak folded his arms over his broad chest.

'Why don't we send Zayid? He might even fall.'

Othman regarded the man with some impatience, although he was careful to keep it hidden. It was not that Said Rak was stupid — he was just too eager to please his leader.

'Said Rak,' Othman replied, his voice displaying the annoyance behind it even though he was doing his utmost to control himself. 'I wish to discover whether it is possible to reach the top of the cliffs — I therefore want a climber to find a path for that retinue outside. It is not my intention to use the cliffs to murder all my enemies. If I wanted to kill Zayid I would do it in a more open and manly fashion — if there is such a thing — and I certainly would not have dragged a thousand witnesses over a three-day march to watch me do it ...'

Said Rak coloured and shuffled his feet. He mumbled something about 'opportunity' and left it at that. Othman took no further notice of him. Of late Rak's breath had begun to smell and Othman found his proximity offensive. The less he saw of him the better he liked it. He felt it a pity that a man like Zayid, who appeared altogether more able that Said Rak, should be against him. Zayid would make a good Master-at-Arms. Perhaps he could persuade Said Rak to retire soon? – give someone else the opportunity to prove himself? Not Zayid. That would be too dangerous, but one of the younger men ...? How stupid – they were all the same age. Zayid, Said Rak and himself. All of them. It was just that some gave the appearance of being older than others.

Jessum interrupted his thoughts.

'We'll find some suitable men,' he said, and left the tent. Jessum had now strapped his paralysed arm to his waist to prevent it from hanging loosely from his shoulder and swinging uncontrollably when he walked. Said Rak followed the builder without a word and Othman was left alone. He wanted, suddenly, to call them back and invite them to his tent later that night. It was not pleasant to be continually alone. Instead he sat on the sponge-soft groundsheet and stared at the stars. The night was a soft one, despite the heat, and star-watching was a pleasant pastime. He could lose his mind, out amongst those bright points of light.

Jessum found two willing men with a little simulated climbing experience and the following morning, after prayers, Allah was asked to guide them to the clifftops without harm. Othman had always encouraged prayer amongst his people. It was comforting to believe at heart and they had fallen into the habit of praying often throughout the day since they had begun their long walk. For one thing they *needed* a divine entity to protect them now they had left the security of their island, and for another it made their rest stops more peaceful than they would otherwise have been. Othman and Jessum encouraged this turn towards a vague religion, hoping that some pattern would form upon which to base their belief in Allah. The senders may have considered they were right to fire their pioneers into the cosmos without a defined religion: those pioneers themselves felt lost without one, especially since they were aware that such a religion indeed formed the main framework of the structure of the society that had sent them. It was inconceivable to Othman's people that such a religion should be denied them. What the eyes do not see the heart indeed grieves over, for nothing is worse than being on the outside of a secret. Such a glorious secret! All they owned of it was prayer and the knowledge that He was listening, somewhere, and that they would meet Him after death – providing He approved of them. But they had no way of knowing whether they were a good, an indifferent or a bad race of people in the eyes of their Lord. For all they knew He could be extremely displeased and angry with them. So they prayed all the more. In that, they were blameless.

The climbers set off, following one of the red-dust dry stream beds, keeping in contact with the people below by means of two-way communicators.

Their first reports were enthusiastic descriptions of the cliffs and the panoramic view of the crust (but as the going became harder and the days passed the reports became abruptly worded complaints about their own physical condition and the physiography of their pathway). That night the two men, one well-built and of a practical disposition, the other lean and dexterous but not normally given to fantasy, spent hours on the communicator because they were afraid in their new surroundings – the high banks threw ugly shapes into their small camp and living creatures scuttled amongst the stones. They spoke in whispers, thereby creating an atmosphere charged with supernatural tension. Rocks began to walk, out in the night, and the ground rolled slowly, carrying them upwards to an unnatural death. The cliffs moaned like wind in the trees: they shifted their feet and leaned outwards, into the night. The newcomers were not welcome on the world's back, and they felt it. Heavy hands gripped the communicator at night and pleaded to be allowed to return: a head spun semi-circles so that its owner should not be attacked, while another twisted in uneasy sleep.

The mornings brought the smell of baked earth to their nostrils and all those moving inanimates of the previous night had reverted to their lifeless states once more. Feeling foolish, the two men informed those below that they felt able to continue, now the daylight had fixed their position in the real world. Nevertheless they intended to get to the top as quickly as they possibly could. Since the daylight on Jessum outran an Earthday by many hours they were able to achieve their destination in three weeks. The way was easy until the last fifty metres, where parts which required vertical climbing gave the men some difficulty in the rarefied atmosphere.

It was cool at the top but there was no snow to be seen, except on the peaks of the mountains around them. Over the surface of the land were scattered giant growths of some nature. They had the appearance of solidified waterfalls that had been turned upside-down and balanced on their tails. Closer inspection of one of these by the braver, smaller of the two men proved the monoliths to consist of hard-packed soil and grit. The place the men had climbed to was at the end of a large river valley flanked by mountains and Othman, on receiving the report on the scenery, was heard to remark that these asymmetrical parasols had probably been formed out of moraine by the pressing snouts of pairs of small glaciers that had met head-on, and fought each other like phlegmatic rams for possession of their chosen paths. The ice had retreated and the pressure with it, but the impression had remained. Closer inspection by one of the two climbers, however, proved them to be insect colonies. The soil and grit were stuck together with saliva from insect-like creatures that grew to three or four centimetres long. Thereafter the umbrellas were given a wide berth.

Othman's caravan began climbing the morning after the men had reached the valley. Fowls ran backwards and forwards covering twice the journey's length, wanting to return yet being driven upwards, complaining and flaring their wings like runaway fires. Pack animals grunted and steamed with squeaking joints towards the thinner, cooler air. Men were glad of the soft cushion of silt that wound between the rocks, and often rested against their women, closely attentive to their spouses whenever an unauthorized rest had become an aching necessity. Smells were left in their wake, of sweat and urine and the excrement of man and beast, but no one cared because this was a one-way path. In the middle of the second week there was an unplanned halt, the reason for which was not expected or wanted by any member of the caravan. They had a visitor.

The visitor came as a heaving oval of light peppered by black windseeds, which swirled in and out of its shape. It stopped, some metres from the entourage, and, pulsing slowly as if breathing heavily after a run, seemed to contemplate the awestruck humans with some interest. Then, without warning, it flashed skywards.

Jessum was leaning against a packhorse, using his good arm to support himself.

'It was watching us,' he said.

'How can you tell?' asked a man. 'It was just a ball of light.'

'I felt it, that's all,' replied Jessum.

He swung round to look at Fdar, who was still staring at the direction the oval had taken.

'He knows,' he said.

They all turned then, to look at Jessum's servant, who regarded them with an unruffled expression. If he did know, the knowledge would stay locked inside him.

Othman first thought privately to himself that it, the thing, might be God. They had asked Allah for guidance. But, though he did not doubt the existence of God, he was suspicious of theatricals. If man wanted to believe his God was contacting him, a ball of fire from heaven was just the sort of spectacular event he would love to witness.

Perhaps the thing had been an illusion? Or an elemental phenomenon – a twist of wind soaked in sunlight? An interaction between two sharply-contrasting temperatures?

Or, not God, but Man? The equivalent of Man, on the planet they were trying to colonize? Not simple stick-shaped people, but a high level of intelligence?

He chose the last idea. At least it would keep him on his toes. Perhaps eventually Othman would be contacted formally and some exchange of ideas could take place. Only one thing worried him: how could one rationalize communication with a whirlwind?

The final leg of the journey upwards was a difficult one. Othman and the more agile of the men scrambled up the face to the top and helped the scouts to construct hoists to lift the women and animals over the vertical stretches. Although some bruises resulted from overhangs, and one man received a nasty bite from a camel which objected to the truss of ropes and leather, the only serious injury was sustained by a horse which fell several feet and broke its leg. Under normal circumstances the medical unit could have healed the leg, but only the light, movable equipment had been brought away from the island – for any ailment this could not handle, the caravan had to rely on the rather dubious skills of the doctor, Malek. Neither Malek nor the instruments available could repair the broken bone and the horse was shot and added to the stew that night.

With his people at last on the cliffs that had haunted his dreams since his conscious life had begun, Othman paused, looking down the valley into the distance, to allow a feeling of self-satisfaction to permeate through his mind. He was aware of Said Rak's presence beside him and made a decision.

'Remove the restrictions from the prisoners,' said Othman.

'Prisoners?' repeated Said Rak. 'You mean Zayid – and your wife.' Othman nodded. 'Of course,' he said. 'I'm not aware of any other prisoners.'

Said Rak looked unsure of himself. After a long while he asked, 'Is that wise?'

Othman swung round to face his Master-at-Arms.

'I'm not interested in your interpretation of the wisdom of my actions,' he said in a sharp tone, 'just in my present mood of compassion.' His voice continued on a softer note. 'I want my wife to see that I am not like one of those distorted mushrooms we see around us – not just an unfeeling, blind, immovable piece of nature. If they – Zayid and ... Silandi, my wife wish – to return to the island, then they may do so. I am finished with coercion.'

He stayed, long after Said Rak had left him, a thick sheepskin wrapped round his shoulders, breathing the thin air and appreciating the unusual beauty of the valley that opened its funnel in the distance. Somewhere amongst the evening shadows was the wreck of their aircraft.

Nineteen

The wreck was never found, even though Othman sent out several search parties as they made their way, day by day, down the long, wide valley. They did, however, make the startling discovery that at least one man may have walked away from the wreck: a piece of personal equipment belonging to one of the crew was found by the tiny stream that followed the valley's course. The stream would have been a river at the time of the crash – more than likely a frozen river

– and it was of course possible that the aircraft had been washed away during the thaw, but the presence of an intact flying helmet by running water suggested that it may have been used as a drinking utensil. If not, why wasn't the pilot still wearing it? The fastening strap was not broken – it had been unclipped. Othman and Jessum decided that the aircraft must have crashed there or near by and at least one of the crew had walked away alive.

At the end of the valley the land rose to form a duck's-foot web of ridges which united the higher mountains on either side. This was the watershed, and beyond it the ground fell away again, into a bowl of dying pampas and bushland. As the caravan moved down to the plains, the stream dried out and water became scarce. Any water they found was from stagnant-looking pools and needed to be purified for drinking. This was a slow process and with the thirst of a thousand people, and as many animals, to quench, tempers were naturally short and Othman's authority hung only on his military backing. One favourable quality of command which could be attributed to Said Rak was that his soldiers did not lack discipline. They were a reserved group of about fifty individuals and their families. Mostly they remained apart from the civilians and always had done. Their simulated childhoods consisted of war-orientated games and military school and they had nothing in common with the tradesmen and professionals of which the rest of the group was comprised. Othman knew that he only had to keep the soldiers satisfied and their support would remain solidly behind him.

Yassim, a site planner by trade, was the first civilian to die by the hands of the soldiers.

It was early morning – just as the sun's scout cut through the lower valleys behind the camp. A soldier named Alim was on perimeter duty, his eyes out on the distant purple rim of the world watching. Soldiers may not be the most intelligent creatures in the universe but they make good use of their grey matter, having more time for thinking than most. Their brains can turn out a multitude of simple philosophies of life, during the silent hours, in the same way that a guru obtains his ascendance to higher planes – by meditation. The planet and the sentry work as one. They turn together, slowly. The day runs the minutes away but when the world sleeps the seconds drip from the darkness like drops of water from stalactites. The soldier sees all things, and hears all the night's small sounds: a beetle scraping a rock is loud to his ears. It is a time when a man comes to terms with his life and vows to be more attentive to his family and to communicate with those people who make him feel awkward and insecure. It is a peaceful time, when delicious sexual thoughts wander in and out of the mind like redhaired canine beasts. It is a time when a man can concentrate, while staring out over the appearing landscape, on the thought of the soft brush of his wife's fur against the trunk of his thigh. It is not a time when a man, even a soldier, thinks of slaying a fellow human.

Alim, his heavy cloak stirring gently in the cold morning breezes, heard a small noise from the direction of stores.

'Who's there?' he called after a while, peering into the half-light.

There was a sound of hasty drinking. Alim's hands gripped his weapon. He had direct orders to shoot anyone stealing water, even a fellow soldier. He moved towards the sound and confronted Yassim, who was indeed pilfering. A cup was at his lips and precious water dripped from his beard. They were about ten feet apart. Alim's weapon was by his hip.

'Put down the cup, Yassim, and come with me.'

The big site-planner was a belligerent person at his best, and the raging thirst he had fended off for several sleepless nighthours had considerably worsened his nature.

'Go away before I break your back, soldier-boy.'

Alim's eyes did not move from Yassim's face and the latter, seeing the weapon was not being raised, smiled contemptuously and continued to drink. Alim aimed the weapon, his finger pressed angrily down on the firing button and Yassim's chest collapsed under the pressure of the air bolt that struck his rib-cage squarely in the centre. Blood from his mouth gushed forth as he staggered backwards. Then he fell amongst the stores with a crash.

'Don't call people names,' said Alim to the dead man. It came out almost as an apology, a reason for killing the looter. Then he took a quick drink of the water before raising the alarm.

The trek continued across the plains and soon no water at all was found. Grasses died beneath their feet and the people became embittered, as Othman had foreseen they would. A woman died of thirst – she had been giving her own water ration to her child. A man committed suicide with a sharpened stave, levering himself bare-bellied onto the point from a rock pedestal, to end the torment in his body. Othman remained aloof, seemingly untouched by the suffering.

Jessum continually warned his leader of the heavy discontent that was present amongst the people and told him that Silandi and Zayid were actively stirring an already flaming fire. The favouritism Othman displayed towards the soldiers, keeping them sufficiently fed and watered for them to remain loyal to him, positively supplied the wind that fanned those flames. He himself could see no way of pushing the people forward except by force. Years of relatively soft living had diluted any stamina they may have had and he knew they would never follow where he led: they had to be driven. Otherwise they would lie down and die.

Jessum's warnings did not go unheeded, but they were not acted upon. Othman had chosen his method – he considered it the only one possible.

Three days before they reached the river, Othman was summoned from his tent by one of his own soldiers. He stepped outside to find Jessum and Said Rak in magnetic cuffs. Fdar had been clubbed unconscious and carefully bound to staves in order that he could be moved without being touched when he regained his senses.

Zayid had taken over.

The short square man, his body hard and faceted like a diamond, stood before Othman and told him that he was no longer in command. The triumph was evident in his gravel voice and his eyes stared expectantly up into Othman's. Othman saw that the man was waiting for his reaction, so he stood without answering, his face expressionless. Out of the corner of his eye he could see his wife on the edge of the gathering and it surprised him that she was taking a back seat in his reckoning. He expected her to be out in front with Zayid, calling for his debasement.

Zayid said, 'The soldiers have feelings too, you know — and families. Their guilt became too heavy for them ... to follow your despicable leadership ...' he spat the final words into Othman's face.

'Let's hope,' replied Othman, 'that you make a better job of it.'

Zayid's spiteful expression changed to one of puzzlement.

'Of what?' he said.

Othman replied, 'Of leading those fools.' Then he turned and went back into his tent, slumping onto some cushions on the floor. Zayid had been robbed of his triumph.

Othman heard someone yelling that he ought to be beaten or killed, and that his officers should be forced to carry out any punishment that Zayid thought fit to award, but there was no general follow-up of this isolated call for revenge and the voices that muttered remained low and dispirited. If Zayid had spoken at that point, perhaps he could have raised some enthusiasm for a blood-letting, but for some reason he did not, and the people were tired. They had no energy for such luxuries as lynching parties. Besides, Othman knew that they still held him in awe to a certain degree, even though he had been pushed aside. He was still the man on the mount – the eremite, needing no one, the detached Pericles of the new world. Othman had been their Imam, and priesthood mixed with kingship is a powerful combination in the mind of followers without a solid religion.

The trek continued, almost as if Othman's leadership was unbroken. Finally they reached the river.

It was a wide stretch of water which had been much wider during the winter years. The liquid that flowed between the banks of red clay was fast-flowing and thick with sediment but that did not prevent it from becoming one of the most welcome sights in the history of the starship's people. They fell in its shallows with screeches of joy and some splashed each other as they drank the muddy fluid in mouthfuls. Many of them became sick, but still they went back for more after their cramped stomachs threw up what they were unused to. Doctor Malek and his instruments saved several lives that day.

Othman at first remained in his tent, disdaining to follow the example of the rabble. Finally, when night fell and many were more concerned with their new pains than with the dignity of a fallen leader, he stumbled out and down to the river bank to soak the hem of his gown in the water and then suck it dry. No one came to him, not even Jessum and Fdar, who were now free of their bonds, and for the first time in his life he felt truly lonely.

Walking back to his tent he stared up at the skies, at the stars. But instead of giving thanks to Allah for his people's deliverance, he softly cursed those who had sent them. Whatever had gone wrong out there in space, whatever had happened to blank their minds, should have been guarded against. All eventualities should have been covered – protection should have been available. Then he realized what he was expecting of them and he knew he was wrong. All eventualities could not be covered.

There was a voice above him and he found he had fallen to his knees on the grass.

'You did what you considered right,' she said. 'And this land is perfect for grazing cattle and sheep ... will be when we irrigate it. There's water, and Zayid says we will build a town of clay, our ancestors once used clay for their houses ...'

Silandi spoke on, softly, and Othman clutched at her legs and pressed his face to her thighs. He felt himself crying.

She whispered over his head, and hugged him to her, and seemed happy. Not because he was broken, he knew, but because he needed her love at last.

Afterwards, when they lay together in his tent she said to him, 'I never did, you know ... with Zayid.'

Othman wondered whether she was telling the truth.

'It doesn't matter,' he replied.

She was silent for a moment. Then she said, 'You don't believe me.'

'It doesn't matter whether I believe you or not. I do believe you, but what has or has not passed these last few years would make no difference to this moment.'

'Do you love me?' Her voice was tight. He could not tell her reason for asking.

'I love you.' He hoped he sounded as if he meant it.

She was apparently satisfied.

'It's enough. You will believe me – about Zayid. When we've been together for a while, you will know.'

But all he could say was, 'It doesn't matter now.'

Next morning the whole camp knew they were together again and many wondered if he would attempt to reinstate himself, but Othman stayed in his tent all day. He only went out when Jessum came running to collect him. The builder was obviously very perturbed.

'Come quickly.'

'What is it?' He could not think of what it was that had disturbed Jessum.

'Just come and look.'

Othman went to the river bank where Zayid and a group of men were standing. As he reached them Zayid silently handed him a viewer which he had been using and pointed over the river.

Othman put the viewer over his head and sighted the far bank, running along it slowly. He passed them without realizing what he had seen the first time – then something clicked in his brain and he found the two thin posts again. For a long while he stared at the objects on the top of the posts, and then he lowered the viewer.

'Well?' said Zayid.

Othman nodded. 'You know what they are – human heads, skulls.'

'And!' said Zayid, in an angry tone.

Othman sighed, before replying. 'And one of them is wearing a flying helmet.'

Zayid continued to stare angrily at Othman, and in the deep silence that followed they heard a faint tune coming from the direction of the far bank. The hair began to rise on the back of Othman's neck as a strong breeze lifted the hood of his robe. Zayid turned his head slowly to look at the skulls, and as he did so the wailing grew louder, until all who were present could plainly hear the mournful singing that came from the opposite bank of the river.

'My God,' said a pale Zayid, 'they're still living! Somehow the monsters that killed them have kept their heads alive.'

All Othman could say, without much conviction, was 'Don't be foolish, Zayid – you'll frighten the women and children.'

But as the skulls continued to pour forth their weird music, it was the men themselves who stood rooted with fear to the soil of Jessum.

Twenty

'Well, what do you plan to do now? Are we moving again?' asked Othman. He regarded Zayid dispassionately and he could see the smaller man was wrestling with an inner problem. Leadership has its rewards, thought Othman, but the dilemmas far outweigh them.

'You realize this was your fault,' said Zayid. 'If it weren't for you, those men might be alive ... we would not ...'

'Yes?' said Othman, patiently waiting as Zayid repressed his anger.

'We would not be here. This is a dangerous ... obviously a dangerous place.'

'In that case you'll be able to prove yourself both as a leader and as a protector – you are a weapon-maker, or handler ... or something of that nature aren't you?' Othman said coldly. 'This will give you the opportunity of displaying your expertise – your craft – to the people. I am sure you will be much admired.'

'May God steal your eyes,' fumed Zayid, using an old saying.

'May God return you yours,' replied Othman.

Later, back in his tent, Othman talked with his wife about the discovery.

'Whatever killed them had the intelligence to put the heads on the poles.'

'Why would they do that?' asked Silandi.

'To frighten away others, I suppose,' said Othman. 'A warning. Earth has a history of such practices. Farmers have hung the dead carcasses of vermin on fences since time began. At one time the British used to leave the mutilated bodies of criminals on the gibbet, or hanging in trees. Even as late as the twentieth century the Americans displayed the photographs of captured robbers in their banks ...'

'But what race,' questioned Silandi slowly, 'put severed heads on poles?'

Othman said, 'I know what you are thinking, but you're wrong. All right, the Arabs did in places like the Yemen at one time, but so did many other races, especially Indian head-hunting tribes. You're thinking that our party was somehow split on landing? Well, I thought of that too, but I've come to the conclusion that it would have been impossible for our ship's people to have been placed in two areas – all the people from our ship are accounted for. No one is missing. And what would be the point of sending two ships? If the senders had seen the need for more colonists they would have built a bigger craft. Why risk the chance of the two ships parting from one another? No, my love, it is a fairly common practice amongst primitive races and all that worries me is that the heads are proof of a new and hostile presence on the planet. One which we may have to deal with in time ...'

But Silandi was hardly listening now, for she had grasped the endearment he had addressed her by, probably the first he had ever used, and the words sang in her head like the tune from a small, happy bird ... 'My love. My love.'

They built the wall to surround them on all sides because Zayid did not trust natural barriers. Another man might have used the river to spare his builders, but not Zayid. There were hostile natives somewhere in the vicinity and he had no intention of giving them an easy entrance into the town. The wall had to be of clay-straw bricks, since rock was not available, but Zayid made up for any weaknesses in the material by building it thicker than the other men thought necessary. The women collected large flints from the river bed and Zayid ordered men to shatter these and place the sharp splinters, some half a metre in length, along the outer edge of the wall's parapet. Zayid also ordered them to haul large stones from the river bed up the inner ramps to the walkways where they could stand ready until they were needed as missiles. The gateway was small – large enough to allow the tallest camel to enter with a bent head and no larger – in order that they could be sparing with what metal they had brought with them in making a gate. Wood was extremely scarce.

The wall took several months to construct, but everyone, even Othman, put all their energies and enthusiasm into its erection. While the building was in progress Zayid ensured that the camp was closely guarded, especially at night. All the ship's people feared the dark – no one would have guessed they were born and raised in the deepest black of space. They never once saw anything to cause them alarm.

Othman's hands were stained red by the clay he had been handling and he inspected them with pride. Jessum was the recipient of his discourse on 'honest labour'. Both men were standing beneath the high walls inside the town. Fdar hovered near by.

'Satisfaction – for the first time in my life I feel satisfaction in a job well done,' said Othman.

'What about your bridge?' chided Jessum, no doubt thinking time and experience had healed the wounds of yesterday.

Othman felt the thunderclouds stirring within him, but he realized Jessum was making an uncharacteristic attempt to tease him. It could not be successful. Even though he and Jessum had been reduced to the same level, the lowest level, in their small society, Othman could not regard the builder as an equal. They could never be friends; Othman was not able to climb down to other men. It was not that he did not wish to: on the contrary, he yearned to be a friend among friends. But something still held him back. He was still the leader. Born to the position. A fallen leader if they liked, but still the haughty Othman of the last few years.

When Othman failed to answer, Jessum cleared his throat,

obviously embarrassed. He too was not a man who found social patter an easy skill.

'No doubt we shall sleep safe in our beds tonight,' said Othman, changing the subject, 'with Zayid's wall complete, and the gate in position. He has a right to feel proud of it ...' He paused, knowing he was drifting back to the bridge again, without being able to stop himself. 'Let's hope it doesn't turn out to be another white elephant,' he finished, allowing Jessum that much entrance to his inner self.

There was a smile and a nod from the smaller man. Jessum's broadness had increased over the years and it served to give the illusion that he was shrinking slightly. Othman knew that Jessum was 'like an ox in bed', bruising his wife's plump flesh with his square hard muscles when they made love. This is what Niandi told Silandi, and Othman's wife repeated these things to her husband who in his turn decided he found them distasteful – not in their basic facts, but because it seemed to thrill women to be able to discuss such details. Othman had no interest in Jessum's battering ram techniques, but it disturbed him a little that his wife, however distant her own interest, obviously dwelled on such thoughts. It meant that he, Othman, was being subjected to a comparison. In this instance, since his wife's tone suggested that Jessum's art was crude (he got the impression that *both* women considered Jessum an oaf), Othman had obviously benefited from the comparison. But what of other men? Some men *did* make an art of lovemaking. (They even practised on other people's wives.) How would he compare to one of those artists in his wife's eyes? Not very favourably he was sure.

'Why are you looking at me like that?' asked Jessum, shifting uncomfortably before him. 'I feel like a worm under the scrutiny of a bird.'

Othman laughed. 'You're no worm, Jessum, believe me. You're built like a tractor – all steel pistons and steam.' The picture this produced in Othman's mind was so vivid and so directly associated with his previous thoughts that he laughed loudly once again. It did nothing for Jessum's discomfort.

'Well, I wish you wouldn't, that's all, Othman.'

'I wasn't laughing at you,' lied Othman. 'It's just ... well, it was the thought ...'

'You were laughing at me,' said Jessum flatly. 'But I don't mind. It's good to hear you laugh. And I am a peculiar man I suppose, with my disability ...'

Othman's tone changed. 'Stop that. I hadn't even given that a thought. Don't start feeling sorry for yourself.' Then he added with a trace of malice. 'If you must know, your wife has been spreading tales about your prowess in bed -- not derogatory tales either, you old ram.' Ashamed of blurting out what he considered to be women's gossip, Othman studied the wall, noting for the first time the gaps between the bricks where birds had already begun to nest. Jessum replied, 'Yes, they do chatter, don't they? I suppose it's the boredom of confinement or something.'

And in that innocent remark Othman recognized that of course the conversations between the wives would be a two-way exchange. Probably not just Niandi but the whole of the town knew what sort of lover Othman was. By God, he would do something that night to give them something to talk about! But he knew he was being childish. Perhaps Silandi merely listened and never shared her own experiences. He shrugged the thoughts away. Jessum was partly right – the women *were* bored. But not only the women – most of the men were too. Zayid kept everyone close to the town – or what was to be the town. They had never been confined to such monotonous surroundings in their lives – not even on the island.

'There – see it? There! There!'

The shout came from the battlements above the heads of the two men and they looked upwards. One of the soldiers was pointing, over the river, at something that had obviously excited two others who were standing by him.

'Yes, I see it – my God, I see it,' came the reply from one of the men.

Othman began bounding up some near-by steps, groaning. 'These fools are inventing fantasies for their tired eyes.'

It was not a fantasy that slid along the landscape in the distance, though Othman had often dreamed of the creature that carried its house over there, in broad daylight. Funny, because after the discovery of the shell in the dark cave, and the incident on the night of the stickmen's dance, he had always envisaged the mollusc as a nocturnal creature – a sinister giant that blackened moonlit landscapes rather than gave them a splash of colour, as this one did. It was really quite attractive in a crimson, sprawling sort of way, this weird mollusc. (Or perhaps another type of creature with an exo-skeleton, not necessarily a mollusc? Just because it had a shell it did not mean it could be categorized neatly alongside similar-looking Earth-type species.) The beast was moving along a ridge in a direction which led it away from the wall. Othman could see thousands of tentacle-like small legs rippling round the edges where the shell met the ground. Two high, waving antennae sprang from the creature's brows and hung like angler's rods before it as it travelled along.

Fast, thought Othman, faster than a camel runs. It sailed a ridge like an upturned yacht. Othman wondered if it had the same kind of nervous system which the stickmen had. He saw Fdar out of the corner of his eye and remembered that the ability was not intrinsic only to the locals – it was a skill that could be transmitted to creatures with a nervous system of any kind, provided that those creatures had a virgin mind.

'Get the men formed into a party,' yelled a guard captain. 'Let's follow that thing. Maybe it'll cross over to us. I'm tired of goat's meat.'

'How do you know you can eat it?' asked someone else.

The captain bounded down the steps and onto a horse.

'We'll soon find out,' shouted another soldier, and followed his captain to a horse and out of the gate. Others joined them, riding out along the river with loud whoops and waving their weapons above their heads. The animal ahead of them disappeared from sight.

Zayid joined Othman on the battlements.

'Where are those fools going?' he growled, running a scarred hand through his long, thick hair.

'They're going to catch ... a *syrinx aruana*,' replied Othman, deciding the thing needed a name, even if it was not a mollusc.

Zayid grunted something.

Othman said, '... which is Earth's largest gasterpod. Admittedly, the Earth *syrinx aruana* is a sea creature – but nevertheless I think the name suits it ...'

'What are you babbling about?' said Zayid.

'Giant snails,' replied Othman calmly. 'Your soldiers are chasing one. I hope it doesn't turn on them. It would seem to me to be a most ignoble death, to be trampled by a snail. They would never believe it back home.'

So the creatures became 'The Syrinx' singular and plural, and were seen occasionally over the river from the town walls in the following weeks. The horsemen did not, at that time, manage to attract one or encourage one to cross to their side of the river. Later they would kill one. Later the syrinx would also have its day. That would be after the people had left the ruins of the town to walk the wilderness once more.

Twenty-one

Night can be a protective place; a blanket of security around its temporary charges; a place of peace where thoughts are unhampered by distracting noises or interruptions; a place where a man can see down the long tunnel of existence to the distant light which he knows is the answer to the question of life.

Night can also be a forbidding place; a frightening hall full of warped nightmares, where running feet slip and slide and fingers fail to grip, or if they do, the handholds turn to steam.

Night can be either of these places. It can change from one to the other with terrifying swiftness.

The people rested within the walls, and although no buildings were complete some had reached the stage where they could support a roof. Many citizens, however, still slept in the maydan, the open square. Animals roamed around in makeshift pens on carpets of hay or slept like their human masters. The camels, strongly companionable, clustered together in one corner of the town. In the walls the birds had pressed themselves deeply into their mud-grass nests.

One of these birds, a large white-plumed creature with a downward curving beak, opened its eyes and stared out into the night. It cocked its head sharply upwards and ruffled its feathers, awakening a neighbour. The first bird stretched on its legs and paused in uncertainty at the edge of its nest, as if deciding whether or not to take to the air. Other birds began to wake and shuffle in their own warm holes. The first bird seemed to settle down on its breast again, and then suddenly it stood and threw itself upward: a large white cross moving swiftly towards the stars. The beat of its wings was rhythmic and unhurried. For a while nothing else stirred. Then the second bird followed the path of the first.

One by one other birds began to leave the crevices in the wall. Without fuss they took to the air and flew silently off into the darkness.

The sentries above them noticed nothing.

Beetles, bugs, spiders and insects crawled out. At first very slowly, then with the birds gone, more swiftly, until finally they stampeded in panic, falling over one another and running headlong into blades of grass which bent like springs under the rush of tiny bodies.

Lastly came the rodents, who hate to leave a comfortable home. Danger has to be very near, very sure, before the rodents evacuate themselves.

Within their pens the domestic creatures (closer to Man than birds, insects and rodents, and cosseted by Man's ability to protect his property – therefore losing that keen edge of the survival instinct owned by the wild creatures) began to moan and shuffle their feet. They too had been touched by the threatening atmosphere somewhere inside the night. Finally the sentries heard, and relying on the blunted but nevertheless reliable instinct of the domestic animals realized that something was wrong. Instantly the danger sounds wafted over them and they were completely awake. They looked outwards on to the grasslands, to see if they were threatened from that direction, but there was nothing out there.

They looked around the walls but still on the *outside* of the town.

Then they looked down, into the maydan, into the mass of sleeping bodies wrapped in nightbags, and they sniffed the air. One of them at last gave the alarm and at the same time opened a vent to relieve the pressure of his fear.

'Fire!' he screamed.

'Fire! Fire!' and the town became pandemonium.

The smell of burning was strong in Othman's nostrils. Wood, hair, rubber and straw. It was so pungent it clogged his throat. His eyes were extremely sore, presumably from the smoke, and he shook his head to try to clear the buzzing inside. Fire! The sound rang in his brain and through the waves of fear which the word had generated within came the thought that if they were to survive they needed to save certain possessions – foremost of which was the animals.

A woman rushed past him screaming, and the signs of an

epidemic of panic were all around him. He shook Silandi roughly.

'Quickly,' he said. 'I must do something. See if you can find Jessum. Come on, woman, wake up!' he shouted into her face, desperately fighting down a desire to run for the gate.

Silandi blinked rapidly and coughed.

'Wha ... what's the matter? I can hardly breathe. Othman!' she screamed the last word.

Othman replied, 'The town's on fire. Calm down and find Jessum. We need the animals.'

A child was crying for its mother and a large man had the presence of mind to snatch it up into his arms as he ran past on his way to the gate.

Zayid was calling for assistance and Othman left Silandi to come to her senses. She seemed drugged by the thick atmosphere and began staggering in the direction of the gate.

Having found Zayid, Othman dragged him towards the camels, shouting at people as he did so to join them. One or two turned – most of them took little heed. Othman grabbed a man, intending to talk sense into his ear, but the other was so terror-stricken that he scratched and bit in his efforts to escape. Finally Othman had to let him go.

Four of them managed to lead a string of frightened beasts to the gate, but the opening was jammed with bodies being pressed still further by people on the inside of the wall.

Zayid and Othman managed to clear the crowd away from the opening by forcibly throwing people aside. The stench of burning was appalling and what frightened them more was that the smell of singed flesh could be detected. Together Othman and Zayid cleared the gate entrance and those on the outside pulled the bodies away once the jam had been loosened. An orderly, though reluctant queueing took place and the evacuees then filed through the gateway. Finally Othman began leading the animals through the hole.

Outside the walls people were lying on the ground or wandering around looking for close friends and family. Some were vomiting. Children wailed noisily. Of those people who had been extracted from the gateway, two were dead. One was a child, the other was Said Rak. Both had been asphyxiated. Othman was saddened over the death of Said Rak. For all that the man had been a fool in many ways, he had had one great virtue: loyalty. It was not something that could be regarded lightly when one ruled from far above the crowd as Othman had done. And what was worse, the poor man had seen the mutiny of the troops of whom he had once been so proud.

Suddenly Othman remembered Silandi and began shouting her name. After a while he saw her lying on a hillock looking very ill and he ran to her, falling on his knees beside her.

'Are you all right?' he asked anxiously. He looked into her face but it was difficult to read her eyes, even though the dawn was now well advanced.

'I think ... so,' she answered. 'The smell ... it was ... it made me feel so sick.'

'I know, I know,' replied Othman, relieved that there was nothing seriously wrong with her. He had, for a moment, had the guilty thought that she might have been one of those people he had pulled uncaringly and roughly from the gateway and then thrown quickly aside. Said Rak had been one of those. He could forgive himself for his treatment of his former Master-at-Arms, but had it been his own wife it would have been a different matter. Even given the expediency of such an act he could not have justified it to himself later.

Other animals were being led out of the gateway, by men whose courage had returned now that a state of semi-order had been restored. They had gone back into the town, cautiously, and had obviously managed to find a path through the flames to the animal pens. Through the fire ...

Othman's thoughts began to arrange themselves once more. The fire. He stared towards the town. What fire? He tried to remember if he had seen flames or even smoke, but his memory was fogged by that awful odour of burning. After a long while he decided he was talking himself into circular thoughts and went looking for Jessum.

'Jessum,' he called out, making several heads turn. Jessum was comforting Niandi, who appeared upset. He heard Othman and left Niandi to Fdar, who then hovered around his master's wife looking extremely ill at ease.

Jessum reached Othman's side.

'Yes?' he said.

'Jessum, what did you see in the town?'

Jessum looked shamefaced. 'Well, I must admit I panicked. Niandi, Fdar and I were sleeping near the gate ... we were among the first few to get out. Later I tried to go back in again – when my fear had subsided a little – but the gate was cluttered with people trying to escape ...'

'What did you see? – why did you run?' persisted Othman.

'Well ... the fire.'

'Did you *see* the fire? The flames?'

Jessum paused. 'No,' he answered. 'But someone was screaming fire – people were running – and I smelt it. Also the smoke was stinging my eyes.'

'You saw the smoke.'

Again Jessum paused and looked puzzled.

'I didn't actually see it, because it was still quite dark ...'

'True,' said a voice from behind them. Othman turned to find Zayid and one of his officers. Zayid continued, 'You smelt the fire like everyone else and you sensed it in every way, except ... there was no fire.'

Othman nodded. 'We have little that would burn except straw and clothes, and both of those articles would flare quite brightly – yet no one, it seems, saw any flames. You have asked others?' he inquired.

Zayid grunted an affirmation. The sun was rising above the rim of the world now and they all looked towards the town. There was no smoke – not a wisp showed above high walls.

Everything looked peaceful and intact. No flames roared heavenward. Yet still the smell was drifting through the damp morning air.

The men walked back to the gate and entered the town, coughing in disgust as the powerful odours penetrated their lungs once again. They found it difficult to breathe as they made a thorough search of all the half-built houses and animal pens. Finally, in a stable near the centre of the town, they found it. The thing was obviously remaining where it was and, judging by the intensity of the foul air around it, was the source of the stench and acrid vapours. They left it quickly, their eyes and nostrils running.

Once outside again they discussed their position.

'What was it?' Zayid asked.

'It was one of those things that we saw at the foot of the cliffs – a whirlwind with black specks in it,' replied Jessum.

'Yes, *but what was it*?' asked Zayid's officer, a tall lean man with a completely bald head.

'You heard,' replied Othman. 'That's all we know. Whatever it is it doesn't want us around. We'll have to leave it alone until it decides it wants to go home. Wherever home is.'

'But ...!' Zayid was obviously torn inside. His beautiful dream of a thriving township was being thwarted. He said, 'What if it doesn't leave?' Othman shrugged. He had no answer.

Zayid said, 'Perhaps that's just a natural odour – maybe those things always smell like that ...'

Jessum replied, 'The other one didn't.'

'But maybe this is a different type,' said Zayid, clutching at straws.

'Maybe,' said Jessum, 'but I doubt it – and so do you. I think it's pretty obvious from the way it chose the town centre that it purposely came to drive us out. It knows us pretty well too – it knows what can frighten us. It knows how to cause a panic. I think we're getting a gentle push.'

Zayid suddenly became angry. 'I see your game,' he shouted. 'You two want us to start walking again – nomad bastards!'

He stormed away, his officer trotting at his heels.

'What do you think, Othman?' asked Jessum quietly. The people were making swift forays into the town to retrieve belongings now. Silandi was on her feet and the colour was returning to her complexion.

'I don't know,' he replied honestly. 'You could be right – but then so could Zayid. What we must ask ourselves is – why the symptoms? The complaint is what we should be looking for now. If we are being driven away from our town we should find out why. Otherwise we're going to make the same mistake again. Pretty soon we'll run out of suitable sites for a town.'

'What do you suggest?' asked Jessum.

'I think we should try to communicate with our friend in the stable,' replied Othman.

Twenty-two

Zayid was suspicious of Othman's motives. When Othman had first suggested that someone – at that time no names had been mentioned – should visit the alien and try to communicate with it, Zayid had thought the idea a good one. Now that the suggestion was being put into practice, he was decidedly of the opinion that he had been a fool to sanction it. It was true that Othman was being accompanied by one of Zayid's most trusted officers but Othman was a shrewd man. By no means did Zayid underestimate the ex-leader's cleverness.

However, Zayid himself was prone to vomiting every time he went near the town and he knew that to visit the stable three days running, as Othman had done, would be a torture he would not be prepared to endure even to protect his position.

Still, the cloud was there and he could not shake off the feeling that Othman was playing some devious game to get them back on the road again. The engineer was definitely a born *Qalandāriyyan* – a man without a fixed abode, a wandering dervish. A person without a home or a true religion. At least he shared *that* much with Othman. Both of them felt that the people were lost without the life-blood of their soul – a meaningful and complete religious background. Zayid knew it had been there, as part of their childhood. It was impossible to divorce a man from a religion such as the one shared by the senders. Yet they, the ship's people, had been robbed of their birthright. It was wrong. He knew it and Othman knew it.

He pondered on Othman's swift rise to power once again. The man was born to be a leader, that much was obvious. In a very short period he had risen from the lowest rung – the prisoner of a new regime – to a fairly comfortable official position once more. It was, in Zayid's view, entirely wrong. But it was happening. And why had Silandi returned to him? She had sworn she hated the man and would draw breath in the next world before sleeping with him again. But the magnetic Othman had pulled her to his side the minute Zayid had considered him neutralized. It was uncanny. There was no fathoming women. His own wife, thank God, was a plain, simple woman with a mind like baker's dough. He liked her that way.

Zayid stood at the entrance to his tent and stared at the town gate. Othman should be coming back soon. He had reported no success to date, but Zayid was of the opinion that the 'thing' was intelligent, and all intelligent beings could communicate in some way or another, given time.

His eyes strayed to a spot, far in the distance, across the river. That was another matter entirely. Perhaps those two failed to keep walking and were decapitated by a ... by what? A razor-sharp whirlwind with black flecks in it? The whole thing was ridiculous. Or would have been if it were not so frightening. Zayid would have liked to get at those heads and bury them quickly to get them out of his sight and mind. Othman, of course, had even solved that puzzle. The riddle of the singing skulls. If one looked carefully through a viewer it was not difficult to see that the jaws of the skulls were wide open. Since the volume and pitch of their singing changed with the intensity of the wind Othman had deduced that there were strings stretched tautly between the upper and lower teeth – possibly gut threads. The wind blew through the eye sockets and mouth creating that horrible hollow wailing.

'Some soup, Zayid?' A voice from the tent.

It was his wife. She was forever feeding him. Trying to make him larger, possibly. It was not his fault that he lacked stature – he was broader than most. Stronger too.

'Not just now, woman. Perhaps later.'

Unkind. He was being selfish, he knew. She was as frightened as anyone by their present situation and hid it in a welter of domestic activity.

'Perhaps just a cupful, to keep the throat lubricated,' he said, cursing himself for his compassion.

Othman came out of the gate, striding tall, and Zayid found himself stretching unconsciously. He swore. Damn Othman and his aristocratic bearing. Why should Zayid feel envious of such a man? A few inches of meat and bone should not make *that* much difference.

Behind Othman came three other men and Zayid's eyes narrowed and a flame of anger flickered within them. Jessum and his servant had accompanied Othman today. That was bad and Zayid had expressly forbidden that the two men, Jessum and Othman, should meet, let alone go on such an important mission together. Othman was dangerous enough alone. With his lieutenant he was positively lethal. They drew up in front of him. Zayid could see his own officer was uneasy about the presence of Jessum.

'Well?' Zayid barked.

Othman answered, 'Nothing, we made no impression on the alien.'

Zayid had not meant that. He was at that moment more concerned about a conspiracy forming.

'Why are you two meeting behind my back?' he said, white with anger.

Othman looked puzzled. 'Behind your ... ? Oh, I see,' he said, as the reason for Zayid's anger appeared to sink in. 'You don't approve of the other ambassadors. Well, I thought perhaps Jessum's man could do something – with his touch language – and since he won't go anywhere without Jessum it had to be all four of us.'

Zayid's anger dissipated. 'If that's the case, then I'm sorry, but you should have asked permission.'

Othman looked weary, but nodded and said, 'Yes, I suppose I should have done. Anyway, the scheme was a failure. Our would-be interpreter here was too frightened to touch the alien – not that I blame him. Every time we tried to get close, the thing glowed red. No heat, but I wouldn't like to bet that anyone coming into physical contact with it would walk away unscathed. So that leaves us cold. We've tried everything – even the lanquonic translators we brought with us did not impress the beast. You can't communicate without a good sample of the native tongue and he spoke with as much fervour as Jessum's follower here. We're stuck. I know you don't want to begin another trek, so I suggest we move up river a little way and start again.'

The new leader felt despair settle in his chest.

'Start again? A whole new wall?'

Jessum spoke. 'Perhaps we'd do better to forget the wall for a while and build the houses first ...'

He did not get the chance to finish. Zayid was adamant about his policy of guns before butter.

'No – we build the defences first!'

Othman said, 'But our enemies float over them – they're worse than useless.'

'No matter!' The tone was emphatic. 'We do as I say. We will start again – but we start the same way, with a wall. I'm not going to have any heads lost through laziness.'

So it was. They broke camp, moved up river and began the whole construction again in the same manner as before.

A few days after they had begun, a companion to the alien in the old town arrived and the winds began. They started slowly and built up in violence until they screamed through the camp, tearing tents from their foundations and lifting people and animals up off their feet, casting them like rags through the air. Broken limbs were an hourly occurrence and blasting grit blinded anyone who attempted to face the onslaught of the storm.

Zayid knew he was being driven away, but he stubbornly refused to accept defeat. Like Othman, his mind was immovable on the basic principles that governed his life. His people were destined to begin a new and settled era on the banks of the river and no one, nothing, was going to force them to go.

The wind was unceasing and finally even the staunchest of Zayid's supporters were begging him to break camp again and move well away from the troubled area. With this kind of opposition Zayid could not hold out for very long and he reasoned with himself that the aliens might be trying to make them move completely away from a zone which was sacred to them in some way or another. Perhaps it was holy ground, or the equivalent of private pastures? – when he stopped to consider, there were endless possibilities for unwitting trespass. So he gave the order to break camp, and bubbles were deflated, the animals laden and the small children were strapped to strong backs. They set forth once again, along the river banks, to a new place where, hopefully, they could be left in peace.

*

Zayid did not get his wish. It was the same whenever they stopped for too long. 'Too long' was when the grazing had ceased to be good, or when the people showed signs of entrenching themselves in one place, or even those times when a feeling of contentment had settled upon the group as a whole. That was the *main* trigger for the winds – whenever men and women lay back of an evening and said, 'This is a pleasant place. I like it here,' the winds would come to dig their sharp spurs in the flanks of the tribe. A tribe was what it had now become. Once, they could have been a group of city people, but since they had begun the long walk they had become more close-knit, more of a family, with each member knowing his or her daily tasks and where they fitted into the structure of the tribe, both socially and officially. The children collected the roots and fruit from the bushes, and scraped the salt from the stones by the river. They fed and watered the domestic animals and helped the women with the household chores. The men sat and discussed the politics of the moment and the wisdom of each action taken by their leaders. They slaughtered the livestock when necessary and hunted the small beasts of the neighbouring countryside.

Slowly Zayid felt himself sliding from favour, and watched bitterly as Othman was reinstated. With each new attempt at planting the tribe in order that it should take root in the soil of a chosen home, and with each new onslaught from the aliens whenever he tried to do so, Zayid's prestige quicksilvered towards freezing point on the political thermometer. One day, after they had suffered a particularly intense week of torrential rain, which raised the river dangerously and forced the tribe to retreat back into the grasslands, he gave up. He retired to his tent the same night and thereafter rarely ventured outside it. Othman's victory was complete, though it rang hollow as a bamboo drum.

To Othman the object in life was not so much to find a place to settle, but to look for it. He was not content to keep pacing the same ground they had covered many times, up and down the river bank. A challenge had presented itself to him – he wanted to cross the river to the other side. Perhaps over there they would find the home they were seeking?

He sent men out to scour the countryside for trees in order that they could make a bridge. Once again he kept the people so busy, so weary that they had no time to consider what they were doing. Othman also whiled away his own time training new falcons. Anything that could help with the hunting was invaluable. This time he trained the birds to carry stones and bomb their prey with accurately discharged missiles. Long hours of patience were finally rewarded and the idea caught on. Very soon hawks and falcons were in great demand: boys and men alike had their favourite 'droppers' which could hit a rabbit-sized creature on the run with a killing blow from a half-pound river pebble.

They swooped on their prey like dive-bombers, or aimed the stones from high above, letting them fall hundreds of feet down onto their victims. A whistle through a master's fingers was the only signal needed.

The bridge reached out with its roughly-hewn arms for the far banks and – a fact which struck some as strange – the tribe was not bothered by aliens during its construction. Othman knew that this was because a bridge is an aid to travellers and not a permanent residence, though some of his people could see no difference between building a bridge and building a wall. They both required a lot of backbreaking toil.

When the work was finished they crossed over the same day and it amused Othman to see how bewildered many of his people were when they left the bridge behind and it dwindled out of sight. They had spent months constructing the wooden span only to use it once before discarding it. It took only a few moments for each person to cross and Othman could almost hear them thinking, 'Surely that's not all? We must be able to do something else with it?' knowing that there is nothing else you can use a bridge for, except to cross a void. Once on the other side you have no further use for it, unless of course, you need to go back again.

Twenty-three

(They had passed from out of the grasslands, away from the constant, noisy attention of the insects of the steppes, to the cooler darkness of the forests at the foot of the mountains. In the woods they were safe from the syrinx, which was a terrible beast indeed ...)

When the people had been travelling for some way, after having crossed the river, a syrinx had been spotted some distance ahead of the main, slow-moving party. Four riders set out to investigate the creature. Othman had warned the horsemen not to approach the animal too closely because Earth's snails had tongues with horny teeth, and the syrinx might use its radula as a weapon to protect itself or its territory – if it had such a tongue. One of the problems on a new world is that of classification. Othman, being human, followed known guidelines, but of course the creatures of Jessum did not have to fall under Othman's specifications. He knew that, but there was no alternative but to draw on *probabilities*: conjecture down any other path was futile because the matrix of *possibilities* covered the whole universe with its nets of lines.

In this instance he had been correct in his assumption that the animal would have similarities with Earth snails, but he chose the wrong similarity.

The riders circumnavigated the creature, watching with fascination the movement of its skirt of tentacles. After their initial awe had disappeared they began charging the creature from different angles, noting with glee its confusion as it turned to avoid the steaming horses bearing down upon it.

But it was faster than they were and made its escape through a gap in their ranks. One man considered the foolery to be over and raised his weapon to his shoulder. What happened next was recounted with horror to Othman when the three survivors rode back to the main party with the body of the fourth draped over his horse.

'He raised his weapon,' said an agitated Sufi, one of the dead man's companions, 'and the syrinx spat at him – not spittle, but the spike you see in his chest!'

A woman moaned. It was the new widow. Othman fingered the object protruding from the staring corpse's sternum, and recalled more of the biology he had learnt at school. What was more disconcerting was the fact that the syrinx appeared to have intelligence.

'Was it coincidence that the syrinx killed the man who was about to shoot – or would you say the animal *knew* it was about to be fired on?' Othman asked the three riders.

They shrugged their shoulders and looked at each other for an answer.

'Never mind,' sighed Othman. His people were becoming dull-witted. It was to be expected, he supposed. Their life of late had been hard and full of privation. They were constantly on the move, there was never enough food and each day was filled with monotonous chores. Only when they were actually walking did the people find time to think, and by then their minds were heavy with drowsiness. They prayed a lot but were short on laughter and cheerfulness. Melancholia was the companion of the caravan.

Zayid and Jessum were among those who crowded round the body. They, as much as any, needed the respite, morbid though it was.

'Zayid,' called Othman. 'I think we'll rest here for an hour or two.'

Zayid looked up and nodded. There was no need to go barking orders. The people had heard and the word would soon spread throughout the tribe.

'Jessum,' continued Othman, 'Please arrange the burial – away from the caravan.'

Jessum nodded and began to organize a party. The widow followed behind, tearfully, through the tall grass. Othman sat down wearily on the ground, and before he knew it he was lying stretched out on his back staring up through the long grass at the sky. For the moment he had privacy – a luxury. But he felt guilty as most of the others were taking the necessary action with the animals: tethering them or hobbling their legs on a good patch of grazing. How well they had settled to the nomadic way of life! How quickly necessity breached the right skills! Even Malek had adjusted to his new, more important role of veterinary surgeon, and was training a young and able assistant – a six-year-old boy with an affinity with the animals. Six Earthyears, that is – after all, they still had no new measurement of the passing time. What did it matter?

A face appeared above him and he started to rise, but it was Silandi and she gently pushed him back again, smiling. Her black hair fell around her dark features like heavy curtains contrasting sharply with the white wisps of cloud in the saffron sky. No one could call her beauty ethereal: there was nothing of the peri, the fairy gossamer touch, to those eyes and lips. More of the sorceress, the enchantress.

The brown stiff grasses crackled in the morning breezes and as she bent lower over him her features darkened until he could no longer see them. Quickly, he pushed her back until he could see her eyes again.

'What's the matter?' she asked, with a puzzled look. 'I was only going to kiss you.'

'I know,' he said, 'but ... I don't deserve it.'

He was not going to tell her that, for a moment, he had been afraid – afraid of witches and dark magic: the things that lurked in his brain when he was alone at night. A throwback to his real childhood in Space, he imagined. Probably something to do with the darkness of a plastic cell carried into manhood. The madness of the unknown.

Silandi smiled again, the hurt look gone.

'Don't deserve a kiss? What silliness is this our great leader talks?'

'You mustn't speak like that, Silandi. I'm not a great leader – I'm a very bumbling, makeshift excuse for one. Oh, I know – at the time I thought I was nothing short of divine. But I'm not the immature boy of thirty that I used to be ...'

'Immature? At thirty?'

'Yes, of course. What experience of life had I had before I tumbled out of the uteri wheel? None. It's not your kisses I don't deserve – it's your love. I treated you badly ...'

Silandi nodded gravely. 'True. You were a beast – a big hairy beast ...' She ran her fingers through the hair of his chest exposed through the slit she still cut in his robes. She allowed no one else to cut the garment of their man in the same way.

He could see there was going to be no serious conversation between them and he raised himself upon his elbows. In the distance, beyond the plains, were more hills – the source of the river they had rediscovered. In those hills Othman hoped they might find a place where they would be allowed to settle. After all, why did the aliens want to keep them moving? Surely only because they represented a danger if they settled and entrenched themselves behind heavy defences? On the island Othman had discouraged the building of a town, and in that he had unwittingly followed the desires of the aliens. He had built a bridge to the mainland, thus communicating to the others his desire to travel.

If, when they reached those dome-shaped hills, they settled in simple huts and made no move to build solid structures the whirlwind creatures might leave them alone ...

(*They built the huts and for thirteen days they watched for the wind, the flood, the fire. It seemed as if they had made it when a hailstorm came out of a clear sky and flattened all their work.*)

After the unfortunate horseman had been buried they set forth again, towards the mountains. This time Othman put out flanking horsemen as well as rear and forward scouts. His caution was wise for the syrinx often travelled in herds and what had begun as a leisurely walk across the plains became headlong flight with men fighting a desperate rearguard action against the giant beasts. Fortunately the syrinx were only armed with one dart and once that had been expended they usually turned and left the field. One, however, continued its charge, like a mad rogue elephant. The men took vicious delight in blasting this beast to pieces as it bore down on them. A soldier called Jem'm, even ran out to snatch a chunk of the shell to keep as a trophy. Once the syrinx had experienced what the men's weapons could do at close range they seemed reluctant to continue the pursuit and eventually the caravan was relieved to see that it had left them behind. It taught both groups a lesson. Both men and syrinx would beware of each other in any future encounters. Both carried deadly stings, and both did not like the results of the other's destructive power.

Once the people reached the woods they felt they were safe. The tree-trunks afforded them a certain amount of fortification. The trees were single-limbed evergreens, their one branch rising straight from the thick trunk and spreading like a brown beaver's tail, but trimmed with a knife-edge of green leaf.

That night they made fires outside the bubbleskin tents and someone composed a song about the fight with the syrinx. If Othman knew that the first stones were being laid in the tribe's culture he said nothing of it. He clapped along with the rest of them, giving the singer a beat to work to – no one even thought about getting a canister of music from the packs, let alone suggested it. They were quite happy making their own entertainment. Even the guests felt the change in atmosphere. The tribe seemed to be more close-knit: more like a tribe should be, if it is to have any unity and its individuals any loyalty to the community as a whole. In the song, Jem'm, who was a bit of a clown in any case, was a comic hero, dashing in between the syrinx for his piece of shell, dodging nonexistent darts. If this is how a situation becomes warped in one day, thought Othman, God help posterity!

The evening advanced and the people slowly slipped away to their tents as the tiring events of the day caught up with them. Probably the only sad person amongst them was the new widow. Othman made a note to see her the next morning. She was, he knew, with friends that night.

Men sat around the glowing charcoals, blowing on them occasionally to keep the redness alive. They spoke of their childhood learnings and of the history of Earth's tribes and nations, and for the first time Othman detected no note of nostalgia or envy in their voices. Without realizing it, his people had dealt themselves a favourable psychological blow, although the small incident with the syrinx had been in many ways similar to other catastrophes experienced by the tribe. The only difference with that day's events was they had scored a minor victory while on the run. When he said as much to Jessum he was reprimanded.

'Things were not quite as you state them, Othman. We retreated, that's true, but it was an organized retreat and for the first time the men were able to shoot at something solid – able to take positive retaliatory action. All those other times the enemy was an invulnerable puff of wind and light. Give them an enemy that stops bullets and they'll love you for it.'

'I don't want to be loved,' answered Othman. 'I'm just glad they're happy for once.'

Zayid was less complimentary, but even he grudgingly accepted that a new spirit of hope had swept through the tribe.

Othman felt good. Tomorrow they would begin to build the huts. If it did not work out, well, they could always move on. One thing was certain, they would never run out of land. He would have a wooden syrinx carved as well – a tribal memento of their victory over what would appear to be an intelligent aggressor. It would help them remember the song.

The charcoal flared and lit the animated faces. Even Fdar, who could not understand all the words, sat enthralled by the talk, listening to the soft, contented tones of men who were men at last. The hands expressed. The eyes told the story of their own accord. And a smile from Jessum was a reward not often given in these times. Fdar did not need oral language, while he still had his sight.

He saw Othman leave the fire and walk towards his tent, to the warmness of his woman, and Fdar felt a little sad that he had no woman of his own to go to. True, he pleased some of the other wives sometimes – those who felt no love, only passion. They enjoyed his electric vibrations. But it was not the same as having the arms and legs of a fond lover wrapped around one's body before falling asleep. He sighed, and one of the men patted his shoulder as if he understood, which made Fdar feel one of them and a wanted person. That also was important to him, and he put aside his sadness to touch a tree trunk near-by. The colours came to him. Fdar was part of a bigger tribe. He was part of it All.

Twenty-four

The hills seemed to rise out of the plains like blisters from sunburnt skin – smooth and weathered. Othman judged that they would take one more day to reach.

'Then what?' asked Silandi. She was busy preparing the fire for the evening meal.

Othman said, 'We'll wait and see. I suppose we could venture in as far as possible – if it seems that it's not going to be easy to reach the far side, then we'll turn back. We have all the time in the world.'

'What are you doing now?' Silandi asked, looking up from her chores. Othman was busy strapping on an ammunition belt and he paused.

'Going hunting.'

'At *night*?' said Silandi. 'It'll be dark in just a few moments.'

Othman laughed. 'That's the whole idea. The sentries have seen a lot of furry creatures running about the plains in the starlight. About the size of a small pig. We want to bag some to see if they're at all edible.'

'That means I'll be sleeping alone tonight – who's *we*, anyway?'

Othman gave her a playful pinch on the buttocks.

'You won't be alone *all* night, woman. I'll be back about midnight – besides, it won't hurt you for once to . . .'

'Don't finish that sentence. I asked who was going with you,' said Silandi.

'Zayid, and a couple of soldiers. Ali and Alrar.'

'I thought you didn't like Zayid – or he you?'

He smiled. 'I don't have to hold his hand. We're only going hunting, you know, not vowing undying friendship. We can tolerate each other's company. That's the difference between men and women – women don't merely dislike each other, they usually hate. Can't stand each other's company. Men are more mature . . .'

She threw a clod of soil at him and he ducked.

'I don't trust Zayid to look after you,' she said after a while.

'Ha! Now then, I thought Zayid was your hero? Besides, I don't need looking after. I'm perfectly competent.'

This time she looked at him seriously and said, 'You're a very competent man – among men. You handle judgements and political decisions better than anyone in the world. But you're not very good at physical things, Othman, despite your size.' She began stacking dried dung on the fire once the flames had caught the grass and sticks.

He nodded sagely. 'There's some wisdom in those words,' he replied. 'I have limitations – I never could play tennis well at school ...'

'Be serious ...'

'All right, I'll be serious. What can harm me out there ...?'

She did not need to answer. She merely stared him straight in the eye. He had been intending to say that the furry creatures were not at all dangerous, but of course there were other things out on the plains.

'The syrinx are diurnal creatures,' he said defensively.

'I know. I'm not saying "don't go", am I? I just want you to be on your guard and not rely too much on Zayid if something happens. He's good – but he'll look after himself first. Whatever you may say about men, he has no love for you, Othman.'

He nodded and bent to kiss her on the cheek. She cooked him a small meal and then, once the darkness had surrounded them and the stars were doing their best to light the world but failing miserably, the other three men arrived at the tent. They had brought Othman's new falcon and each had a satchel of round pebbles for the birds to use as missiles. Othman's bird had been named Mufti by its owner. A Mufti was a professor of law on Earth and Othman had called the peregrine that because of its 'scholastic expression'.

'Come, come, come,' said Othman, holding out his wrist for the hooded creature. It climbed from Alrar's arms to his own, unsteady in its temporary blindness.

'I've heard *that* expression somewhere before,' said Silandi, then realized she had overstepped the mark. There were other men present.

Othman gave her a black look full of promises to be carried out later, and she turned and walked through the bubbleskin, hoping he would forget before morning came.

Zayid grunted, 'Best be away.' He was wearing a half-cured sheepskin cloak which must have been warm on such a balmy night, but he maintained that he could use it as camouflage.

'They'll smell you a mile away,' said Ali. 'Just don't get upwind from me, that's all.'

'You watch your tongue, or I'll rip it out at the roots,' growled Zayid, turning on him.

Ali gulped rapidly and did as he was told. It took a brave man to face the stocky little Zayid and outstare those hard eyes behind the broken nose.

'Gentlemen,' said Othman. 'Let's save it for another time. We can't have bad feelings amongst us before we go out there ...' He nodded to the half-lit grasslands.

Ali mumbled, 'I was only joking,' but Zayid had already turned away and was threading his way between the tents to the edge of the encampment.

The starlight shone on the grass like silver and flashed as the breezes turned the blades this way and that, as if displaying them to a purchaser. Occasionally a running bird would dash out, pause on one leg as if undecided about the direction of the danger, its beak and eyes glinting as its head clicked from one side to the other, then just as swiftly it would disappear back into the grasses. The men were not interested in such small fry. They wanted joint meat, not fowl.

Zayid was pleased when he saw them first. He never failed to get a thrill during a hunt and it was always the front man that got the best kicks. He motioned for the others to be silent. Ali nodded and smiled when he too saw the creatures bumping along on top of a hump like huge rabbits, occasionally pausing to munch on a weed. There were about a dozen of them.

'If we spread out we may be able to get them all,' whispered Zayid. 'Aim for the head. We don't want a mess of stew, we want good solid meat.'

'What about the falcon?' said Othman. 'I don't want him hit.'

Zayid replied softly, 'Save him until last. If it looks as though any are going to escape, then release the bird – okay?'

'Right,' Alrar whispered, and slipped away to the left. Othman and Ali went right, and Zayid settled where he was, taking aim at the nearest animal. He was going to make sure of at least one, even if one of the others bungled it and made the others bolt.

His cheeks rested on the cold metal stock of the weapon which had two crutchlike supports clipped to his upper arms. Beyond the nibbling creatures he could see the horizon and a bank of stars, a cluster of them closer together than a bunch of berries on a bush. Zayid was not in any sense a poet but he did have a certain appreciation of raw beauty and that star bank was beautiful. On the night of Kadar, the night he died, he would like to go to those stars, perhaps become one of them. The thought pleased him. Better to be a rough-cut chunk of silver ore in the heavens than a patch of pretty weeds on a world below them.

The animal in front of the stars lifted its head and Zayid's fingers tightened. Were the others in position yet? They ought to have arranged a signal.

Suddenly, the animal he was about to shoot jumped high in the air with a squeal and fell shuddering to the ground. Zayid's heart jumped too, despite the fact that he should have expected that one of the others would fire at the prey he himself had picked out as a target.

He quickly shot at another that was scampering in his direction and scored a hit on its flank. It fell over, kicking, and then he fired at the profile of the head, this time killing it instantly. He looked around for more. So far he had only heard the plopping of his own gun. Perhaps he had not been paying too much attention. He listened. There was an ominous silence. Wait! No, that was just the breezes in the grass. The star bank was still ahead of him, unblinking, but the hump was empty of the animals they had come to hunt. A hand clamped on his arm.

'Wha . . .'

'Quiet!'

It was Alrar. He looked frightened and Zayid suddenly realized he had not heard the noise that killed the first animal, which was why he was surprised.

'There's something out there,' whispered Alrar in a strained voice. 'I saw a man.'

Zayid was puzzled. 'A man? What, someone from the camp?'

'No, no,' Alrar's voice croaked as he tried to get his fears across to Zayid and at the same time keep his voice low.

'It was no one from the camp. I saw him crouching in the grass. He had no hair and was naked. Then he suddenly ran, out into the taller grass – *and he ran like a man, on two legs.*'

'An alien? A human?'

Alrar shrugged and shook his head in confusion. The incident had obviously shaken him up very badly. Humanoid was probably the correct word, thought Zayid. He had to do something! He suddenly wriggled forward through the grass, leaving the trembling Alrar behind, and finally reached the first animal that had been killed. He tried to flip it over but it would not turn – then he saw why. From just below its throat a small arrow protruded. He ran his hand along the shaft. Wood flighted with some kind of hard scale or a thin slice of bone. He crawled back to Alrar.

'Are you all right?' he asked.

Alrar nodded. 'I'm fine now. Just the shock of seeing – well, whatever it was. Shall we find the others?'

Zayid had forgotten about Ali and Othman.

'Yes, I suppose we had better.'

They discovered Ali lying face downwards: his head had been split open and the blood was seeping into the ground. Othman was nowhere to be found, though the two men threw away caution and were running around in full view of any enemy. Finally they realized that they needed help and they had to get Ali to a doctor. Between them they carried the dying soldier back to the camp, half-running, half-walking because the man was heavy.

A search party with torches was quickly formed and they went out again, led by Zayid. He had asked Alrar to see Silandi as he had a dread that they would not find Othman alive. He wanted Silandi prepared for that. At the same time he had no wish to see her himself – he knew she would blame him for Othman's death.

Towards morning they found the weapon – quite a long way from the spot where Ali had been found, but they did not find Othman. Zayid's spirits were slightly lifted by this. It meant that Othman might still be alive. After all, why would the aliens take him away if he was dead? And if the weapon had been dropped *en route* as it appeared, it meant they were heading in the direction of the hills. So be it. He would find the man and bring him back.

He was right about Silandi. She attacked him bitterly for failing in his duty towards her husband. At least, that was how she herself put it.

'Why did you let him out of your sight – you know he's not the same sort of man you are,' she accused.

'Woman!' cried Zayid, exasperatedly. 'It was only supposed to be a hunt. Men don't usually *need* to be looked after on a rabbit hunt ...'

She hung her head, fighting back the tears. 'You should have known there would be other dangers. He's only a boy when it comes to things like that ...'

Zayid put his hand on her shoulder and motioned for Niandi and his own wife to come and comfort her.

'If he's alive, I'll bring him back,' he said bluntly. 'You can be sure of that.'

'If he's alive,' she mumbled in a hopeless voice.

Jessum had insisted on joining the rescue party, although Zayid had wanted to keep the numbers down and had planned on taking only the toughest of the soldiers with him. There was no stopping Fdar either, of course. They left the camp and made for the hills. Fdar would track for them, Jessum explained to Zayid, as his skills had been learned on the island where he had had to follow trails left by his companions. He was also closer to nature than any other member of the tribe; he could feel where the grass had been disturbed; the broken bush cried into his mind, and there were other signs, an absence of small creatures which will not cross a path smelling of people.

They followed the signs into the hills, which, it was found, were giant mounds of red clay. Zayid had no time to reflect upon what might have caused such geological freaks. In the fertile valleys between the mounds, where dark, wind-blown soil had collected in thick rich abundance, fruit trees grew, and ground fruit, and nuts. The men paused to inspect these treasures before riding onwards.

Zayid left the main party in one of these valleys and he and Jessum began to climb up towards some caves they had seen. The evidence of the alien's presence somewhere in the heights above was unmistakable now. The paths were well-worn and here and there a step had been cut to assist a climber up a particularly steep stretch. The whole time they climbed they were alert, their weapons covering both sides of the path above them. One thing was in their favour. The slopes were clear of any kind of cover, which meant they could not be surprised. It also meant they had no protection themselves, but since they expected to have the superior fire power they were not too concerned.

Just let them show themselves in daylight, thought Zayid. *I'll hit them so hard they'll think the end of the world has come.*

Twenty-five

Othman had felt such pain before, when in his childhood he had lain with a bullet-shattered chest on the banks of the canal.

The savages had strung him up between four green-wood poles, one limb tied to each, in a star position above and facing the ground. Buried in the clay beneath him, point-uppermost, was a half-metre-long dart of a syrinx. The spike was just a centimetre too long: this fraction of its length was buried in Othman's breast, just below the sternum. The pain was a continually stoked fire in his chest, and it was all he could do to stop himself fainting. If he moved at all, the spring-like poles bounced him gently up and down on the spike and he needed to keep the whole framework taut to stop his chest arching downwards and burying the point even deeper. Eventually his muscles would give out and go slack, and he would relax into his death. Or the wind would rise and make him sway on the poles, boring a wider hole in his chest until he blacked out and finished the job. His hawk, half-choked, and the hood still in place, had its talons deep in his lower abdomen – forced there by the savages as a small diversionary torture. The bird dangled, wings outstretched, limply below him, and occasionally one of the humanoids would touch it with a burning twig to make its reflexes work. Its claws would tighten, making Othman squirm, and, in turn, the poles bounce.

Jessum and Zayid reached a point on an adjacent hill from where they could view the aliens without being seen. It was truly an awesome sight – the hills were covered with thousands of caves, and outside each large cave sat three or four families.

'My God,' said Jessum, his eyes taking in the scene. They

had only one viewer between them and as he was using it Zayid had to be content with hearsay for a time.

'What is it? Have you found him?'

'No, but we'd better stay nice and quiet while we look for him. I estimate at least a hundred thousand people within the range of the viewer, and the mountains might have several colonies like this one. How do these people manage to feed themselves?' His eyes followed down the line of hills and he found a graveyard of syrinx shells. No wonder the syrinx were so aggressive with this kind of harassment. Well, that was the food problem solved. Part of it, anyway. If they ever got out of this place alive they had better get *well* out.

'What's happening?' asked Zayid impatiently.

'Nothing, I'm still looking for him. I hope the men below aren't like you. We don't want this lot down on our heads. I ... God's face!'

'What now?' cried Zayid.

Jessum took the viewer off. He looked ill. Zayid waited to see if he was going to speak and then snatched the viewer. Putting it over his head he searched the tiers. Ledge over ledge came to his eyes as he scanned the hills, and upon those clay platforms were thousands of people – naked people with red matted hair and red skins – all milling around engaged in daily tasks.

'You realize,' he said, 'that as soon as they've killed Othman and cut off his head, they'll go back for the other body. Judging from the way the heads of the crew of the aircraft were displayed it's obviously a ritual with them. Then they'll find the camp ...'

'I should be very surprised if they don't know where the camp is already. We're all earmarked for their game ... see that tall hill with the double hump?'

Zayid took the viewer off and followed Jessum's finger. 'Got it,' he said and fitted the viewer again. The hill sprang forward towards him.

'Third ledge down,' said Jessum.

Zayid obediently followed the ledges down, then said, 'Yes – what in God's ... he's dead. No – wait a minute ... those bastards are torturing him on some kind of rack. If he isn't dead now he soon will be. There's nothing we can do ... God snuff them! They've tied a cockerel to him!'

Jessum said, 'That isn't a cock, it's his falcon – and I don't think it's tied to him.'

Zayid brought the image closer and his head snapped backwards as he realized what the hawk was doing there.

'You're right of course – but I still can't see any way of getting him out of there. We'd be cut to pieces by that lot, even with our superior weapons.' This was delivered in a quiet tone. Zayid obviously expected an argument from Jessum, but Jessum could give him none. He was well aware of their position and knew that to go in with a contingent of men would be to sentence them all to death. For a start the hill could only be assailed from the bottom – there were no adjoining ridges – and he doubted if they would manage to get halfway to Othman before a hail of missiles cut them down from above.

'Unless of course ...' began Zayid.

Jessum gripped his shoulder. 'What? Unless what?'

Zayid's profile was etched with hard light: his brow lined in thought. There was a determination in his face which had been a characteristic of his during his anti-causeway days.

'If he could hold out until nightfall ...'

Jessum's hopes released their grip on his heart. For a moment he had thought that there was a chance. He said, 'He won't last an hour – let alone all day. There's a stake ... well, you can see it. Could you last out? Could anyone?'

Zayid took off the viewer. His mouth curved in natural relaxation. 'Can you presume to know? Perhaps Allah has decided that Othman's body shall contain an ember of life for more than a day? At least we could end his suffering. I know

— I agree,' he said as he saw Jessum about to protest. 'The man's all but dead now, and from the look on his face the pain must be — well, unbearable. If he manages to survive till nightfall though — could you go away now, knowing that he *might* have been alive? And in the knowledge that you did nothing?'

Jessum wiped his hands on his robe. They were stained red from the clay.

'No,' he said at last. 'What should we do then?'

Zayid replied, enthusiastically now, for he was a man who loved to be attacking the improbable, 'You go back to the camp and get the women and animals on the move. Send them south with an escort of, say, a third of the men. With the rest I want you to try to round up some of those syrinx and drive them this way, in the valley. Don't get too close to them — make a lot of noise. Use explosives. We don't want to lose any men to those harpoons they shoot out. When the natives leave the hills to kill the beasts, the soldiers and I will climb up and get Othman . . .'

Jessum gripped the sleeve of Zayid's robe. 'Will it work?'

'It'll work — but be assured, Jessum, he'll be dead. For our sakes and Silandi's at least, we'll be sure he really died. The other way, just to go, would have left us forever in doubt.'

So Jessum left the small force of men under Zayid's command and rode back to the camp. There he comforted Silandi as best as he could without raising her hopes too much. In private he told Niandi there was *no* hope and that she should gradually bring Silandi round to this point of view.

Then he and the majority of the men rode out, leaving the others to break camp and hustle the females into a hurried departure.

Jessum and his group rode hard and long that day in search of the syrinx. Now that they knew the animals were not of a high level of intelligence and were merely aware of humanoids and the danger they represented, they were quite easy in their minds that the task would not be difficult.

They found a herd and drove the beasts before them with squams and thunderflames towards the people Jessum had already named the Plinthites. The beasts rolled the grasslands under them in their panic to escape the noise, and flattened bushes and trees. As they came close to the mountains it was already growing dark.

The herd went sliding into the valleys like the comic, though terrible, circus animals they were. Jessum and his men managed to keep well out of range, so far out that the beasts had no real sight of their enemy. The squam tubes threw their spinning packets high in the air and these exploded some two to three metres above the ground on the downward flight. One lord of the plains did turn and came headlong back in the direction of its tormentors, but Jessum's men just parted ranks and allowed it to sail through as they stood hidden in tall grass. They watched it swaying left and right in its fury as it searched the country in front of eyes that waved like bright red flowers on their tall stalks. Finally it disappeared, making quick sucking noises in its frustration: the sound of water being drawn rapidly down drainholes.

The Plinthites went mad with delight. Their drums, cymbals and horns sounded through valley upon valley, and they poured down the darkening slopes, red skins gleaming in the light of the torches they brandished above their heads. There were more than a million of them.

Their method of hunting was simple. They would fire flaming arrows at a single syrinx until it finally took exception to being the only one of the herd to be persecuted and charged the archers. One man amongst the others would stand his ground, yelling and screaming and rocking from side to side like a mongoose facing a snake, ready to leap one way or the other at a split second's notice. Occasionally a split second was not enough time and the speciality of cavorting out of the way of a syrinx harpoon, for which the Plinthites had been training for months, died with its owner.

The syrinx only carried one harpoon. It took several weeks

to form another, out of hard mucus and hair, and the Plinthites knew that all they had to do once this spike had been discharged was surround the animal and with sheer weight of numbers force the urgent-sounding beast on to its back. Even here some men were crippled or killed if they were caught under a syrinx that fell heavily back onto its aggressors. Never were the hunters so numerous, nor the prey so tank-like in speed and weight. If an Earth equivalent needed to be found, it was like monkeys playing tag with mad elephants. The night air was full of screaming, laughing, crying voices.

Zayid took his men up the slopes, away from the furore below, and made for the ledge upon which Othman was held. He was attacked once, by a woman with a sword which took a slice the size of a coin from the crown of his head. One of his men dispatched the Amazon with a blow behind her ear. Zayid snatched up the sword and stuck it in his belt.

They found Othman hanging over the harpoon and, holding him free of it, cut the thongs that bound him. His body was limp and apparently devoid of any life.

Women screamed and threw stones at them but so much noise was going on in the valleys below that no notice was taken of the females by their spouses. Their red faces were twisted in malevolent anger and they continued to harass the group as they climbed down the hillside again. One or two of the soldiers silently crushed the front rank of women above them with automatic weapons but those behind only clawed the remains out of the way to get a better aim at the retreating men.

Once on their horses the men rode out onto the starlit plains with Plinthites running past them like underworld gnomes, intent only on getting their share of the available meat.

Jessum had already arrived back at the caravan and Zayid was greeted as a hero. Never before had he felt so proud of himself. It had been *his* plan and he had carried out the most dangerous part of it – successfully, for Othman's heart was still beating. He was the man of the hour, and no longer did he wish to lead – he was happy to be the one at the sharp end, the front line. He had proved himself and he was happy.

Malek was astounded as he carefully removed the claws of the falcon.

'Still alive? After being roasted a whole day under a hot sun with a wound like that...?'

The hole in Othman's chest was indeed ugly, and it would take a lot of grafting to replace the lost skin. Zayid had forbidden Jessum to let Silandi enter the tent until the wound had been padded, but she soon stormed past both of them.

'Do you think I'm a child?' she said. 'Never try to keep me from my husband – I've seen blood before.' But she was not prepared for the ashen face, so near to death, and the fluttering heart visible through the wound. Her own complexion lost its natural dark colouring.

'Please leave,' said Malek, not looking up from overseeing the medical unit. 'We cannot afford to stay for more than an hour – the savages will be following us shortly.'

Whereas Zayid and Jessum had no influence Malek was a professional man and women are snobs. Silandi left quietly but her pale face registered a determination to return before long.

Zayid followed her out and said, 'Let me say now to you, for I would never say it to him, that I admire him more than any other man. He had mental courage surpassing any I had thought possible in anyone. To have kept himself alive through all that pain – death should have claimed him hours ago.'

'Thank you, Zayid,' she replied, 'but I will tell him.'

'I don't *like* him any the better, you understand,' Zayid said hastily. 'I still thing he's a pig.'

Silandi was not listening any more. She said quietly, as if to herself, 'Yes, the pain. He died once before, long ago – and no one dies of a pain the body has withstood once already. It's the will to live that pain destroys, and Othman knows what it's like on the other side ...'

With that she walked off, towards Sham-san, her restless horse, leaving Zayid mystified. He watched her walk away under the faithful starlight and fingered the handle of the short sword in his belt. The sword from the Plinthite woman! He took it out and examined it. It glinted wickedly along its crudely-honed, curved cutting edge. Steel! He weighted it, stroked its cold shiny length. Good steel. A nice finger-firm grip of compressed plastic. Just another mystery for Othman to solve when he recovered, for though Zayid knew what it was, he had no idea how the Plinthites had obtained it.

The object in his hand was a lever from a starship tractor.

Twenty-six

Close to death, he thought. Every man should be a breath away from death and survive, just once in his life, in order that he should *know* what it all hangs on. Why those badly-shaped coagulations of cells and chemical matter strutted around shedding dry epidermis and flakes of dead flesh, waste hair and slivers of nail. Why they breathed the air at all, poisoning their own atmosphere with foul gases and excrement. Finally becoming a mess of putrid, rotten meat. It might have been ugly, if it were not for the fact, or rather the belief, that the animal, man, produced beautiful works with its hands and mind. He wondered though, what a goat thought of a richly woven carpet. (A barely digestible meal?)

If only men found their art beautiful, was it that the other animals were lacking in soul, depth, awareness, or was it that sentimentality made a fool of man? Othman suspected the latter.

Close to death, though, you saw it all. Realized where the futility lay, and where the importance was to be found. Twice Othman had been holding hands with the other side: the first time he had wanted to cross over completely, and could not; this time he was pushing at the cold fingers, to keep himself inside warm flesh. The drowning man, the faller cushioned by tree branches or a bank of snow; the cured incurable; the pieces of an accident sewn together, still pumping blood and sensible thoughts around the body; the brain dangling in a bath of fluid. They knew what the feeling represented. Some of them even went back for a second go. Even brains connected to oral devices had been known to stay silent as their fluid drained through a crack in the tank, waiting patiently to see if alarm would wake the sleeping nurse.

The experience clarified the contents of the mind.

Othman had an answer for most things now. Sometime he would tell Silandi when he was better. When he was able to talk for a long time without experiencing a feeling of nausea.

Zayid had been to visit him. The visits were strictly formal as each man was well aware of the other's dislike. Zayid had seemed agitated, telling Othman about the Plinthites – how they had attacked the caravan daily and had to be beaten off. Now, when the battles were at their height and Zayid was cutting down the enemy with heavy weaponry, the whirlwind creatures would intervene with a dust storm or a rainstorm – almost as if they did not mind conventional hand-to-hand fighting, or even the use of small arms, but drew the line at sophisticated aerial whizzbangs and heavily destructive armaments. Because of their superior weapons, Zayid's men had suffered very light losses – one man dead and five wounded. The Plinthites had dead numbered in hundreds. Perhaps this was what the whirlwinds objected to? The slaughter of natives? Othman had his doubts about that.

They should be a fair distance away from the red hills now,

thought Othman, but still the Plinthites followed them, would not allow them a peaceful passage from the country which they considered their hunting grounds.

As he lay on his bed, half-doped (but not fully dosed because he had warned Malek that he wanted to *feel* his wound healing – if there was just a numbness the boredom of waiting would have been intolerable) he could hear the sounds of the camp awakening. Soon they would come to carry him out on the stretcher and in his drugged state he would fall asleep under the warm sun. On the cushions covering the floor Silandi snored softly. Somehow her noisy breathing was sensual rather than irritating to him, even though it had kept him awake for some time. He tried to visualize making love to her, to arouse himself, but was unsuccessful. The problem was that his mind was still occupied with a recurring dream. The dream was of Earth.

At the time the intelligence units, the teachers, were being destroyed they had been droning about Jupiter, the largest planet within the solar system shared by Earth. There was a red eye to the planet Jupiter which dominated Othman's dream. The eye grew to an angry flaring, until it covered the whole of the planet with its searing crimson – it was a hot redness that Othman could feel scorching his skin as it crept over the surface of the giant planet. There was a dizziness, a whirling sound accompanied by a roaring around his ears – the sound charcoal had made in the punctured can which as a boy he had spun about his head on a long wire, so that the coals should glow fiercely, catch fire, in hand-created winds. So, in his dream, did Jupiter orbit his shoulders and grow a furious whistling fire like a beard around its shape. Othman's head, between the sun Phoebus and the sun Jupiter, burned black over its surface, and the life therein began to die.

He knew his head was the Earth. He knew why the senders had catapulted their unborn children into space – they had known what future Earth held in store for them. It now remained to find the last piece of the puzzle.

A donkey brayed in the stillness outside the tinted bubble-skin walls of the tent and Silandi stirred, mumbling in her sleep. The strong smell of sleeping, unaired woman wafted up to him – a feminine smell which could be unpleasant, or welcome, depending upon the mood of the recipient. Othman accepted it with disinterest. He could do nothing anyway, in his condition.

A slap, loud and distinct. Someone had hit the donkey on the rump. Probably the sound of the hollow braying had woken the man. There was a splashing noise then which triggered thoughts in his brain. Suddenly Othman felt thirsty.

'Silandi,' he said.

'Yes?' She was awake. Probably had been for a few minutes since the din outside was growing in intensity.

'Could I have some water, please?'

She sat up and yawned, leaning back on her deeply tanned arms. The breasts were bare, and perhaps less firm than they had been on that first evening on the planet, when he had lifted her robe. They had been like her spirit then: high, haughty, indignant. Now they lay across her ribs, still full, but quivering at her slightest movement, the dark brown tips no longer like pebbles but more like the softness of upturned mushrooms. She seemed unaware of his gaze and stretched her legs, still attempting to throw off the sleepiness in the limbs.

'I'll fetch it now,' she said, making no attempt to rise. She then added, 'I'm not very pretty in the mornings. Not these days, anyway. Perhaps I used to be – are you searching for what used to be, Othman?'

She had noticed him staring.

'I was just thinking how lovely you are growing with the passing time – a different loveliness to your first few years, but you have no need to be jealous of an earlier Silandi. There's a softness about you now that's difficult to define, but I like it. We all change, some of us look older, some of us just look different. No one could call you undesirable ...'

She stood up now and slipped on her robe.

'Now *that* I understand – no wonder you've been inspecting me for the last ten minutes. You're not well yet – heaven knows I'll be the first to ... well the *only*, I hope ...' She appeared to become tongue-tied, which made her seem foolish rather than coquettish. She had always been an amateur at womanly techniques. It did not worry him unduly, though occasionally it caused some embarrassment in bed when a falseness crept into their lovemaking. Only occasionally.

The wall parted and Zayid stood before them.

'How's the patient?' he inquired. His voice was dull and he was clearly only carrying out what he thought to be his duty. His mind was obviously on other things.

'I've only just dressed,' flashed Silandi. 'Please shout or something before you enter our tent.'

'Sorry,' he said, sounding genuinely surprised. Othman realized that even if he had caught Silandi in a state of nakedness it would not have registered. The man quite obviously had problems which outweighed all other considerations.

'What today, Zayid?' asked Othman. 'Are we still running?'

'Oh, they'll be here, don't you worry,' replied Zayid, becoming agitated again as he had done on an earlier visit. 'And those others – they'll all be back. But the Plinthites – they seem bent on destroying themselves, and us. They would jump down the barrels of the guns if it meant getting some of us. Stupid fools. Anyway, I'll do my best for them – kill a few today.' His eyes looked wildly around the tent as if searching for something.

'But those other things – got to do something about them. Can't bully us forever.'

Then before Othman could reply he was gone, out through the self-sealing wall, and Silandi shook her head.

'Even Jessum's getting worried, Othman. We *can't* just keep running, and killing those savages as we do so.'

Othman suddenly felt sick and leaned over the edge of the raised stretcher to retch into a bucket which had been placed there for the purpose. His stomach pulled on emptiness and the muscles sang out with pain. Silandi stood by, waiting for the bout of nausea to finish.

Outside Othman's tent Zayid stood turning over in his mind what lay ahead. He wondered why he felt so much antipathy towards the Plinthites – or those other things, the clouds of black dust. They had every right to protect their territory from invasion and he knew he should not feel resentful – but he did feel it, which was why he had not moved completely out of the Plinthites' sphere of influence. Without Jessum realizing it, for Jessum was no navigator, Zayid had managed to lead the tribe in a semi-circle around the mountains, staying within reach of the Plinthites, instead of steering a course directly away from them. Perhaps Jessum *did* realize – after all, the sun and stars were easy enough to follow. He hadn't spoken of it. Maybe Jessum felt the same anger that Zayid did when he thought of how snug and cosy life was for the Plinthites in their clay spelaeans, while the ship's people were made to wander the world, never knowing a home.

Well, soon there would be a reckoning! It was no good, Zayid had realized, just killing patrol after patrol of Plinthites. They were being slaughtered in dozens but they were not learning the lesson and they were numbered in thousands. Zayid wanted them to be beaten. He wanted to see them abject before him. Instead they died screaming and yelling, and spitting rage at him with their last breath. That was not the way it should be at all. Why, only yesterday he had walked among their mangled bodies and one, crippled and blind, but still alive, had grasped at his ankle and dug his filthy nails in, bringing blood before the hand was hacked off and the locked fingers prised open.

They resented intrusion, he could see that. Well, he resented their resentment. Why should Zayid move out of the way of some low form of life, even if it did resemble a human in outward appearance? It was essentially an alien savage, a beast, with alien organs driving alien blood around unEarthly tubes. A superficial likeness to an intelligent race, that was all. Outside, skin and hair cast in a similar mould to Zayid. Inside, a jumble of twisted alien anatomy: strangely shaped hearts, perhaps five in a row: perhaps no heart at all? Maybe within, they were so different as to defy all Earthly description: a sickening mess; a hollowness filled with foul gases?

If the Plinthites resented intrusion, the whirlwinds represented it. Wherever the humans went they were dogged by those clouds of dust, acting like the guardians of a sacred trust. Well, perhaps he, Zayid, could put an end to that!

Twenty-seven

The battlefield was sprinkled with the corpses of the Plinthites lying like red stones on the grass, and Jessum felt a surge of triumph as he called his men to move forward. It was not the triumph of achievement, it was the satisfying feeling of striking out in blind, helpless anger and finding the solidity of a target at last. He knew, of course, as most of the men did too, that they were moving carefully around the Plinthites' spelaeans, and that if they moved out of their territory they would not be followed, but they needed to vent their frustration on something, someone. They were human, and humans have always needed victims. Besides, war alleviates boredom. The causes of war are often complex and inextricably entangled, but the wave that bears those high-sounding reasons on its back is born of boredom and of frustrated, everyday, monotonous lives filled with repetitive chores. The tradesmen drop their tools, the managers their pens. Eagerly, they take up other tools and other administrative tasks and it is only later that they find them just as boring, just as frustrating.

Jessum and Zayid had not reached that stage in the cycle. They had found a way to hit out and be felt. The sense of power tuned their bodies to a pitch of energy they had not known before.

But today Zayid was edgy, Jessum had seen that, before the attack had come. He could see him now, on the adjoining slope, standing with his hands up his sleeves, like a Chinese mandarin, looking very anxious.

At first Jessum thought Zayid was going to remain in that same statue-like pose while his own men surged forward unsupported on the right flank, but Zayid suddenly seemed to awake from his brooding attitude to wave his own men onward. Just as that happened the whirlwind aliens appeared between the humans and the fleeing Plinthites and Jessum knew that they would be thwarted once again. The men knew it too, and halted their charge, their battle cries tailing off to disappointed moans. Dejected, they began walking slowly back, calling down abuse on the aliens. After their inventiveness began to wear off their voices fell to discontented grumbling.

As the sounds wafted up to Jessum there was a loud shout and he turned to see Zayid running down the slope towards the whirlwinds. Jessum was stunned. What was wrong with the man? Had he gone mad?

Zayid blundered through the ranks of his own men, scattering them, and ran full tilt at an alien.

'Zayid!' yelled Jessum, but the shout was lost in the explosion: Zayid had thrown a grenade into the very centre of a whirlwind. There was a look of total satisfaction on his face. The supreme moment had come to the weapon-maker, for the whirlwind had disappeared, blown the way of four winds.

'I did it!' shouted Zayid to his men, and they began to wave their weapons above their heads. Then came the dreadful noise which Jessum would not forget for the rest of his life. It was the high-pitched shrill squeal of a dying rabbit. Men put their hands over their ears and even some of the Plinthites in the distance stopped and turned.

At first Jessum thought the noise was coming from the alien and then, since it was so loud and penetrating, from all the aliens' kith and kin. It was neither of these and Jessum bit hard into the back of his good hand to stop from screaming himself as he realized the sound was coming from Zayid's own throat. Then Zayid's body imploded and fell like a limp sack to the ground.

Not a man moved for at least five minutes. They just stared in terror at the misshapen skin lying at the foot of the slope, and then they turned and began walking quickly back to their camp. They had had enough of war for one day. They did not even send back for the body.

On one of the outer planets of the system the body of the Manipulator that had destroyed Zayid stirred fluidly, filling its iced-over mound as it contemplated its action. Its contemporaries had confirmed that the destruction was inevitable and therefore it was really unnecessary to project its mind along the feeler wand and out into a space between the stars to contemplate the act. However, this particular Manipulator had never before needed to use its feeler wand, the thin beam of energy controlled from within its thick casing, in the unnatural and normally abhorrent employment of life-taking. It was an effective destructive device but life was beautiful and irreplaceable in its individual fragmented forms, and why eradicate beauty? The Manipulator was a young one and as such it had an intensity of purpose. It needed to meditate.

The creature that it had killed had (of course) not harmed the feeler wand with the explosive device but the potential had been there. It was all right, to a certain degree, for these bright new creatures to interact violently with one another –

that was part of the cycle – but showing hostility towards their hosts was another thing completely.

Around the young one older, more established mounds lumped the frozen wastes of the huge planet, using each other to ricochet their own feeler wands on to the surfaces of other worlds and out into deep space. It had been one of these wands that had fused the intelligence units of Othman's starship. The creatures within the mounds led a simple existence which produced a high level of intellect. When all activity consists of growing old and slowly gelling it leaves much time for development of the mind.

They charged their viscous, immobile selves directly from the sun, by bouncing their feeler wands from moons and space debris directly into the sun's bright maw. Very occasionally they remained too long with the ecstasy of the charge and in sizzling happiness boiled their casings dry. Several cracked mounds offered themselves as evidence of the dangers of overcharging. Others, that had died of old age, were now solid from their casings through to their roots in the planet's mantle upon which they had originally anchored themselves.

That they, in their love of life, were artists was evident in the attention they lavished on the fourth world from the sun. One of their manipulative interests was ecology – a natural area of study for a static race. The tips of their feeler wands materialized in clouds of charged particles as they moved them over the surface of the fourth planet, encouraging migratory habits or, as in the case of the Plinthites, merely relaying a curious psyche to watch the roots of existence at work. Technology, beyond a certain safe stage, was disapproved of. Organization was discouraged. These two aspects of intelligent life led to far-reaching, destructive forces. The Manipulators survived by holding all else down. Highly mobile and heavily armed starfleets cause more than palpitations amongst a race whose individuals are imprisoned inside immobile hills.

*

Silandi and Othman moved into the shade of the fustic tree that pointed its thorns, accusingly, at various places on the ground. She said that he had started to become too fond of his own company once again. She had had enough of lofty, introverted husbands and now that he was helpless she could do something to make him more sociable: force society upon him. So there he sat, under the spikes that occasionally dripped a harmless but irritating yellow fluid onto his shoulders, saying hello to passers-by and generally being sociable. He spent the time contemplating the birds that darted with wasp-like, sharp-angled flight paths above his head. Occasionally one of them would drop suddenly into the bare branches of the tree, to pick at the berries that grew under the protection of the finger-long thorns.

This world, he thought, so full of new life – at least, new to the Earthman – yet they had not even begun to study it in general, let alone classify the individuals. They were so busy with their own survival that they had no time for such civilized pastimes. More than a pastime, for classification is said to be the basis of science. Perhaps Malek had done something? He was always fiddling with flowers and things like that. But one man could not make any impression on a whole new world of life, surely? Each grain, perhaps each atom, was new. Possibly there were more elements on Jessum than on Earth? Maybe the cell structure of animals was wildly different? Possibly there were magnificent crystal formations to be discovered.

What a lot they were missing, Othman and his people. Opportunities were slipping away with age. He was still fairly young, but the style of life was harsh. How long could he expect to live in such a manner? Boys became old men overnight in such conditions.

He stared moodily into the distance, then sat up sharply, causing himself some pain. There was something out there. The hills! They were still there, barely visible through the heat haze but there, on the horizon. Surely they must be some other, similar range? he said to himself. No, they were the same rounded red hills. That damned Zayid had remained within striking distance of the Plinthites – God only knew why. God, and all the rest of the camp, except the stupid ones and the women. Not Silandi, though.

He called her and demanded an explanation. She replied that she had argued with Zayid and he had seemed adamant that the Plinthites should not drive them away, although even to him it was obvious that if they attacked in full numbers they would over-run the camp. The whole idea was insane but she had not wanted to worry Othman, who could have done nothing anyway.

So, thought Othman, the idiots were playing at soldiers, remaining just far enough away for the Plinthites to send out expeditionary forces but not near enough to constitute a threat to the whole community.

Silandi went away and he sat back in his chair, realizing that after all the time he had spent with them he still did not know his own men – least of all Jessum, who was normally a sensible, sensitive man. Still, this latest madness would suit his purpose. He could unveil a mystery once and for all.

It was while he made his plans that a bird landed suddenly on his arm. At that moment his heart jumped, knowing his system could not take a shock like those given out by the local fauna. But no jolt followed and he realized that it was not he who was touching the bird, but the bird that had landed on him. He stared at the dappled creature, hardly daring to breathe in case it flew away. He felt he had at last made contact with the planet and its life. There was a moment of exultation before a guilty thought formed in his mind. They had brought life from Earth – pet birds, domestic animals, hopefully nothing smaller. God forbid not spiders, or insects of any kind. Frozen fleas? It was almost a humorous thought, except that if such creatures of Earth were introduced to Jessum they might interfere with the whole balance of nature – totally upset the native ecology. Let loose a handful of locusts and destroy a world. (Let loose a handful of humans and destroy a universe?)

The bird flew away just as Jessum entered the camp, followed by Fdar and the soldiers. Othman saw at once that something was wrong and waved his arm to attract Jessum's attention. His companion came straight to him, his face registering dismay.

'Zayid's dead,' he said as he drew near. Othman took this in and then said, as Jessum fell wearily by the seat to sit crosslegged on the ground, 'People get killed in battles. Sometimes it's the leaders.'

'It wasn't the Plinthites,' said Jessum, in the same dull tone. 'It was those devils that hound us – that have chased us over the world. The whirlwinds.'

Othman's eyes opened in surprise.

'They killed him?'

'I think so,' came the reply. 'They didn't actually touch him but he had just thrown a bomb at one of them – he seemed to go berserk and the alien just disappeared. Whether it actually killed it, the explosion I mean, or whether it reformed somewhere else' – he shrugged – 'who can tell? Anyway, they didn't like it. They didn't actually touch him, or even go near him – he just collapsed inwards, a mess of skin and bone, that's all.'

Othman nodded. Jessum was obviously very shaken. He had no desire to push him over the edge. Very carefully he said, 'Did he say anything, Zayid?'

'He screamed like a woman,' said Jessum. 'Worse than a woman.' He shuddered violently.

Othman put his hand on the man's shoulder and said, 'Help me up.'

The other pulled away sharply.

'You can't get up. You're not well enough.'

Othman replied, 'Help me up – then go and fetch that weapon-handler, I forget his name. The one that used to follow Zayid around – big fellow with untidy hair.'

'You mean Al-Alam. But, untidy hair?' Jessum almost laughed. 'You must be joking surely? Have you seen your own lately – or anyone's? We're not the spick and span cherubs that crawled out of our uteri now, you know.'

Othman ran his hand through his own matted clump.

'Yes, I suppose you're right, but this Al-Alam is particularly bush-like in appearance. Anyway, I wish to talk to him, and to you – and don't say anything to Silandi.'

'Why?'

'Because she'll know I'm plotting something ...'

Jessum opened his mouth and Othman stemmed the protest with 'I'll tell you soon enough. Get the big man now.'

After Jessum had left him Othman made tentative plans in his head. He needed Al-Alam to help him because he was still physically very weak. He needed someone to lean on, a hod carrier. While he was lying above that stake up there on the mountains, he had seen something, a flashing in the sun, and slowly over the past few days he had juggled with a theory – not a brilliant one for most elusive mysteries have simple foundations – a theory concerning their reason for being on the new world. This theory coupled with delirious dreams, visions of the past thrown out from behind the id by a fever and drugs, had given him a story he was prepared to offer his people. There was nothing terribly startling in the story. It had begun long ago with the planet Jupiter flaring into a new sun. A shadow fell over his own. Silandi was behind him.

'Are you rested now?'

He had to get rid of her before Jessum returned with Al-Alam. There was no way he could explain to her that he needed to go for a midnight ride that night, to prove a theory to himself.

'You've heard about Zayid?' he said.

Her face fell, and he felt a twinge of jealousy. Quickly he quenched the small flame – to be jealous of a dead man was almost like admitting he was not of the living himself. A dead man can only be a rival to another dead man.

'Yes, it's sad, isn't it? He was such a serious little fellow too.'

Like me, mused Othman, except that I am not small and the phrase 'a serious man' hangs better on a taller person. The bigger the man the more at home it appears – a small man always *looks* as though he is trying that much harder and people are suspicious of those who try too hard to get somewhere, be something. Probably, he finalized, that's why so many small men are clowns. It's more acceptable to their contemporaries.

'What are you thinking about?'

Silandi again. God, she had to be out of the way.

'Zayid's widow – have you been to see her? She must be lonely.'

'I shouldn't think so,' said Silandi rather spitefully. 'She didn't seem to pay much attention to him when he was here. She . . .' Silandi pulled up abruptly.

Othman was staring at her hard and she said, 'You're right of course, we're all guilty of something like that, especially me.'

'I didn't say it.'

'You *looked* it.'

Othman shrugged.

'Someone's with her already – there's no need for me to go,' said Silandi.

'There *is* a need for you to go – you are the wife of the leader of the tribe – the uncontested leader now. That gives you some responsibilities. I would like you to visit the widow and offer your condolences.' He could see Jessum on the edge of the camp, walking towards him with Al-Alam.

'Yes, I will go,' she replied suddenly and then, noticing Jessum approaching, said, 'Here's Jessum ...'

'We have something private to discuss – concerning the safety of the tribe,' Othman said quickly.

Silandi raised her eyebrows and turned and left them all the same. He wished he had said that in the first instance, instead of attempting to use guile. He was never good at subterfuge. That had been Zayid's forte.

Twenty-eight

The horses were ready at midnight – dark-coated like their riders. Al-Alam had secured a brace to a camel saddle and had strapped them both to a sturdy but tolerant mare. The horse had withstood the burden of packs over a period of time and the saddle was just another such encumbrance: a necessary irritant. She was to be Othman's mount, the furniture was for his support.

Othman had kept Silandi talking until late, knowing that she was already very tired having answered his demands for service throughout the day. She did not wake when he stepped over her and through the wall of the tent, quickly, in order that any breeze outside should not have time to blow through the gap he caused.

They climbed on to their mounts outside the camp, and set off under the starlight towards the hills. Othman kept his pain to himself. He knew that Jessum would insist on turning back if he showed any serious signs of physical weakness. He knew also that he was strong enough to cope with the journey. The truth was not worth his life, he was well aware of that. Slung over his shoulder, as well as a weapon (which he realized would be of little use in the hornets' nest of the Plinthites) was an instrument bearing several dials.

Groups of stars, so close together that they almost formed one silver flash on the horse-dark forehead of the night, lit the Plinthites' trails through the grasses. Othman's mind ran over the line from an old poem. 'Deserts are there, and different skies and night with different stars ...' Earthworld, the ship chose you well. I could be crossing the grasslands of Africa, or South America, or even the Russian Steppes. You may have different stars but you are similar enough to Earth for one who has never seen her. The other is the dream, you are real, he thought.

The night was lulling him into a lethargic mood with its tranquillity and he began a softly-spoken conversation with his companions to ward off the subtle persuasiveness of the warm air.

'Can you smell the grass, Jessum? It's a good smell – an aroma, one might say.'

Jessum said yes, and Al-Alam sniffed hard and loud, but added nothing. Othman said, 'You do not appreciate the acuteness which the night gives to our senses, Al-Alam?'

The big man grunted. 'I smell the sudor of the horse and the still damp crap on her left hind leg. I smell the fear from my own armpits and from windward an unknown scent, probably the musk of a dangerous beast. My senses are sharp but I do not find them pleasant, any more than I like this ride into the mouth of hell.'

Othman had not realized the others would be afraid, but of course he had not told them where, exactly, they were going. He spurred his horse on, talking in undertones, 'We are not going into hell tonight, we're going to learn what created it.'

The three horsemen reached the foothills some time later and Othman led them down many paths until the instrument he carried indicated that they were going in the right direction and that the readings were growing stronger. At one point the trail rose steeply to pass between two large rocks and like a gate between these, supported by tall posts, were several gonfalons of hanging bones and rags.

'What's that? – what are they?' whispered Al-Alam in fear.

'They're the guards to the spirits of Earth,' said Othman cryptically.

Dismounting, they led their horses between the posts, beneath the dangling skulls, and into a large bowl which nestled in the centre of the red hills.

Looking down they were blinded by a blaze of reflected starlight which took Othman's breath away. He had been expecting to see them, but the multitude of objects that stretched out, wave on wave of silver fire before his eyes, made him forget even his pain with the wonder of it all.

'My God,' said Jessum, with a catch in his throat.

'There they are,' said Othman simply. 'Tractors, cranes, aircraft, ships – vehicles of all kinds. The dismembered starships of our enemies the Plinthites – the very people we were sent here to defend we ended up slaughtering.'

Al-Alam was still in a state of bewilderment.

'But what does it all mean?' he asked.

'It means,' said Jessum, 'that we were a single ship amongst many – this is the main fleet. We somehow became detached – right, Othman?'

'Wrong. We were never part of this fleet – they too are from Earth but we were sent on ahead. Guns before butter. Zayid's favourite line. We were meant to build the defences ready for their arrival. Those red savages are the clay-stained farmers, shopkeepers and businessmen of the new world.'

Jessum said mildly, 'We let them down – we failed them.'

'We failed no one,' replied Othman. 'These people are no more capable of building a colony than we are to defend them as they do it. They're what they are – half-crazed savages. Whatever interfered with our teacher units, and produced our morons, did the same to theirs.'

'At a different time in their development,' said Al-Alam, with some perception at last.

'Somewhere in their early childhood perhaps. But what about their cattle and horses?'

Othman shrugged. 'My guess is that they ate them. It wouldn't take long, you know, especially if one doesn't know how to open a canister of stored food. At least we know where to steal from if we ever need anything in future.'

The three men stared for a long time at the glittering junk heap, which would be idle in the hills until its individual components rusted into the soil. Jessum suggested they return and take some of the vehicles for their own use, but Othman shook his head.

'Equipment such as this is only of use to a stationary civilization. We are nomads, by force as well as by choice, for it's what I choose to be. A Bedu. If you think back, Jessum, to when we were on the island? I was the one who had itchy feet. I wanted to be on the move. Why? Because the teachers instilled in me a desire for travel as I was the man who would make the roads between the missile sites. I was the man who would inspect the defences. Out each day, on the move ...'

Jessum took up the theme. 'And I was the builder who would follow your lead – carry out your orders. Your wife and Zayid, they were the townies – people who worked in one place, homely types. Some of us would have stronger feelings than others, depending upon how receptive we were to the teaching ...'

'But his wife?' said Al-Alam, puzzled again.

'Weekends – odd days, here and there,' replied Othman. 'She was meant to be my stabilizing influence. Possibly that is why we fight so much – our temperaments are not compatible and we were never meant to see too much of one another.'

The three men remounted, Othman with some difficulty. Al-Alam helped him onto the framework and held him steady as they made a rapid retreat from the dangerous hills. They had no wish to be caught out in the daylight. Not in that vicinity. Their brothers from Earth would take them prisoner and do un-Earthly things to their bodies before decapitating them, in the old style.

Othman capitulated to his weakness and allowed Al-Alam to keep a supporting hand on his shoulder the whole way back to the camp. He wanted the tribe to be on the move at sunrise, having no wish to fight further with the Plinthites. He wondered where the whirlwinds fitted in to the scheme of things. Perhaps they were the ones that had destroyed the teacher units? Or, more likely, they were the servants of those that had committed the act. Perhaps they were some kind of machine, only not machines because they weren't mechanical, but something of that nature – insentient, cold robots.

What of the motives then, of the mysterious, unseen aliens that were so zealous in their efforts to keep the planet free of settlers? He had a theory about that too – his sickbed had spawned many ideas.

When Othman was a boy he had visited a palace, the *Qasr al-Hayr al-Shargī* – an old building with a walled parkland in which wild animals had once roamed. What if they, the people from Earth, had landed within such a *hayr*? Perhaps the whole planet was a park, or sanctuary, where the beasts were allowed to play out their lives in their natural ways – the carnivores killing the herbivores and one another, mating, wandering, loving, dying under the order of a conservationist-minded species within the same solar system? Within the same galaxy?

If this Intelligence had seen the ships of Earth heading towards their exotic garden what would their reaction have been? To destroy the alien ships? Othman had tried to surrender this in the light of *not* being what he was – a human – which was, of course, impossible. However, rational thinking told him that if they (the Intelligence) were concerned with the preservation of life, and they had a way of containing these intruders, the newcomers, without destroying them utterly, then they would take the less drastic of the two courses of action. After all, they could always do their worst later. Why not guide them down to a remote spot, an island say, and study them for a while? Let them use up their energy in natural curiosity. Then decide whether they were worth allowing to survive. If they didn't try to plant a civilization on the soil of the planet, then there was no harm in letting them live. They might even make a useful and interesting addition to the *hayr*.

Othman decided not to communicate these thoughts to the rest of the tribe. It might upset them to think that they were regarded as wild beasts, although there was no reason why it should.

The three men arrived back at the camp in the early dawn. Silandi and Niandi had awoken and found the messages left for them. They greeted the men as they entered the camp, making a mental note to scold them later. Silandi told Othman to go straight to his bed, but he ordered the people to decamp. Silandi began to protest, backed up by Niandi who thought Jessum looked exhausted as he was led away by Fdar, but Othman said, 'Don't heckle me, women! We're moving now. I don't want anyone else to die – not today, not tomorrow. I will say no more.'

Silandi could see that Othman would listen to no arguments from her or anyone, so she went to do her share of the work. Al-Alam helped the heavy Othman from the makeshift saddle and carried him to the shade of the tree under which he had sat the previous day. Then the big man settled the horses with food and water. Someone took Othman a cup of hot tea and he drank it under the soft coming of the sun, thinking, *it will be a good life*. A slow, hard, private, but *good* life. Lacking in material comforts, but not in reward. They had stories to tell, a religion to grow and a tradition to found.

A cool breeze touched his cheek as he sat and amused himself with pictures of a pastoral existence. The weather was turning – soon it would be winter.

Later, on the move, Othman told Silandi what they had found in the hills. She then saw the significance of the tractor-lever sword, and was pleased with herself for pointing out to Othman that the seeds of the qat plants, and others, on the island must have come from the stores of the Plinthites – carried unwittingly to the island by birds. Othman nodded seriously and said he expected she was correct. It was all falling into place for her – the perplexity of Malek who, beforehand, never could get people to understand that the discovering of a duplication of Earth's flora on the new world was an event to cause scepticism.

She wondered, sadly, whether the morons and stickmen had managed to find a new home – or whether they had perished out on the sea of quicksand. Othman had said that the weather was turning. The crust to the sea would soon disappear. She sighed. It was strange how all the aggressive men had died, leaving only the gentle ones. Yes, she even included Othman, for whatever else he might be he was definitely no warrior. Cold, detached, hard, but gentle-natured just the same. Now he was a shepherd leading a nomadic tribe into forever. She had known a shepherd once, long ago in her childhood. He was just such a man as Othman, uncompromising. Men like her two shepherds were easy to misunderstand. Shepherds. They had trodden worlds since the dawn of time. Arrogant, gentle creatures, like their sheep.

Twenty-nine

In the light of the evening sun the boy played with the sands of the oxbow lake, knowing that this was to be his last chance at his favourite activity before the tribe moved upland once more for new grazing ground. The upland rivers were rocky and had no silt with which to make shapes. He made a castle like the one Grandad Jessum once taught him to build. Grandad had been good at making things out of sand. Now he had died and had gone to Nanna, who had been a little woman, sometimes loving, sometimes scolding, sometimes both at once. Al-Othman had cried when Grandad Jessum had died, and that only proved to young Jessum that his Grandad was a very important man because Al-Othman was very old and very wise. Anyway, the world was called Jessum, which was *his* name too, so that also made *him* important like his Grandad.

The boy let the silt trickle through his fingers, and a small pattern ran lazily through his nerves to his brain, creating a fuzzy picture there. Looking down he saw it was a sandworm with thousands of little legs that he had touched. He let it fall to the bank because it seemed alarmed at being so high off the ground. That was a *new* picture. The boy looked up at an old man sitting in the weak sun and called, 'Uncle Whitehair, I had a new picture. It was a ...' The boy hesitated, he had not the skill in word power to describe what he had felt.

The old man nodded and smiled. His hands were clasped in front of him and he was watching the boy from a squatting position, peering through his knees.

Uncle Whitehair could not speak much – only a few words – he said it was because his brain was clogged up with pictures. Uncle Whitehair had taught Jessum how to talk with pictures and patterns though, and the other children too. They could all exchange with one another. Uncle had told them it was a secret language for the children. Parents were not to know. '... it was frightened,' said young Jessum.

Fdar nodded again but was paying less attention as a pair of birds was overhead. The boy looked up too, at the white shapes that winged across the yellow sky. He could trace the patterns of their bones through their feathers as the light shone through the translucent wings. Uncle Whitehair was always touching the birds and he wanted the children to do likewise. Uncle had belonged to another tribe, long ago, that went wandering on the sea-desert in high summer. He was sad because they might all have been lost and never reached land before winter came and the sea-desert's crust changed to quicksand. So he touched the birds to try and find out if they had pictures of the lost tribe in their minds. Birds were silly creatures, though, thought young Jessum, attending to his sandcastle once again. Their pictures were often mixed up and sometimes hard to understand. They really were silly things.

Suddenly, without prior warning, a large forkwinged bird landed by the boy and snapped up the sandworm with its hard beak. Jessum, startled, jumped backwards – the bird was taller than himself and it had fallen like a large rock dropped from high above. However, the creature was not alarmed at the boy's sudden movements. It was certainly not going to be moved from the place where Jessum had been digging and began rooting around in the upturned sand for more delicacies.

Jessum watched it for a few minutes before stretching forth a hand – gently, because it was a very large bird and sometimes the creatures could overwhelm a small boy's patterns with their own. Out of the corner of his eye he could see Uncle Whitehair rising slowly to his feet. The small brown hand touched the white-feathered neck and stroked slowly downwards, along the plumage, gently, gently. The patterns came – only the fresh ones, for old patterns were erased in the minds of simple creatures as a new series entered the brain. The chances of finding a bird that had recently been touched by a member of Fdar's morons, or stickmen, were extremely slim.

'Uncle Whitehair!' called the boy, and turned to see the old man scrambling towards him. Then suddenly the smooth face below the cloud-like head creased in an expression of agony, the breath began hissing between the thin lips which had long since turned blue and, as the old man lunged forward in a desperate effort to touch the bird, he slipped and collapsed. He lay groaning on the ground as the creature finally took flight to join its mate.

'Uncle Whitehair, Uncle Whitehair,' cried the boy not knowing what to do. He tried to lift the old man to his feet by his clothes but found him too heavy. Then, with tears of fright streaming down his face he began running uphill, to fetch Al-Othman. Fdar's eyes had closed.

In his tent Othman was busy thinking. When Silandi had been alive she had, in later years, taken him to task for sitting and doing nothing, not realizing that he was busy. He knew she was afraid he was becoming senile but she had forgotten that even in his youth he used to sit in his chair for hours at a time indulging in the same activity. Now she had gone he had all the time in the world, and found he did not really need it because no one listened very much to his ideas now. There was a new leader of the tribe – a younger, stronger man whom Othman loved as the son he had never sired himself. Being a strong man, though, he obviously followed his own opinions and paid those of Othman only slight heed.

That was the way it should be, thought Othman. Silandi would have said so.

Theirs had been a stormy relationship throughout their lives but Othman did not regret a minute of it. She had once told him that although she found him hateful and exasperating at times, she never found him boring. What better compliment could an old man in his declining years ask for? I have had my fill of life, thought Othman. It is these poor wandering people that have to face the monotony. Only the moron and himself were left now, and he, Othman, should die before the moron because he was certainly a good few Earthyears older. In fact he was disgusted with himself for hanging on so long. He was positively ancient. The children were frightened of him. Even some of the adults stepped quickly out of his way when they saw him hobbling along. Was he held so much in awe? Was he a wizard to frighten young children? Or did his old crumbling frame look grotesque to the lithe creatures that scampered from his path? Probably it was his acid utterances that drove them away. He was inclined to be testy, he admitted to himself, but, God's teeth, who would not be with a rotting frame?

Still, his life had not been wasted and, as his wife had been fond of telling him, the gentle shepherds had won the day.

He was nodding his head, almost asleep, when a small boy came charging through the flap of the goatskin tent.

'Al-Othman, come quickly! Uncle Whitehair is ill,' gasped the youngster.

It took some seconds to register in his slow mind.

'Ill? Then send word for the doctor, boy. Don't come bursting into my tent like a waterfall.' Uncle Whitehair – that was what the children called the moron.

'I think he's dead, sir,' said the boy, trembling and beginning to cry.

Who was this lad? Jessum's grandson, wasn't it? Quite a sensible youngster – or used to be. How old was he? Seven Earthyears? Six?

'Send someone for the doctor, boy, then get me a mule,' he said, as kindly as he could make the words sound.

'Yes, sir.' The boy went running out again and Othman struggled to his feet using his bony hands to lever himself up.

Damn that moron, he thought. Why was he dying now? It

was ill-mannered of all these people to drop away like this leaving Othman looking old and foolish. If Othman had died when the tribe was young they would have revered his name. They would have remembered his fine qualities of leadership. Now there were none of the ship's people left and the new ones, those born on Jessum, only knew the stories of how Zayid had gone out, gloriously, in the midst of a bloody battle. Oh yes, they repeated stories like that with bated breath. But who wants to hear stories that have no real substance? Tales of good, dependable leadership and the encouragement of art, literature and religion. Dry stuff, that. Not worth talking about or listening to.

The boy came hurtling back through the flap and Othman said, 'All right, all right. I'm coming.'

He needed help to climb on the mule and the boy then led him down to the bank of the lake, saying that the doctor was coming. The doctor did, in fact, arrive before them. It was getting dark but even in the poor light Othman could see that Fdar was fading out.

'Damned inconsiderate moron,' Othman said, as the doctor rested Fdar's head on a rolled blanket.

'It's his heart,' said the doctor, peering at Othman through the dimness.

'Silly old fool, always did overwork his body,' Othman murmured. 'His eyes are still closed. Can't you get him to open them? I want to say good-bye.'

It sounded callous but the doctor was used to the truculent Othman. He replied, 'If I give him something, it might do him more harm than good.'

'Will he live until morning anyway?'

'No,' answered the doctor. 'It's unlikely, but our drugs are running short again. I really shouldn't waste them.'

Othman grunted. 'Give him the stimulus, man. The youths can make another raid on the Plinthites' stores – plenty of drugs there that the red devils don't use or don't know how to.

It'll give our young thugs something to do. Get rid of their aggressiveness.'

The doctor hesitated, then shrugged. Othman was still very much respected in the tribe despite his own misgivings on this subject. The surgeon injected Fdar quickly, before anyone else came down from the camp.

Gradually the moron opened his eyes and Othman stared at his face from a few inches away.

'What's the meaning of this?' he demanded softly. 'Couldn't you wait for me? Don't look away, I know you can understand me – you're not the idiot you pretend to be. Seducing our young people with that nasty magic of yours.' The moron's eyes looked back at him, full of comprehension.

'Yes, that's right, isn't it? Well, I hope you've done the right thing – and me allowing it when I knew what was going on. I just wanted you to know that I'm not stupid either, before you go on that premature trip to Allah. We've created a new breed of Man between us – let's hope it's better than the last one.'

Fdar smiled at him although Othman could see the pain in his eyes. Then the moron saw the boy and he tried to struggle upwards, beckoning.

'Come, come,' he rattled in his throat. It was obvious he desperately wanted to touch young Jessum.

'Come ... Uncle,' he pleaded.

The doctor pushed the reluctant boy forward and Jessum touched the fingers of the dying man.

'Bird pictures,' he said. 'Please?'

There was silence. Night had descended and the stars were out. The mottled skin of the wrinkled hand touched the small dark fingers of the boy. Along the mound above, the tribe had gathered and were watching. There was a stillness in the air.

The moron suddenly cried out, 'It is!' Then he slumped backwards. The smile had returned to his face.

Othman rose, stiff-jointedly, from his kneeling position and the boy Jessum ran to his parents on the hillock. The people still waited, watching.

'Another soul is learning the secrets of the night of Kadar,' Othman called. 'It will not be long, God willing, before I too have that revelation.' He looked up at the bright, blazing patches of silver above and repeated, 'God willing,' in a voice that crackled like old paper.

Then he bent over the body of Fdar and whispered a prayer into the dead man's ear.

'Tell her I'm coming soon,' he said.